LAST CHANCE

CHANCE

STOP

LAST CHANCE STOP

SARAH FJELLANGER

atmosphere press

Dedicated to all those who have ever been asked:

"Tell me, what is it you plan to do
With your one wild and precious life?"

from "The Summer Day"
By Mary Oliver

CHAPTER 1

Turning Twelve in 1899; the Age of Change

Da's crop was ruined again. Though I tried, that truth could not be squished as I pushed my feet against the porch floor and listened to the rungs of the rocker send their squeak into the night. In the distance, the Northern Lights danced above the mountain range of my home in Norway. Night had brought on a coolness, and I pulled the quilt tighter around my shoulders. Mother had pieced its multicolored pattern some unknown time ago and written my name, Kristi Ann Monger, on one of the squares.

A whiff of pine pierced the night; the fireflies came out to float on the breeze. I imagined their blinks to be a song sung by a huge choir of voices. A wolf howled in the distance. Another answered his lonely call. Far above me, the clouds passed across the face of the full moon like wisps of a broom. Light from that pumpkin-colored heavenly surface reflected off the icy cold waters of the fjord that caressed the base of our mountainside. Though I'd never seen all the creatures that swam in its deep waters, I truly believed that monsters existed. *Maybe they will disappear tonight when I stop being a child* is the hope that ran through my mind while goosebumps, like an army of centipedes, walked across my arms and legs. I pulled the quilt even tighter against my body.

The stroke of midnight on that late August eve in 1899 would usher in my twelfth year. I believed that I'd be an adult if I surrendered all my childish ways, including stories filled with dragons, trolls, fairies, and Cinderella. *I should have done it two years ago* I thought as I recalled the first appearance of the earworms. There weren't many that year, but wherever they gorged on corn, they left behind a blackness that turned the remaining golden kernels to a milky substance. I hadn't thought too much of it back then except to notice that after the harvest, Da seldom dropped a krone into the can sitting on the shelf above the stove. Mother started cooking soup instead of making meals with lots of mashed potatoes and lefse. The white cutworms had invaded the garden and destroyed many of our root vegetables. Potatoes, carrots, and onions, the few that we had, could freely swim in the cloudy broth. The subtraction all happened so slowly that I failed to recognize its true effect on my family.

At supper that evening, my da, a man slow to share his thoughts, had quietly sat with his shoulders slumped forward like a roosting bird. I'd positioned myself across from him, both of us slurping our soup and sopping up the last of it with a small slice of bread. In some ways I wanted him to get angry at the failed crop and slam the door, like he had when his best friend fell from a wagon and landed on his head. The man had died that night and Da went off into the darkness, alone, his fists held tight by his side. At least then I'd seen his anger. This time he merely went off to bed without a word to either of us.

After our meal, Mother went to sit in front of the hearth, its fire unlit. She needed no light. Her hands moved in rhythm as she tatted a long-remembered pattern using the thin floss she'd wound and rewound many times. It made me think of the day we'd gone to the village and stopped in at the General Store. There she'd picked up a multicolored spool and casually said, "Now wouldn't this make a nice doily to sit under your da's Bible?" She had held it reverently, pulled it in against her chest and lifted her chin as if to pray. After a deep breath and one last look, she returned it to its place on the shelf. I'd never heard my mother ask for anything and knew the want of this thread would never cross her lips. It wasn't her way. Complaining was something she'd never do either. She had too much respect for Da.

On that night, as I sat thinking about the approach of the midnight hour and the beginning of my twelfth year, I considered how Mother, like me, had only two dresses. Both had started to hang from her shoulders. The effect made her look like a scarecrow or someone shrinking back into child size. No longer did she resemble the person in the framed tintype that sat on their bedside table. That beautiful woman, who'd married my da ten years before I came along, now had hands that often bled from the hours she spent keeping ahead of the worms in her garden.

"If those pests are left to their own devices, they'll destroy all our root vegetables," she often said. "We need to eat some of the vegetables now and put up many jars for the winter months."

Most of the jars that lined the shelves of our root cellar still had nothing to fill them, and that worried me. Winter would soon be upon us. My parents had always found a way to provide, but this time, I sincerely wondered if they had answers.

Our three hens seldom laid more than one egg apiece, so Mother had no extras to sell in the village. I'd grown taller and added curves where none had been before. Mother let the seams of my dresses out in all the right places, but still they did not fit properly, and I felt self-conscious.

When I woke the next morning, my sadness and self-pity had faded. Da had already gone to do chores. I came from behind my bedroom curtain, wished Mother a *god morgen* and expected no cake or gift this year. I eased myself onto the bench seat by the table just as Mother turned from the stove and handed me a small dish with an entire boiled egg. In her other hand she held a half-full bowl of gruel with a pat of butter in the center and a lake of cream spilling down each side. My parents had remembered. They had sacrificed the cream for their coffee so I could have this treat, and I smiled.

"*Mange takk*," I said, then rose to embrace my mother, praying the seams of my dress would hold.

Two days later, I hurried through my chores. School would start at 8:00 and I needed to be on time. Da had given me an old piece of leather to tie around my chalkboard and the study book our teacher, Miss Robinson, had delivered the week before. He surprised me with two newly sharpened pencils and a small box of chalk that he tucked in my coat pocket just as he grabbed me for a big hug.

"Have a good day, learn all you can, and remember I love you always," he said.

Mother wasn't much for hugs, but a kiss on the cheek she always enjoyed. Da liked to stop her from what she was doing, squeeze her from behind, and plop a big kiss on her lips just as she turned to scold him.

"What if someone sees?" she'd say and then he'd laugh.

The excitement of the first school day dimmed a bit as I walked by our field and caught sight of Da. There he slowly inspected his perfectly straight rows of corn, looking for any cobs that the worms may have missed. I didn't wave or holler to him.

Ever since I was five, that one-room white-washed building that I called school had served as a place of escape. It overlooked the village and had originally been built by the men who believed in learning. Mother had told me that not all of them did and I couldn't imagine why.

Miss Robinson, who I considered a kindred spirit because of her love of learning, knew how to reel our minds back into the world of study. Never once had I heard her dampen someone's dreams because of their age or present circumstance. I studied her every move.

When I entered the building, I immediately noticed that the other girls, including Astrid, my best friend, had also outgrown their dresses and the pant legs on the boys hit closer to their knees. Twelve desks filled the room, but only eight were occupied on that September day. The older boys had stayed home to help harvest the few ears of corn or heads of wheat that survived. Their mothers, friends of my mother, would insist they come later. I even knew of a couple girls who'd gone through the fifth grade and now were kept home because their fathers believed too much learning made the girls think high and mighty thoughts. I agreed with the part about the thoughts—but I also wondered what could be wrong with great ideas coming from a woman. I'd need to ask Miss Robinson as she, unlike my parents, never sidestepped the most delicate of questions.

At the end of our first school day, I waited for the others to exit the building before I approached her desk.

"Miss Robinson, for a long time I've been thinking and have decided I'd like to someday be like you ... a teacher."

"If you want to teach, Kristi, I'll need to give you extra assignments to prepare for Normal School in Oslo. That way, when you are sixteen, you'll be ahead of the others, and it'll be easier for you."

She hadn't hesitated and I wanted to jump for joy, to run all the way home and share the news with my parents. Instead, I thanked her and slowly headed back home, my thoughts stacking up like bales of hay in a barn.

For the last two years, Miss Robinson had lived in the village during the school year but spent the summer months in

Oslo where her parents resided. I couldn't remember a time when she'd been crabby or unable to handle a situation. Maybe that's why I studied her every move throughout the day. She'd play ball games with the boys and often joined in private talks with us girls as curiosity grew, and our bodies changed. She secretly helped Sissel when, at only nine, her bleeding began and Sissel's mother had never explained about this event. No subject frightened Miss Robinson. But she could be strict too, like when Elmer picked on Clarence, who loved to draw. I'd watched her pull Elmer aside and threaten to inform his parents of his behavior. I saw the look on his face. He knew she meant it. After school that day, I stayed behind to ask her about the incident.

"How can you be sure Elmer will behave now?" I asked.

"Kristi, I will never threaten something unless I am willing to follow through. Over time, I've learned that Elmer's da is a man with a bad temper and might whip him. I reasoned he'd rather behave than take a whippin'."

Every day I learned new things from Miss Robinson and when I shared them with Mother, she often called them *common sense solutions*.

"If you learn about a person's life, and I mean their life at home not just at school, it often clarifies the 'why' of their behavior. We are all a puzzle, Kristi, not just one thing," Mother said.

That day, I'd started toward home but remembered that Da wanted me to pick up a flier from the General Store. What I found there sent tremors throughout my body.

Nebraska, The Garden of the West
50 million acres of grain and grazing land
Offered to actual settlers for $1.25 per acre outside of Railroad
Land Grant Limits
10 years credit

The words, printed on a one-page flier, came from a railroad company in America and caused a fresh sprout of worry-weeds inside me. Only a few days before, I'd overheard my parents discuss some men from the area who spoke of leaving Norway for America. Their crops had failed, too. Never, though, had my da mentioned doing such a thing.

A monstrous fear took hold in my belly as I read every word over again. Had Da decided to go to America because his crop had failed for the third year? We couldn't leave. None of us had ever lived anywhere else. This was home. Grandpa Carl, Mother's da, was here. My aunties, uncles, and cousins farmed nearby. No family member lived in America. We just couldn't go—even though our cow had ribs that poked against her hide and recently she had stopped mooing when hungry. I wanted to talk to Astrid. She would know what to say. She had turned thirteen, been an adult for a whole year even though her parents, like mine, never treated her as one. She'd always listened to me, made me feel better in the worst of times and now—now I just couldn't for one minute think of not having her in my life.

That evening, when Da came to sit by the table, I handed him the flier. I made no mention of its contents nor my dream to teach. Surely that dream would be ruined if we left. Small talk passed between my parents, but nothing of importance. I thought that twelve years of age made me an adult, but if it did, they'd not noticed. So, I went to bed with fear racing around inside me. In the dark of the night, a rabbit screamed, and I cringed. His life had been taken. Mine lay before me and no flier could take that from me.

CHAPTER 2

Time Drags On

In late September, Da began to harvest what little corn had survived. He saved the best cobs for Mother to shuck and grind into flour. Even those would make only a few loaves of bread if we had yeast, maybe more if we fried it. The rest of the crop, I figured, wouldn't be enough to feed our cow and the chickens for the whole winter. I wondered where Da would get the money to buy extra feed this year, or if any was to be had from other farmers.

Not many days thereafter, and before the sun had risen over the mountaintop, I awoke to the sound of someone walking across the floor into the kitchen. It had to be Da. The boards let out a heavy creak, boot laces slapped against its surface, and a chair gave a scratchy sound as it was pulled back from the table. A heavy breath escaped when he bent to tie the laces. As he stood, a soft cracking sound filled the quietness of the morning air. Grandpa Carl had knees that did that too, but I didn't know why. He pulled at the swollen sill of the screen door, but it held tight for a moment. When it was released, I could feel the unusually warm air rush in under the curtain to my bedroom. At his exit, the door slapped against its frame; a habit Mother hated but Da never changed.

Sleep eluded me. Worry, questions without answers, and no friend beside me to talk to made my heart race. Where would he be headed so early in the morning and why hadn't

Mother gotten up when he did?

With the first rays of light, Mother stirred, then came from behind her curtain and headed into the kitchen. I hurried to get dressed before pulling my curtain across its rod. In front of the stove stood Mother, straight as a statue. Clothed only in her nightdress, she stared out the window as she stirred the morning cereal. I thought it strange that she hadn't changed into her housedress. She was a very proper lady and wouldn't want to give anyone a reason to talk about her in a bad way. If a neighbor were to stop by to look for Da, she would be embarrassed.

"I can stir the gruel while you get dressed," I said in the strangeness of the moment.

Slowly, she looked down at what she wore. Her hand flew to her mouth, and she rushed behind the curtain of their bedroom. When she returned, I casually went outside to do my chores.

"It seems Jenny has stopped laying eggs, and the others only gave two this morning," I said as I came back into the house. "It's at least two weeks since anything rested in her nest."

"One of these days, that hen will find herself in our soup!" Mother's harsh verdict flew into the air like a dart shot from her tongue.

But hens and their demise held little importance for me that morning. I wanted to know where Da had gone and why. It took time, but I found the courage to ask. Mother's lips immediately pursed. I knew that meant she'd not reply, so I picked up my books, gave her a kiss on the cheek, and headed off to school.

The smell of chalk dust greeted me as I entered. There, in the front row, sat seven-year-old Millie, the youngest of those who came faithfully. She loved to draw and as usual had leaned forward to concentrate on her next piece of art.

Aric, seventeen, sat in the very back seat on the right side of the room. Maybe because he was older than most, some of the boys liked to tease him when he couldn't properly read out loud. He'd mix up his words and get angry, sometimes slamming his book on the desk. But Aric wasn't dumb. Miss Robinson had figured that out right away. Numbers crowded his mind. He could tell you how many seeds were in an average bag of corn, how long the rows should be, and how much should be left over as profit on a good year. He needed no paper. It all came from his head. I marveled at him. But even more, I wanted to have the gift of insight like Miss Robinson. She stopped having him read out loud except to her, early in the morning, before the others arrived. She praised him for his skill and used a Bible story to teach that everyone can't be an arm or leg. We need all the different parts if we want to make a complete body.

As the room began to fill, I quietly approached Miss Robinson with a new idea. "Do you think I could get my teaching certificate by the time I'm fourteen instead of sixteen?"

"Well, the earliest you can enter Normal School is fourteen, and the classes take two years. I did it that way and I'm sure you could too. For now, you could practice the technique I taught you last week and help the younger students with their reading."

At the end of the day, she and I went into the back room where her coat hung.

"Is something bothering you? Is there a reason you want to hurry to Normal School?" she asked.

I shared the worries about money, crops, and even Mother's desire for the colored thread. "It just isn't fair that bugs should make our life so hard. And look at me. I've grown up and we can't make a new dress. It isn't Da's fault, nor Mother's. But I see others who leave the only home they've ever known, and

I don't want to do that. I love it here. I can run in the forest, up and down hills, into the bogs for strawberries and cloudberries, watch the sea eagles skim over the water's surface and pluck a fish. Nothing could be better than this. Nothing. I don't want to ever leave, so if I can make some money to help, maybe my parents wouldn't listen to those who are leaving."

I cried hard that afternoon and blew my nose on her handkerchief. "Dry your tears now, Kristi. We can't control the bugs, but we can work hard on your plan to teach. It's a good one, though a way off. For now, I want you to concentrate on studying all the worksheets I will give you. Slowly, you'll feel better about your journey to teach. For now, your family, like others, may sacrifice some things; but in the end, working it out together is what counts."

After our talk, I raced home to share the news with Mother. But as I entered the house, I instantly stopped. There she was on her knees scrubbing the floor, not for cleanliness but in a way that told me she needed to sweat out a fear. *Fear feels like little bugs crawling all over, biting you in places you can't reach*, she once told me. *The only way to overcome it is to sweat, to work so hard you can't move anymore.*

Her dress had sweat lines growing from under her arms and patterns of wet on her back. Her hair looked like she'd come in from the rain. Droplets ran down her cheeks and fell into the suds that bubbled up as she pressed the scrub brush against the wooden floorboards. She seemed unaware of me as she wiped away the salty drops threatening to enter her eyes and without thinking, I'd let go of the screen door, allowing it to whack against its frame.

I promptly explained my plan, hoping it would get her to stop for a moment. "I'm older now, Mother. I'll be able to help even sooner," I added, then waited for a reply.

Eventually she sat back on her haunches and looked up at me. "I'm glad you like your studies and have goals. But you should know that women have limitations."

I scowled, pulling back in disbelief. "Limitations? What do you mean by that?"

She went back to her scrubbing. I began to think she might not answer. After what seemed like forever, she lifted her head, stared straight into the empty air, and explained it to me.

"When I was ten, I too wanted to be a teacher. But my mother took sick. I had to quit school to care for her and my younger brother. I never went back after she died."

For a moment, she looked down at the pail, held the scrub brush like she wanted to throw it, then turned to look me square in the eye.

"Women are not allowed to teach after they marry." The words came out like a man spitting snoose.

I drew back. "That can't be true."

"You have no choice. It's the law. Now run along and do your chores."

I never knew what had put Mother into her own basket of fear, but by the next day, Miss Robinson had confirmed Mother's statement.

"If you fall in love with a man someday, you'll have to choose him or teaching. You can't have both," she told me.

"No, I won't choose. Once I'm old enough, I'll work to change the law."

· · · · ❀ · · · ·

By the time supper was done, I seriously worried about Da's absence. I tried to act cheerful for Mother's sake. I didn't know if she felt more worried or angry by then; her silence kept that answer locked away from me.

"I'll clean up the kitchen while you go sit on the porch and watch for Da," I cheerfully said, then handed her one of the lanterns. "Here, you'll need this. It's a new moon tonight."

Reluctantly, she went to sit on the rocker and turned to face the pathway that led down the hill, her elbows perched one on each arm rest, her chin leaning on her raised and folded hands, her eyes peering into the darkness. She did not grind the rung against the floor, but I wanted to do it for her.

The Milky Way and Big Dipper had popped through holes in the coal black sky by the time I came outside. When I pointed at them, she didn't raise her eyes. I had always loved the night sky in Norway, its clear brilliance framed by mountains and often colored in the green or pink dances of the mystical northern lights.

Mother's attention stayed focused in the direction of the village, but my eyes followed the pathway. Eventually, a lone twinkle of light caught my attention as someone moved up the mountain and toward our house.

"Is that Da?"

I couldn't wait. I picked up the lantern and headed into the blackness.

"Kristi Ann, get back here," Mother said in a scratchy voice.

I stopped. Waited. Scanned the darkness. When the light illuminated Da's frame, I hardly recognized him, he looked so disheveled. He stunk of fish entrails and his clothes had stains of blood.

"Where have you been?" I said as the inappropriate words of a twelve-year-old fell from my mouth. Still, by habit, I reached out to hug him.

"No hugs tonight," he said, putting his palm up to stop me.

My heart hurt. Da always hugged me, even when he'd been doing chores in the smelly barn or a dusty field. From behind me, the old rocker let out a groan as Mother rose to her full height.

"You'll not come in this house smelling as you do. Go clean yourself up."

Who was this woman who'd spoken so harshly? Her fear had evidently become rage, and I wanted to defend my da. But he gave no argument. He simply walked over to the pump where he filled a pail with cold water and dunked his head. I was overtaken with a fresh outbreak of fear. My parents never fought as I had heard that others could do. Da was a gentle man, quick to laugh, willing to shake a man's hand and hug a child. He never complained of hard work, nor a night when a man from the village showed up because he'd lost his way. That man slurred his words, shooting spittle toward Da, but he said nothing unless the Lord's name was taken in vain. That brought out the preacher in Da and the man was silenced. More than once, I'd peeked around my bedroom curtain to see him hand a fresh cup of coffee to the man and set a bowl of soup and a slice of fried bread on a plate. Later, he'd walk the man home. Astrid told me her parents wouldn't let that man in their house because he drank too much. Neither of us knew his name, nor asked our parents about him. For me, I knew that Da believed in doing God's work whenever the need presented itself.

Mother, on the other hand, had a more reserved nature. It took time for her to allow you into her private world. Still, I thought of the kind things she often did for others. She came first to offer help when someone died, last to leave the loom where the church ladies stitched a quilt, and always available to nurse the sick when family members just couldn't. She taught Sunday School because they had no rules about a married woman. Her education had gone only through the fourth grade, so much of what she knew had been self-taught. Our house was always spotlessly clean, and she made sure I knew how to be a respectful child. But when Da would try for a stolen kiss in front of me, she'd push him aside and I'd hear her whisper, "Not here, Ole."

My thoughts were interrupted as Mother brushed against me and headed in to get some fresh clothes for Da. Upon her return, she placed them on the fence rail along with a towel.

"Come in now," she sternly said to me as she made her way to the house. I followed; a bit embarrassed because I'd witnessed Da begin to remove his shirt.

Inside the still-warm kitchen, I reached out for a chair, but Mother stopped me. "Go to your room now. Your da and I need some time alone."

I felt like a naughty child who only wanted to be included, but instead got sent to a corner and out of the way. In the privacy of my room, I quickly donned my threadbare nightgown, then sat perfectly still on the edge of the bed as the words of my parents came around, through and under my bedroom curtain.

"Come. Sit with me, Johanna," Da said after he'd entered the kitchen. "Let me tell you about my day."

I hardly breathed. I needed to hear him too.

"You see," he began in a tired voice, "I left early this morning because I've been so worried about our spoiled crop and the little money in our can. I needed to find a job. We both know farming is getting worse each year."

"I know that. But why didn't you share your plan with me?" she asked, her voice beginning to crack.

Da remained silent for a time before his words came out. "I am a farmer. I neither know nor love anything else. But I must care for this family, and this year's crop will not be enough for us or the animals over the winter.

"At first, I only intended to walk and do some thinking. But when I got to the dock, I met a trawler captain who needed help right away. I had to jump on board or lose my chance to earn some money. I'm so sorry I worried you."

From that night on, Da worked on the trawler. He never went back into his corn field, not even to pull out the air-dried stalks. I offered to do it, but he waved my idea aside.

"No use, Kristi. It's just no use. We'll let the land sit for a bit. Maybe the bugs will die out," he said, though the tone of his voice didn't match the lilt in his words.

From time to time, Da would bring home a large fish. Mother made stew with some of it and the rest he dried. The drying had to stop when the darkness of winter came on. That process needed sun and it wouldn't come back for several months. Da's pay didn't add excess money or food like I'd hoped. He hadn't the heart to kill all our animals, so much of his pay went to supplement what he hadn't been able to grow. He'd bring home bags of feed and when I asked where it came from, he said, "America." Mother continued to make meals that did little to ease the hunger we felt—both in our stomachs and in our hearts. Our only hope was for a better life come spring.

CHAPTER 3

The 1899 Winter Sets In

Snow began to fall sometime in mid-October, though the fjord had not yet frozen, so Da continued to work. It made me sad when he'd come home with his hands blue from the cold of icy water and winter winds.

On the last Friday in November, I came home from school to find Mother sitting by the kitchen table, her body tensed, her face etched in worry with red-rimmed eyes. Moans came from behind their bedroom curtain, and I could tell they belonged to Da.

"What happened?" I asked without looking at Mother.

"Your da slipped on the deck of the trawler this morning," she said. "He fell hard against a cleat and broke his leg. The captain brought the trawler back to port so his shipmates could carry him home. Dr. Fjelstad is in there with him now."

Mother stared as if she could penetrate the thin curtain of their bedroom. Her hands shook and I knew they must be cold. *A cup of coffee, that'll warm them*, I thought, but the fire inside the stove had dwindled. Thankfully, Mother had shucked some cobs the day before. I dropped three of them into the fire box and watched as the flames took hold and started to sound like the snap of whips against the interior of the charred metal surface. So many thoughts ran around in my mind from every direction and acted like a fly buzzing against a window he could never open.

As the stove began to heat, I lifted the lid of our blue speckled coffeepot. There at the bottom lay day-old grounds suspended in murky water. The shelf where we kept a new supply for that soothing black drink held nothing but an empty container. *I'll pick up Da's pay in the morning, then buy a quarter pound at the General Store*, I thought as I added more water from the pump, crumbled some herb leaves into the mixture, and stood waiting for it to boil.

"Kristi, your boots are dripping on the floor," Mother said in a voice so soft I could hardly hear.

I'd forgotten to remove both them and my coat. With those garments off and the puddle cleaned up, I became aware of the damp chill in the room. The fire in the hearth had burned down, so I took the poker, shuffled the log jam to keep the flame from totally dying, added another chunk of wood, and watched to make sure it took hold. I wanted the room to be cozy for Da.

"I've given him something for the pain," Dr. Fjelstad said as he exited my parents' room. "I'll not lie. The break is a bad one and it's going to take a long time to heal."

The doctor, who cared for all things from birth to death, went over to the sink, washed his hands, dried them on his pant leg, then sat down to face my mother. Her vacant look made me question if she'd really hear or understand any of the instructions that the doctor would give.

"Don't let him lie on his back too long," he continued. "Kristi can work with you to turn him every couple of hours. We don't want bed sores to take hold. Later, when he feels up to sitting in a chair, make sure you have someone else to help move him. Maybe one of his brothers or a friend from the trawler."

Mother and I had been silent up to that point, but when he added that it would be spring before Da could work, her eyes opened wide, and she gasped. I held my breath.

"I have no money to pay you," she said as a tear ran down

her cheek. "Would you accept a couple of chickens for now? You could choose the ones you want."

A couple? I thought. The idea of their subtraction sent a lightning-like arc of panic inside me. Eggs. Meat. Even at my age, I knew we'd need them to survive and now, without trawler money, how would we get by? My thoughts were tied up in knots.

"Don't worry about a thing, Mrs. Monger," Dr. Fjelstad replied as he reached to pat her hand.

Instantly she drew back, lowered her head, and turned away from his gaze. Her shoulders curled in on themselves. Normally, Mother faced life head on—but not this time, and I sensed Da's accident had broken her like an iceberg calving. Cupboards void of staples, empty jars in the cellar, and no money coming in; she must have felt the heaviness in our future. I casually offered the doctor a cup of coffee to break the silence that had descended on the three of us. He declined, lit his lantern, and walked off into the darkness carrying only Jenny, the scrawniest of our hens.

That night, while Mother sat holding Da's hand, I filtered out some broth for him and made fried bread for sopping. The rest of the winter, Mother slept in my bed so she wouldn't disturb Da. I insisted on sleeping by the fire so I could stir it if the logs broke down. Each day, I brought more in and filled the metal basket by the hearth, but it seemed that the pile outside never went down, only grew. It took about a week before I came home from school to find Uncle Andrew, Mother's brother, unloading a wagon full of logs.

"Use the oldest first," he said without further explanation. "I've made a separate pile here for these newer ones that have only been sitting a year. Never use green wood, Kristi. It'll cause a fire in the chimney."

I tried to thank him, but he'd already turned his back and headed toward home. I told Mother and she cried.

There were others like my two aunties who came to cheer

Mother during the days I spent at school. They knew she'd never accept what they couldn't spare, but still they gave, sometimes leaving a helping of cheese, some lefse, or a few portions of chicken for our soup, but never so Mother could see. I'd hear a soft knock in the night, find the gifts on the porch, but never did I catch anyone. I knew it had to be family watching over us.

There were a couple of times during that winter when an uncle or Grandpa Carl would come by to be with Da.

"You women need time to yourselves—outside. It's not healthy otherwise."

I have no memory of who told us that truth. I only know that Mother and I came home from our walks with rosy cheeks, spirits lifted, and a peace that couldn't be explained. Those times always began in parts of the forest where no one else had been. Snow, sometimes knee deep, had fallen on the mountainside. We'd clasp hands, stand perfectly still just shy of the open valley, and speak not a word. I was sure that angel wings brushed against us whenever a breeze slowly wove its way across the sparkle of those diamond-like flakes. Deer would calmly appear outside the tree line, seeking the last greenery buried beneath the white. Sometimes an arctic fox leapt upon an unsuspecting field mouse and though I felt bad for the mouse, I knew he'd be taken back to the den where the kits hungrily waited. Our sight line also allowed us to watch the sea eagles soar and dive above open areas of the fjord. Rabbits that had changed their brown fall coat to white remained hidden until they moved. I knew that some of the boys trapped them in the fall and used their fur to make hats. I never could.

On school days, everyone spoke of being hungry. I noticed that some came with a slice of bread slathered in grease, but only if their family had given up feeding an animal and could render out the fat. I knew of families that had moved in together to share what little they had and not heat two houses. The breath of their animals filled a common barn. Elders, even my Grandpa Carl, would go live a short time with each of their family members. I remember he refused to stay too long at any one place, thinking he'd become a burden.

Though my uncles came faithfully to spend time with Da, it was Ellert, his friend from the trawler, who brought him the most joy. Ellert had no wife or family and hadn't lived very long in the village. Whenever he arrived, he'd hand Mother a gift of food before entertaining us with lots of stories and laughter.

"These are just some extra things I found hanging in my cellar," he'd say, doling out a few carrots or sometimes a potato with its eyes popping out. One time, he brought a small bag of flour, but that gift came in the darkness of the early morning. His footsteps made a crunch in the new fallen snow and a loose board creaked when he came up the steps. No knock sounded. I waited for a time, then quietly opened the door and found the bag leaning against the doorjamb. The footprints in the snow were too large to belong to anyone else, but I swept them aside before Mother could see and tell Da. He tended to get grumpy about what he thought came as a handout. Only once did he snap at Mother.

"A man should take care of his own!" he'd said.

"Family takes care of family," was all she could muster before turning her back on him and going to sit in front of the fire to read her Bible.

For several days, Da had refused to get out of bed and into the chair. The uncles even tried to convince him, but it didn't work. However, when Ellert came, that man, his friend, allowed no excuses. He hoisted Da up in bed, swung him over the side and onto the chair where Mother had placed a cushion.

"You need to get out of this bedroom," he firmly said to Da before he left us that day. By the next morning, Ellert returned with a solution.

"I've attached wheels to this chair, Ole. Now you can move

about. I've even shoveled a space on the porch for you to get some air."

Though Da protested, his arguments fell on deaf ears. Ellert wheeled him outside, rolled him a cigarette, and the two sat in the darkness of a winter day talking as only men can.

By the spring of 1900, both would return to work. Mother had moved the buttons over on the waistbands of their trousers and taken in the pant legs so they wouldn't trip. At the approach of summer, Ellert felt the urge to move on to another village, though not one of us could pry a reason from him. Doc Fjelstad was the one who told us that Ellert was sick and didn't want us to know.

CHAPTER 4

Mid-1900; Her Farewell Gifts

On a sunny morning in early May of the following year, a neighbor passed by me as I walked to school. Alone in his oxcart, he headed toward the village, his eyes locked on something in the distance, the lines in his face drooped, and I knew he was still sad. Six months ago, Mother had washed and prepared his wife for burial. Dr. Fjelstad had been unable to save the woman. Her labor had lasted over two days. In the end, she'd birthed a dead child. I kept watch as dust rose from behind his wagon. At the base of the mountain, he turned left toward Bergen instead of right to go into the village. No doubt he too had read the fliers about America, but I couldn't imagine making the trip alone.

Later that morning, I had a feeling something wasn't right with Miss Robinson. She smiled, trying to be cheerful, but it looked like an effort instead of a pleasure. She stared out the window a lot and didn't reply right away when someone asked a question. Her nose wasn't dripping, and she didn't cough, so she wasn't sick. She still hugged the little ones but no longer placed her hand on someone's shoulder when checking if they had properly done her assignment.

At recess, I shared my thoughts with Astrid, but she hadn't noticed a change. So, at the end of the day, I stayed behind pretending to work on an assignment. Miss Robinson busied herself with the next day's lesson plans. I, not sure how to approach, waited quietly at my desk.

"Kristi, is something wrong?" she finally said.

I hesitated for a moment before blurting out, "I think you are sad, and I need to know why."

My ears rang with the chiding I would receive from my parents for asking such a question of an adult. Thankfully, my teacher answered in the kindest of ways.

"Like you, I'm an only child," she began, "and my parents are older. They need my help, so I plan to join them in Oslo when the school year ends next month."

"But you always go there for the summer."

"Yes, but this time I won't be coming back to teach."

I can't be sure of it, but I think my mouth gaped open. Her confession truly knocked the wind out of me. Losing her did not fit in with my life dreams nor the plans for learning to teach. School, my special place, had always included Miss Robinson, our long talks about life or a school subject. I'd even told her of my worries about Da back on the trawler, how everyone seemed to shrink in their clothes, and the one boy who often came to school with a bruise on his cheek. She sometimes shared life's hidden side with me but always tempered it with encouragement to keep pushing toward my dream to teach. I told her what Mother said about being married. Her reply was, "Don't let that hold you back. You have a gift and must use it as God intended."

"I'm so sorry," she said. "I know you wanted my help to get your certificate and become a teacher."

"I guess our parents will have to find another person to teach," I said as if that solved everything.

She shook her head. "Crops have failed for too long. That affects everyone, and now no one has money to pay a new teacher."

Air. It had been sucked out of the room. I couldn't think. I couldn't put her words together. I couldn't hold them still in my head.

"Here, you keep this," she said as she handed me the big book that always sat on her desk. "Study everything in it. When times get better, your new teacher can quiz you on the questions they'll ask when you apply for entrance to Normal School."

"But when will times get better?"

Her eyes lowered and I knew she'd not answer. Eventually, she hugged me and said not to mention our talk to the others. "I'll tell them when the time seems right."

I cried all the way home.

Everyone came to school that last week, even the boys who should have been planting crops. "Our mothers all insisted," Aric told me. Before Miss Robinson rang the close-of-day bell on the Thursday of that week, she gave us some instructions.

"Be at the main dock in the village by nine o'clock tomorrow morning. Not a minute later."

Everyone had questions but she shook her head and shooed us out the door. Our anticipation of something unknown and special helped to brush aside the sadness of knowing that we were losing Miss Robinson. Instead, excitement filled the air.

When morning came, I rushed through my chores, kissed Mother goodbye, and ran down the path toward the fjord. There, on the dock, stood Miss Robinson, silhouetted against a haze rising off the fjord. Behind her, a moored ferryboat waited for passengers to board. Our teacher refused to speak until all had gathered around. Finally, with an impish grin on her face and a sparkle in her eye, she handed each of us a boarding pass.

"Today we will all go for a ride on the ferry. These tickets allow you to board and sit anywhere you'd like."

"But where are we going?" Aric asked for the second time. "None of us has ever been on a boat like this before."

"Hurry on board," she said without answering his question. "I'll explain later. The captain can't wait for those who lag."

No one dallied. We all rushed to the front where we found seats organized as if it were a school day. Before the motor on the ferry could roar to life, Miss Robinson came to stand in front of us and said, "I wanted to do something special for you before I left. So today we will ride down the fjord to a village about an hour from here. It's called Mundal. Have any of you ever heard of it?"

No one had. "Well, many years ago the people of Norway decided they needed a way to share books because not every village could afford a library. Someone came up with the idea that, once read, books should be sent to a central location where they could be organized and sold throughout the summer months. Mundal is that location. I want you to see this, to know that the experience of learning is never-ending."

The idea fascinated me, but what was the use of just looking at so many books?

As if she'd sensed my questions, Miss Robinson explained, "In honor of the hard work you've done this year, each of you may choose two books. One will be to keep at home and the other is to share with your classmates. I will pay for them as my gift to you."

Everyone, even Aric who I thought would never like reading, burst into excited chatter just as the ferry's engine came to life. The captain steered the vessel into the center of the fjord and away from the mountain walls that rose high above us. We all gazed and pointed as occasional rivers of water flung themselves over the rims of mountain tops and into the blackness below. He told us the names of those veils of water and why they were different colors. Cloudy meant water coming from a melting glacier. Clear meant it originated from an underground spring.

The village of Mundal came into view just as the captain

had finished one of his stories about Viking ships. Small, much like my own village, it had only one street and that pathway ran parallel to the fjord. Homes and businesses lined each side, maybe a dozen of them in total. Miss Robinson began her instructions while the captain slowly snuggled the ferry against a dock barely long enough for the vessel.

"At four o'clock, the captain will come back for us. You must be here on time. Until then, you are free to wander about and inspect the books in people's homes, in stores, and on front porches—anywhere you see a bookcase."

"In homes?" I asked.

"Yes, if their door is open or they have a 'Come In' sign, then you are welcome."

Everyone raced off the ferry and toward the main street where our search for treasures would begin. Even the boys, who usually fussed about reading, seemed overwhelmed and at one point I noticed they'd all gathered in the section labeled mystery and suspense. I soon lost count of the number of bookcases, some stacked too high for me to see the tomes on the top shelf.

Dreams are made of places like this. The words circled inside my brain whenever I lightly touched a new row of books. And though I wanted to be seen as an adult, I was unlike my friend Astrid who thought only of love stories. I still clung to the ones that pulled your imagination into peculiar worlds.

The perfect treasure for me came when I found the book *Alice's Adventures in Wonderland*. To it I added *Little Parsley*, a collection of poems I thought Da might enjoy. He had little schooling and none past eighth grade, but when I was young, he'd recite some of his favorite poems for me as he milked the cow or worked in the field. I hoped this book would cheer him up. I hadn't seen him laugh or even smile in so long.

It was well past suppertime when the captain snuggled the ferry back against our village dock. Miss Robinson, first to exit, stood off to one side and hugged each child, whispered words of encouragement, and sent them off with pencils as another gift. I, the last in line, tentatively approached her and found her eyes had begun to fill with tears. My hug seemed longer than the others. After she released me, she removed a small package from her purse.

"You cannot open this until you get home," she said.

I thanked her in a voice sounding on the edge of tears, then ran up the hill. That night, alone in my room, I carefully removed the string and brown paper to reveal a leather-bound book containing blank pages. On the first of them Miss Robinson had written, *Never give up your dream no matter the trials that come your way.*

No one saw Miss Robinson leave that next morning. She was just gone. I felt lost, so after chores I wandered toward the school. There I found Lennert, a boy close to my age, kicking a can around the grassy yard. He told me that his family was planning to leave for America.

"Do you really want to go to America?" I asked in disbelief. "And aren't you sad about leaving?"

Without hesitation he replied, "My da said land is almost free, and he can have his own farm there. We'll have all the food we can eat."

"My family already has lots of food," I lied. "More than we can eat. We don't need to leave."

"That's not true. I saw your mother last week and she's so skinny ..."

Before Lennert knew what hit him, I'd smacked him in the middle of his nose. Blood spurted. And I ran.

CHAPTER 5

The Solstice Picnic

In early June, sometime during the night, our barn cat left a gift on the porch. No doubt Da had merely stepped over it when he went to do chores before heading to the trawler. Mother, however, let out a scream that sent Da running back from the barn. I came up behind her, looked at the gift, then covered my mouth so the giggle didn't escape. I reasoned that the sweet creature knew of our need, not just for food, but for something to cheer us up.

Later that evening as Da and I pulled our chairs up to the table to eat, Mother spoke up. "I've been thinking," she said. "There's entirely too much sadness in this house. We should plan a picnic and invite everyone in the family. No one has done that in ages. What do you think, Ole?"

Da pretended to ponder the thought for a long time. I wanted to jump up and down with excitement. Instead, I forced myself to wait for his reply.

"Let's do it," he finally said, then added a slap on the table-top. "Your brother and I could make a table for the food to sit on and if we put it by the spruce tree, it'll leave plenty of room for folks to set their blankets on the ground."

"Could we do it on the night of the summer solstice?" I asked. "That way we would have light all night."

They loved my idea and, though I didn't mention it, on

that day I'd only be two months away from becoming a teenager. Maybe then they'd recognize how grownup I'd become.

As the night of the summer solstice drew near, Da took his trawler pay, bought only a quarter pound of coffee instead of a whole pound, and surprised Mother with an extra bag of flour so she could make her famous cloudberry pies. He also added a block of Gjetost cheese because she loved to put a slice on the pie wedges. Harvesting the cloudberries and delivering invitations for family members were my assignments. It didn't take long to learn how an event as simple as a picnic can bring joy to everyone, no matter the circumstances in life.

Mother's first thought was to clean the house as if she expected King Oscar and Queen Josephine to arrive. I helped but couldn't stop thinking how different the two of us were. I had a creative mind and hers had strict rules. When it came to cleaning, I often became distracted and would miss an entire section of the house. I could cook but neglected to add an important ingredient. Mother would cook, clean, wash clothes, and still find time to sew an article of clothing, mend a sock, or stitch a button on Da's shirt.

On the morning of the picnic, I awoke to the sound of Da and Uncle Andrew laughing as they put the finishing touches on the bench seats for the table.

"No one wants splinters in their backside," my uncle said as he pushed the sandpaper against the still rough surface.

In the kitchen, Mother busily added leaves she'd designed from the thinly rolled pie crust. They would rest on the latticed surface of her pie masterpieces. I went to milk our lone cow.

"Take whatever cream there is and put it in the churn," Mother said as I entered with less than the cow had given the day before. "Andrew brought some too. I've already poured that in so it should make plenty of butter for any bread people will bring."

I loved making butter, something we'd not had in a long

time. Without any need for instructions, I rhythmically pumped the dasher and listened as the contents sloshed about. When they hardened, I removed the cap and there the pale-yellow goodness had formed. I scooped it into a bowl, covered it with a towel, and set the golden goodness in the ice box to cool.

"I think we should decorate the food table with a bouquet of flowers," I said to Mother.

"That would be wonderful. Why don't you gather some off the hillside and put them in the vase from under the sink?"

I ran straight up the hill and into the tall grasses where my feet and legs chased aside the bees buzzing in search of the best nectar. Lavender fireweed, blue artic willow, and yellow buttercups filled my hands when I returned; just enough of them for the cracked but beautiful pink vase.

Dust rose from behind the first cart as family began to come up the pathway. My girl cousins, four of them, all younger than me, climbed up and over the back of the cart as soon as their da pulled the horse to a stop. Little Per, who'd just turned ten months, eyed me from the safety of his da's arms. My auntie handed me the food gift which I brought to the table so she could go inside and help Mother with the last of the preparations. By the time all the others had arrived, the top of the table held plates of lefse, flatbrod, bits of chicken, smoked salmon and cod, a dozen hard boiled eggs, pickled onions, and some cheese. Dark breads, all arranged on two cutting boards, looked like centurions waiting to capture a heaping scoop of the chilled butter.

When everyone had eaten their fill, the air came alive with words, mostly expressing the joy of being together. I felt wrapped in the cloud of love that we had not touched in a long while. It was then that I went over and hugged Mother from behind as she cleared empty plates. "Thank you," I whispered. "You've made everyone so happy." Still, it was clear to me that each family had sacrificed much to bring food to this event.

While adults sat on the blankets and talked, I entertained the cousins with the game of hide-and-seek. But finally, no one could help spilling talk of failed crops, people leaving, and promises of good land in America. It tamped down the liveliness until Da called out.

"Andrew, let's get some ice chips from the cellar."

Bursting with curiosity, the cousins and I followed the men. One of them lifted the door to the underground cellar, then each ducked their heads as they descended into its darkness. We watched as straw was pushed aside to expose the ice block. Da took his pick from the hook on the wall and began to chip small pieces from its surface. As those slivers fell, Uncle Andrew scooped them up and layered some around the outside edge of a metal cylinder housed inside a round wooden bucket.

"Something wonderful will come from this machine," Da said in a teasing voice as he carried the bucket of ice back to the table under the spruce tree. That's when Uncle Andrew took the fresh cream, poured it into the metal cylinder, put a lid on top, and began to turn the crank. The ice crunched. It crackled as it settled, and the cylinder turned frosty cold. At first, they allowed the cousins to help turn the handle, but before long the men had to take over and even they had to use all their muscles for one turn. Finally, the crank held tight. No more could anyone move it. Uncle Andrew removed the lid, and we peered inside the cylinder. "Ice cream," he called it.

"Everyone, come and get a scoop of this delight. It'll fit right on the top of your favorite dessert," Da called out, trying to raise his voice above all the oohs and aahs. "Hurry, before it melts."

A strange feeling came over me as I watched everyone gather a dessert. I couldn't identify its source, and neither could I say why I searched the tree line like a deer on high alert. I said nothing to anyone. But like in the Bible where a voice is described as coming from a cloud, I had the strong sense that this scene, this gathering, needed to be locked in my memory.

When all had finished eating, the cousins went off to play on their own. I sat on the top step of the porch petting the husky who belonged to Joe, Da's bachelor cousin. Behind me the men had gathered to roll a smoke or light a pipe while they talked a bit. I listened.

"Martin, my neighbor, has given up," one of them said in a husky voice filled with worry. "He doesn't want to farm here anymore. And he showed me several different fliers that described the cheap, sometimes free, land in America. You've seen them too, haven't you?"

I looked up to see who had spoken, but noticed everyone, including my da, nodding their heads. No one offered a response.

Finally, Uncle Theo spoke up. "It's a shame. He has a wife and child to feed. He'd need a sponsor in America, if that's where he's thinking of going."

From the tone of his voice, I sensed that leaving Norway was a sin to his way of thinking. The women pretended not to listen, but I knew they'd heard. The very suggestion of going to America made all of them look down at the quilt block they held in their lap. None would ever add an opinion. Like my own mother, they'd keep their feelings private until later when they could be alone.

"Enough of this talk," Da said as he stood and slapped his hand against his leg. "We're here to have fun, so let's make some music."

Without hesitation, Uncle Theo pulled a harmonica from his shirt pocket; Da went to the house and returned with his Hardanger fiddle; Uncle Olav had brought a shepherd's willow flute; Uncle Louis had a squeeze box in the back of his wagon, and Uncle Andrew had a drum. Ballads about warriors and the dragons they slew (*Skillinsviser*) is what they played first. Silly songs came next and brought on peals of laughter from all of us. Everyone joined in when the strains of a favorite folk tune cut through the night and echoed off the mountainside. The women rose, joined hands, and formed a circle, their voices harmonizing with the men. Uncle Olav finally spoke up to call out for some foot stomping music and that's when Mother grabbed my hand.

"Come with me. It's time for you to dance."

Around the yard we twirled, first one way and then the other. As we got closer to Da, I turned to call out to him, but changed my mind when I saw his eyes had locked on Mother's. A twinkle shone in them, one that I was too young to understand at the time.

"Give me that fiddle," Da's bachelor cousin said as he gave a pull on Da's well-worn shirt. "It's time for you to dance with that beautiful lady."

And dance they did as all the while Da held an elfish grin on his face. The two of them glided across the grass as Mother's dress flowed behind her, making her look like Cinderella at the ball. When the music stopped, he leaned in to kiss her forehead. The gesture made her cheeks color, and she gently pushed him aside. He let out a hearty laugh, something I hadn't heard in quite a while, and the sound of it cut through the brightly lit night.

After everyone had headed home, I went to my bedroom and opened the blank book from Miss Robinson. There I wrote: *Today we laughed, but tomorrow the cupboards will still be bare.*

CHAPTER 6

The Announcement
(August 1900)

Six weeks later, after finishing my chores, I sat on the front porch fanning away the August heat. The aroma of Da's favorite tobacco weaved its way through the open window and I knew something must be wrong. Mother never allowed smoking in the house. The orange barn cat had come to sit on my lap and without hesitation placed his paws on my shoulders and leaned his head against mine, an unusual gesture for him.

A little pop sounded as air slapped against the inside of Da's pipe. I was sure that one of my parents would say something. Instead, their silence dragged on through several more puffs. Finally, Da spoke.

"I've been thinking."

He stopped. Cautiously, as if contemplating the worth of each word, he resumed thinking out loud.

"Crops have failed for too long. And the pay I get from fishing will never be enough to feed this family and our animals. It would be hard work if we went to America like the others from around our village. First, I'd need to break the land. A sod house, that would have to do until our crops were flourishing." Again, he paused, though no sound came from the pipe. "Here we barely have enough to eat. And eventually, it will ..."

"Don't say it, Ole," Mother interjected in an unsteady voice. "We can't leave my father. And what about ..."

"I've already spoken to him. He won't go. He says he's too old to travel that far. Your brother Andrew will watch over him."

Mother hesitated before continuing. "Are you saying that we will no longer try to farm here, and are now going to America like others have?"

"Yes," he said. "I've thought long and hard about this. We must be on the ship that leaves in a week. It's the last one until next spring and I want to be on the land before then."

Numb. I couldn't move. My entire world had just crumbled at the sound of those words, and yet, I couldn't make a single tear. My emotions bounced from fear to excitement and then landed on anger. No one had asked me how I felt. I would have told them.

But then, as if Miss Robinson had come to stand beside me, I recalled her final advice to our class. *Be strong. Move forward. Find your dream no matter where it may lie.*

That night, I made another entry on the blank pages of my journal: *Da wants a farm. I want a school. I don't know what Mother wants. Maybe she just wants enough food for the pantry.*

On the morning after Da's announcement, he tried to give Mother his usual hug, but she kept her back to him, her neck stiff, her hand slowly moving in circles to stir our morning cereal. Even his "I love you" came out weak as if he knew she'd not reply in kind before he went off to sell what he could. I tried my best to be helpful so I wouldn't upset Mother. I believed she felt as lost as I did though she never shared that with me.

Everything my mother did had a purpose. Organization, her God gift as she called it, came naturally. Without a word to me, she set two kettles of water on the stove to heat, then ordered me, and I do mean ordered, to gather all the clothes and dump them in a pile. "I want the clean ones there too," she added, and I didn't dare ask why.

"These all need to be washed." The answer flew into the air carrying an exclamation mark, or at least I heard the words that way.

When the water for washing was ready, Mother began to scrub each item on the rough surface of the washboard. I knew her hands would start to bleed again, and we had no more bag balm. The container Da bought earlier in the year sat empty in the barn, a reminder that we needed more for our cow's relief and Mother's chapped hands. It was the only thing that healed the cuts by her fingernails.

I volunteered to do the washing, but she wanted only for me to rinse each item in the cold-water tub and wring all of them out before I pinned them on the clothesline. I don't know why, but I always loved helping in that way. This time though, I wanted to slow the drying process. I wanted the absence of wind. I wished for a rain cloud to come by and dump its drops on the freshly laundered clothes. And every time I pinched a clothespin, I felt more and more like a demented mouse looking for a path out of a maze. I didn't want us to leave, I needed my friend Astrid, and I almost cried.

"Get the suitcases from under the bed," Mother said when I came in from hanging the last of the clothes. "I'll need to wipe them out before we pack."

How does anyone pack a lifetime into a small case? The question kept circling in my head as I took out the thin-sided travel boxes, their exit path bringing along dust bunnies that I'd missed on the last cleaning day. What should I put in my case? Clothing, of course. But to me the only other important things consisted of the journal from Miss Robinson and the book she bought for me in Mundal. I'd read the poems to Da, so that book went to stay at the school, and I'd kept the other, the "Alice" one in perfect condition.

By midmorning, Mother's level of agitation had increased. She repeatedly wiped down the open-mouthed suitcases, but the trunk Da had brought in proved a tough assignment. It smelled musty from sitting too long in a damp corner of the barn.

Da used the morning to sell the remaining hens and our cow who, by then, looked as if her bones were all that kept her upright. No fat. No full udder. Just a limp bag. It made me sad to think that I hadn't considered her suffering, only ours. The few kroner Da brought back from the sale landed with a clink at the bottom of the empty can.

My hands trembled as I ironed, then folded the bed sheets into perfect squares. Air stirred when Da passed behind me on his way to their bedroom. Upon his return, I noticed he held the watch and fob that had belonged to his da, the only treasure that remained of my grandfather who had died weeks before Da turned seven.

"No, Ole, not those," Mother pleaded with a shake of her head. "Here. Take this instead."

She placed her wedding ring into his open palm and pressed his fingers over it. "We are married with or without it."

This time I felt a heaviness in my chest, and I called out as Da headed to the door. "Wait, I have something for you to sell."

A look of confusion crossed his face as I rushed into my bedroom. I came back with two books, *Alice's Adventures in Wonderland* and the heavy book from Miss Robinson that I needed to study for my teaching certificate.

"Take these. The study book will be important for someone else with a dream like mine and the other book is in perfect condition."

Da looked at me, the lids of his eyes heavy, and squinted in concern. "Both you and I will find our dreams on the other side of the ocean," he said as he lovingly ran the back of his hand down my cheek. I hoped he'd be right.

Again, I tamped down my tears as he started a second trek on the path to the village. Mother stood forcing the pump handle down and watched as water filled her scrub bucket.

"What are you planning to do?" I asked.

"I'll not leave this house in disarray. We may lack some essentials, but we have always cared for the things God gave us." Her words came out with a sternness I'd not heard before. I didn't think she had meant them to be aimed at me, they just needed saying.

She wouldn't allow me to do the scrubbing nor add hot water from the kettle. I thought she used the cold like monks of old used whips on their back. She couldn't stop what she feared and hated, the leaving of everything she loved. So, like a madwoman, Mother scrubbed the countertop as she screamed out the unfairness of life.

"Poor. That's what some people would call us. But poor is not about money, nor about the soup with only an occasional chunk of carrot in its murky water."

I studied this woman like someone I didn't recognize. Again, she uttered her deep-seated fear. "Poor is the emptiness that can claim a heart and change a person, take away their pride. It's a demon. No one will come in here and accuse us of being poor or slovenly," she declared.

Helpless to add or do anything, I listened to her. Overnight, the twists and turns of life had put my mother into a vulnerable state. Her shoulders sagged and I wanted to comfort her. Dropping down to her hands and knees, she grabbed the scrub brush with its brittle spikes, pressed down on it with all her might, and vowed to rid that corner from an invisible speck of dirt I'd already scrubbed away.

Around midafternoon, Da returned to drop a few more kroner into the can. I spotted a white area on his ring finger and guessed he'd sold his wedding ring, too. Before Mother could have a chance to notice it, he told her, "We have enough for our passage and a little extra."

She dumped the contents of the can onto the table and counted the money. "Certainly, we will need more than this," she said, hands on her hips and looking Da straight in the eye.

"Yes, but two things remain to be added. I have a buyer for the cart and oxen. The man has agreed to bring the money tomorrow. On Sunday, he'll meet us at the Bergen harbor to take possession of them."

"But we have no oxen. We share them with my family."

"They are a gift from your da and Andrew," Da replied. Mother opened her mouth to speak but Da raised his hand for silence. The discussion would not take place.

When we'd finished the last of our evening meal, Da spoke up. "I have our exit papers in my suit pocket. They are very important. If we should miss boarding the ship, another may not sail until spring. The process would need to start all over again."

I slept very little that night. Out in the forest, a lone wolf called his pack; a rabbit's scream pierced the night air; an owl hooted from a tree farther up the mountainside. I loved the night sounds. They belonged to my life, to my home, and I wondered if America had them, too.

In the predawn light of the Sabbath, Da placed the wooden collar on the necks of the oxen, hitching them to our two-seater cart. Mother rose early to fry slices of bread made from the last of our flour. Only six slices lay in the middle of the shabby towel that she folded over them. She had already added the cooking utensils and bedding to the trunk. The last of our carrots, a few meager onions, and some potatoes that had escaped the cutworms made me aware of just how little we had to survive on. I noticed a twitch on her fingers as she nestled those staples into the corner of the trunk next to the small bag of fixings for our gruel. I vividly recall Da reaching from behind her to place the smoked fish wrapped in butcher paper.

I must not have hidden the concern from my face because Da said to me, "Don't worry. With any luck the ship will make the crossing in good time." Still, I knew we would have to ration our portions until Da could buy more in America.

I too had gotten up before dawn to review the contents of my case. The dress Mother brought home after her friend Mildred died over the summer lay atop all the other items. It had been pulled apart and re-sewn to fit my body changes even though no more life could be found in that dress fabric than in the one whose seams now stretched tight across my hips and bosom. I checked my undergarments, socks, rags, a hairbrush, a sweater growing thin with age, my journal, and two pencils Da had sharpened for me. I'd have to wear my coat even though our weather was still warm. No room remained.

The metal latch on the trunk sent out a loud click as Da snapped it tight. He hooked straps around it like he would a belt on his trousers, then proceeded to hoist it onto his shoulder. Before he came back for our small cases, I surveyed the only home I'd ever known. We'd have to leave behind the ticks on our beds that Mother kept filled with clean straw, the rocker passed down from Da's people, the table where we came together each day to eat our meals or offer a friend some coffee, the doilies made and remade, the two cups with painted-on blue flowers used only for company, the empty jars for canning, the bucket, the broom, and so much more. Memories clung to everything. Da had even left his Hardanger fiddle sitting in the corner by the hearth. Maybe Uncle Andrew would take care of it.

"We should arrive in Bergen by noon," Da said casually as he helped Mother up onto the front seat.

I sat directly behind her, closed my eyes, and breathed in the scent of the pines. But what would forever be etched in my mind was the thud of the swollen front door when Da yanked it shut for the final time.

The seat of the cart groaned when he sat down. His back seemed unusually straight and reminded me of a board measured against a plumb line. His face pointed at the road ahead. He inhaled a big breath, then slowly let it out.

"Don't look back," he said without turning toward either of us.

CHAPTER 7

The Journey Begins
(August 1900)

The oxen, held in step by a wooden yoke atop their massive shoulders, began their amble down the hillside path. Before we reached the village, we passed the Andersson farm. That family had left Norway a month before. I'd been so consumed in our life that I hadn't noticed how rapidly the farm had fallen into disarray. *All things will be reclaimed by the wilderness if left unattended*, Da had once told me. Now I saw what he meant, but I refused to apply that thought to our home. The uncles would watch over it. Still, no one would live in it except any mice that the barn cats couldn't catch and eat.

I thought about the hour Mother had allowed me to spend with Astrid. I'd gone to her house and we both cried and hugged, then promised to write. But I knew sending letters could be expensive and I had no way to get money for paper or stamps. Maybe Da's crops would be as good as the brochures claimed, and he'd give me the money. And yet, as I returned to my family, the finality of that last wave felt like reading the final chapter in a favorite book. The story had ended without my approval.

Bergen church bells rang as we crested the top of the hill and caught our first glimpse of the city. It was many times the size of our village. Houses had a multitude of colors. All of them that faced the waterfront were built two to three levels high with adjoining walls and roofs that looked like inverted Vs.

Three large ships were moored against the longest dock I had ever seen. Their tall wooden masts with unfurled sails called up mind-images of pirates, buccaneers, and lost treasures. One even had a carved wooden mermaid at the bow, her arm pointed straight ahead. I hoped that ship would be ours.

"There sits our ship," said Da as he pointed to the end of the line. A surge of disappointment rose up inside me, but only for a moment. Everything here had a newness to it, and that included what I noticed on the dock—scantily dressed men with dark skins, one of them a striking ebony color. Some of those men worked to check the strength of the giant ropes that held the ship in place while others helped load cargo into the belly of the floating vessel. Mother had noticed them too and fixed me with a look that meant, *Don't stare.*

On the top deck of the vessel were women holding parasols and strutting up and down the walkway. I could only describe their dresses as elegant. Yards and yards of material. I had always wanted a dress with a skirt that could go straight out when I twirled. Mother would think it a waste, but I tucked that fantasy away for another someday.

Da located an empty spot beside a large pine tree and there he maneuvered the team into the shade. "Kristi, take the blanket out of the trunk and spread it on the grass for your mother." I was used to Da asking kindly, but this time it sounded like an order.

Before he could head to the ticket booth, the man who'd bought the cart and animals came to take them back to his farm. He helped Da unload our suitcases and trunk and wished us God's blessing before leaving. His son, a boy not much older than I, drove their horse and buggy back up and over the hill.

Da headed to the queue to get our tickets, and I settled Mother under the shade of the tree. Suddenly, I realized we had no way to change our minds, to go back home, and I felt trapped. I wanted to ask how much our passage cost and would Da have money left to find his farm, but that topic, too, was off limits to me as a mere child only days from thirteen.

"We have our berths on the steerage level," Da said when he came back.

Grandpa Carl had explained to me that steerage meant we'd sleep below deck. "It costs less than a cabin on the main or upper level," he'd said one night when he and I sat together on a hay bale in the barn. Not for a moment, though, was I able to picture what the term would come to represent.

Da soon noticed that the line had formed for passengers to board, and he said, "Hurry, gather up our things. We don't want to be last in that queue."

I folded the blanket, put it back in the trunk, and fastened everything. Da lifted the beat-up container onto his shoulder, offered Mother the crook of his arm, and together they led the way to the line that ended in front of a desk. There sat a sour-faced man, his grating voice like fingernails on a blackboard. Repeatedly, the man dipped his feathered quill into an ink well. He wrote things on a large paper that covered the entire desk. When we were close enough for me to view his script, I noticed that he had been taught the Palmer method of cursive. Each letter perfectly matched the example cards Miss Robinson kept on the wall above the blackboard. Astrid and I had been the only ones to always get the curves and lines just right because we'd spent one whole Saturday practicing.

I tapped my da on the shoulder and asked, "What is he writing on the paper? I can't see from here."

"It's the ship's manifest. Every captain is required to have a list of all passengers who travel on his vessel."

"Is that man the captain?"

"No, just a recorder."

When we came closer to the desk, I also noticed the man's hands. No calluses on them, just a softness I'd not seen before on any man. It bothered me that he wouldn't lift his eyes to look at anyone. His slow and deliberate manner of speaking made me think he considered himself superior to everyone else. I did not like him even though Mother had counseled me not to judge other people.

"Naaame?" the man said as he dragged out the word when Da approached the desk.

"Ole Anders Monger."

"Country of origin?"

"Norway."

"Marital status? Financial resources? Any medical or mental problems? Are you sponsored?"

Da answered all the questions except the last one where he hesitated. "No, we have no sponsors. But I have written to a friend in New York, and he will teach us what to do when we get there."

That last answer finally prompted the man to raise his head and look directly into Da's eyes. "You won't make it past New York without a sponsor," he said with an air of certainty. Then, as if chasing off a pesky fly, he motioned us away from his desk.

The muscles in Da's face tightened, and a redness moved up past the collar of his shirt. Wisely, he said nothing. He merely ushered Mother and me to the walkway as if everything were fine. The weasel man, as I chose to think of him, had given Da a small pile of tags. The numbers on them would match up with our sleeping quarters. The larger cards were for our suitcases and trunk; the smaller ones had to be pinned on our clothing before we changed vessels in Hull, England.

On every single step up the ramp, I could feel an unseen force pull us forward. Home, the only one I'd ever known, rested on a faraway hill somewhere behind us. "We'll never go back," ran through my mind as my foot landed on the wooden deck of the ship.

CHAPTER 8

The Wooden Ship
Journey Begins

Sweat rolled down my back as Da led us onto the main deck and toward a cave-like opening on the left.

Steerage Compartment
No Candles or Lanterns Allowed

"This is a wooden ship," Da said in answer to my unspoken question. "A fire on board means death to everyone. Our next vessel won't be wood."

I followed Mother and Da down the extra wide stairway. Odors of bleach and vinegar made my eyes water and my nose felt like it was on fire. At the bottom, I stopped to survey our dim surroundings. No portholes. No way for light to enter. Row upon row of double-stacked beds were crammed into the compartment, each displaying a number painted in red. Da walked forward until he came to number 57 on the bottom bunk and 58 above it. The beds looked barely wide enough to hold one person. I would later discover that some families had as many as five who rested there because they couldn't afford more bunks.

"I'd like you to sleep on the top bunk," Da said as he gingerly lowered the trunk from his shoulder.

Though Mother looked weary, she immediately began unpacking our bedding. I took out the clean, thin sheets and covered the straw-filled tick on each bunk. Next, I fluffed up the old goose down pillows we'd brought with us.

Mother gave me half slices of bread as she said, "Put one of these under each pillow. We'll have them for our evening meal."

With a final thin blanket placed in each bed and our next meal stored safely away, Da took charge of the suitcases and trunk.

"They'll slide all over in a bad storm if they aren't stored in the hold," he told us.

When he returned, he stood by the beds without speaking; the shadows of the compartment outlined the worry lines that had formed on his face.

"We should have a word with the Lord," he said.

All day I had tried to be brave, but his words lit a spark of fear in me. *My da only ever prays at mealtime*, I thought, as we bowed our heads and listened to his supplication.

"Father, we ask that your loving arms surround us on this journey. Grant safe passage and your faithful presence when we arrive in America."

He waited in total silence. I took ten deep breaths. I know because I counted them. Finally, he said his *amen* and like the lighting of a lamp, I had a flash of what courage requires. It needs the faith that another power, greater in wisdom than you could ever be, is there to walk beside you on the journey.

A loud screech cut through the air and set the hair on my arms at attention.

"What's that sound?"

"They're raising the anchor," Da said. "Let's all go topside and watch as the ship moves out to sea."

Mother chose to stay below and rest. I now think she couldn't say goodbye to our land. She probably believed we would never come back. Maybe that's why she wouldn't allow

Grandpa Carl to see us off that morning. Goodbyes made her cry.

I followed Da to the deck where a faint breeze mussed up his hair and I giggled. Though I hadn't wanted to leave, I couldn't deny that the adventure excited me. I hurried across the freshly polished deck toward the rear of the ship.

"Be careful," Da called out, but it was too late. I had already slipped, and my body was in a backward fall. Luckily, he reached me in time, but his face carried a look of disapproval. I knew I'd worried him. I had promised my almost thirteen-year-old self that I would act like an adult. I failed. Sheepishly, I thanked him for catching me. Without running, I made my way to the stern where I watched the final raising of the anchor and listened to the snap of the sails as men hoisted them into place. They billowed in the wind and pushed us out to sea. I tried not to cry when the Bergen coast became nothing more than a distant outline.

Da studied the sea. I studied the people on deck. Some still waved even though land had long ago disappeared. One woman caught my attention as she stood alone in a corner by herself. A kerchief covered her hair and a moth-eaten sweater hung around her shoulders. Her arms crossed over her chest as if locked in place. A man came to stand beside her. He whispered something in her ear, and she flinched.

Da interrupted my spying. "I think I'll go back and check on your mother."

"May I stay a little longer?"

"Yes, but don't dally. You'll want to find your berth before darkness falls."

"Oh, I can find it. I counted the steps from our beds to the staircase."

Da chuckled and walked into the mouth of the steerage opening. I pictured Alice sliding down the hole into another reality and I wanted some paper to write a story on. It would involve Pegasus helping a noble prince leave the enchanted forest with his rescued princess. *Maybe I'll never grow up, I thought, shaking my head.

A sign drew my attention as I resumed my scan of the deck. I had seen the same message printed on a board behind the weasel man.

Ship Rules
Keep things clean
No smoking below deck
Do not consume more spirits than you should
Card games and dice are not allowed because they lead to argu-
ments

The list went on at great length and I truly judged it a waste of good paper to say things that should be common sense. How could adults not already know these things?

A tickle of cooler air crossed over my shoulders as the vessel moved into open water. Several of the passengers headed below but I stayed to take in details for when I wrote back to Astrid or Grandpa Carl. Besides, I wanted to learn new things. I hadn't known, for example, that a large V would trail behind us as the bow of the ship plowed the waters. And for the first time, I witnessed the sun become an immense ball of red hovering just above the horizon where it met the water. Da used to tell me that the sun sizzled when it sank below that line. I believed him. And although childish faith no longer abducted my mind, sending it to a pretend world, I still liked remembering those stories.

A darkness deeper than any I'd ever known enveloped us. Clouds rolled across the heavens and blocked the sliver of moonlight. My heart sped up when I contemplated our ship floating in water deeper than the fjord. Creatures could rise from the depths at any moment. A lump rose in my throat and a wave of sadness overtook me. Truth came. I'd never see my Norway again.

I didn't want to be alone anymore. I held tight to the railing and walked toward the steerage stairway. At the top, I stopped and looked up into the sky just as the clouds parted and a single star appeared. That small beacon of light made me smile, and I breathed in the last of the fresh air for that night.

Below, our windowless compartment had taken on additional odors: unbathed bodies, dirty nappies, vomit from those who had already become seasick, and chamber pots that needed to be emptied. With great care, I counted the steps to our beds. I climbed the ladder to my bunk and drew the thin blanket over my head just as Da emitted a deep snore.

By noon on the second day, when the shoreline of Hull, England, came into view, I was ready to get off the ship. Living in small spaces with people I didn't know made me anxious. A forest or a mountain, that's where I belonged. Da had come on deck and when he found me leaning against the railing, we listened together to a sailor shout the instructions through his megaphone.

"Passengers preparing to disembark here at Hull must have assigned numbers on all luggage as well as on any outside clothing. A person will stand at the end of the walkway to direct you to the train station. Families must stay together. Those who dawdle may miss the crossing."

Da and I hurriedly made our way back to Mother. She had already started to fold the bedding. Da scrambled to retrieve our trunk and cases from the hold. There'd be no hot gruel that morning, a reminder that fires weren't allowed on the deck of a wooden ship. Instead, we had the other half of our fried bread and a tiny portion of smoked fish.

Da and I carried the cases and trunk up to the deck. He went back to get Mother while I stayed to guard them. His plan had been well thought out but failed to account for the man who staggered toward me with his finger pointing in my face.

"You stole our trunk," he said, spittle flying from his lips.

His breath reeked and I took a step back, but the railing left me no avenue of escape.

"The trunk belongs to my da," I asserted, noting his red-streaked eyes.

That only made him angrier. He moved even closer as I covered my mouth and averted my head from the sourness of his breath. He spoke again, but this time his slurred speech sprayed droplets of spit right in my face.

"Go away," I demanded shakily. The man terrified me. My legs wobbled and I had butterflies in my belly.

That's when Da arrived and noticed my predicament. He released Mother's arm, then inserted himself between me and the man. "Sir, move back from my daughter," he said sternly.

"She stole my trunk," the man persisted as he tried to stand without listing this way or that.

"This is clearly our trunk, sir," Da said in a controlled voice. "Number fifty-seven. Yours will be fifty-nine, the same as it says on your coat tag."

"I'm not stupid," the man hissed as he leaned in toward Da and started to raise a fist. "I can read."

"Dear," a woman called gently. She held the hand of a young girl who looked no more than five. "Our trunk is over there by the suitcase. It's green, remember? Theirs is navy."

"Come on, Daddy. Hold my hand and we'll go find it together," the little girl said.

"Sure, sweetheart," he slurred again. "We'll go over there away from these bad people."

By the time the family headed away from us, I was building up to holler at the man. Da could tell, so he held his palm up for silence.

"Kristi, there is no use trying to reason with someone who

has had too much to drink. Best to let the turmoil die down and just go on your way. Tomorrow he will feel ashamed."

"He should," I said through gritted teeth.

"Everyone deals with life's changes in a different way. It's not for us to judge."

I rubbed hard at the places where the man's spit had landed. Anger still controlled me as even more passengers came on deck. Eventually, I lost sight of the family but then I felt like icy cold needles were piercing my skin. I was starting to panic, to look for a way to get off the ship. Breathing became difficult. Mother noticed and rotated me toward the sea.

"Take a deep breath. The fear will pass," she said. Her voice was calm even though the hand she'd placed on my arm was shaking.

CHAPTER 9

The Train to the Next Stop

"Train station to your left," shouted the rotund man standing at the base of the walkway. He had long bushy eyebrows that stuck out over the lip of his forehead—I felt an urge to clip them with some scissors.

"No time to waste," he added as I passed by him.

We'd been told that vendors came to the docks, but I hadn't expected as many as presently lined the far side. All manner of food items lay across table after table. The first ones, filled with loaves of bread, emitted their fragrance as a tight ball knotted in my empty stomach. Racks, more than I had time to count, were covered in fillets of cod hung to dry. When we passed by the sweet cheese blocks of Gjetost and sharp wedges of Jarlsberg, it was more than I could bear. But Da kept up a steady pace without even a glance at the food. It made me wonder how much money he had left after buying the tickets for our passage and if we'd continue to feel this hunger.

Locating the train station proved an easy task. Its red-topped roof had a smooth metal surface to allow the snow to slide off. A huge black engine that breathed out puffs of smoke sat on the sidetrack ready to pull a long line of cars. The closer we got, the more the red cinders coming from the firebox stack became visible. Air currents cooled those sparks which became flakes of black soot that coated the ground and the side of the station wall closest to the engine. They didn't smell like a wood fire, but rather more like the oil Da used to grease the connections on the oxcart wheels. Mother and I waited on a bench outside the station until Da was done speaking with the man at the ticket counter.

When he returned, he announced, "We're in car number three. The agent told me they don't assign seats, so we can choose where to sit."

Da looked proud when he lifted the trunk back onto his shoulder. Once again, he offered the bend of his arm to Mother. The two of them walked past a car piled high with coal and on to find the exact one listed on our tickets.

I followed but soon became distracted by all that happened around me: conversations, even ones in languages I did not understand; people, pushing and shoving in a hurry to board; and especially a well-dressed lady who struggled with a large travel bag in one hand and her suitcase in the other. She stumbled as she walked across the rocky terrain in her high-heeled, high-topped shoes, a type I'd always wanted but dared not request. Her feet twisted about, and I felt sure she'd fall.

"Oh, excuse me," I said to a man I had just run into.

Suitcases fell from my arms with a crash, one of them landing at the edge of the platform next to a giant train wheel. The man, dressed in a pinstriped suit and bowler hat, stopped to face me, whereupon he brusquely issued a stream of quite improper curses. I wanted to cry. I'd become separated from my parents. I didn't know the number of the car I stood beside. And underneath my dress, sweat trickled down my back and into my bloomers. There was a tightness in my chest.

"All abooooard!"

The conductor, in his navy-blue uniform with brass buttons, made his way through the crowd and toward me. I lifted my head and searched the side of the car for a number. Six. I needed to backtrack to find number three. Salty sweat dripped into my eyes, causing them to sting, and I couldn't see through the blur. I wiped my face and picked up the cases, aiming myself back toward the engine, which was still spewing cinders.

Da stood on the top step of number three. I called out to him, but he couldn't hear me above the station noise. Frantic, that's how I felt as I elbowed my way toward him. Courtesy would have to wait for another day. Finally, he saw me and ran to wrap me in his arms. Without speaking, he picked up the suitcases and took them into the car. My legs shook so badly they hardly held me up. My arms felt weak, and a sob escaped.

"I'm so ... sorry ... I didn't mean ... to worry ... you," I said between hiccups.

Mother looked at me, her eyes all red and puffy. The sight of them felt worse than a scolding. Da instructed me to sit in the seat across the aisle from them. I shivered as he spoke in a stern voice.

"You worried your mother—and me," he added. "You let your thoughts wander again. We could so easily have been forever separated, you left behind, and I don't know what would have happened then."

The mere thought of being alone made me envision falling into a dark hole where I'd search and search and search but never find my family. I apologized again.

A loud blast from the train's whistle brought us back to reality as our coach lurched forward and the engine strained against the weight of its load. For the next four hours, I stared out the window at the English countryside with its stone fences and occasional castles that ignited my daydreams. Still, nothing could erase the fear-filled sting of my failure to pay attention.

"We're coming into Liverpool," Da said as the train started to slow.

The conductor entered our car and instructed everyone on how to get to the ship. When he left, all the men set about to efficiently organize their family trunks and cases. I listened carefully because the possibility of missing the ship's crossing had caused great anxiety for my da. We all crowded into the aisle to wait for that final rush of steam as the engine glided to a stop.

Balancing the trunk on his shoulder, Da helped Mother down onto the platform. Though I tried not to, I couldn't resist a glance in the direction of the harbor. Our ship, the SS Eldorado, was moored there and passengers were already clogging the walkway.

"Kristi," Da called out in a sharp tone.

A man behind me yelled, "Move on, girl!"

Embarrassed, I hurried to catch up. At the ship's queue, everything came to a halt, and I could safely examine our ride. Da had been right. Steel instead of wood framed its length and breadth, both larger by half than the ship from Norway. In addition, it had two levels for steerage. On the first level, some passengers might get lucky enough to have a porthole window. Above the main deck I saw two additional levels, complete with center cabins that opened onto a walkway. Already some of the rich people had boarded and found their assigned locations. Women had begun to walk the promenade deck to show off their finery while the men with their fancy walking sticks held big cigars between their fingers, taking a puff now and then and flicking the ashes over the rail.

As we neared the entrance to the ship's gangway, I said a silent prayer for Mother to get a bunk by a porthole. Da checked that we each had our numbered tags pinned to our coats and straightened Mother's just the smallest bit. "You won't be allowed on board without them," he said.

"*Neste*," called out the blue-eyed man behind the desk. Da stepped forward.

I immediately noticed that this man took time to glance up at people's faces and ask them questions not on the list. At the end of his conversation with my da, he added a sincere smile before saying, "I've assigned you some decent bunks on the first level below deck. And they are right next to a port-hole. That way, when any of you wants to read, there will be light close by."

"That's very kind of you," Da replied. He tipped his hat and shook the man's hand.

This man reminded me of Mr. Bjornson at the dry goods store. He'd always let us children come in and look, even though we had no money to buy anything. He knew we all loved the hard candy. So, at Christmastime he'd allow us to select one piece without charging our parents' accounts.

Neither Mother nor I had slept on the train. I could tell that she was exhausted. Dark bags of skin sat under her eyes and her cheeks had no color to them. She gripped the railing as Da helped her up the walkway. Still, she kept her back straight, lifted her head, and faced forward. I mimicked her stance and thought to myself, *I hope that someday I can be a woman as strong as she.*

When we reached the main deck, Da took us off to the side and suggested we take a moment to look at the city. Liverpool presented a much different view than we had seen in Bergen. Here the streets didn't just have horses pulling carriages and carts, but automobiles, too—something I'd heard of but never seen. Their drivers navigated the muddy road rippled with tire ruts. Sometimes a horn warned pedestrians that they'd soon be splashed if they stood too close to the puddles. Smoke poured out from the factories and climbed skyward to form a blue-gray haze. I instantly disliked it.

But then something came into my head that Miss Robinson had once said: *Not everything can be a fairytale. Life has bumps and we all must learn to work through them.* Maybe my first impres-sions were too hasty. I'd have to learn to navigate them like a ship going around a rocky coastline. But I didn't have to like it.

"Some say that New York is even bigger than this," Da said. It made me think of how I felt when studying for a big test. My worry seemed important then. But Da's task now, his decision to go to America, had no room for wrong answers. "I think we should find our bunks and get unpacked," he added without further explanation.

Many more people made their way on deck while we lingered. Weaving our way around them proved a challenge. I did, however, notice a small area in the middle of the ship a step above the main deck. There, neatly spaced, sat three sand piles and each of them had a tent of wood in the middle.

"Only the crew can light the fires," Da said in answer to my puzzled face. I wondered, but didn't ask, how everyone could possibly cook with only three fires.

This time our berths were a third of the way back from the bow and, just like the man at the desk had promised, Mother had a porthole for light. Water often splashed on the glass which caused salt to build up in the outside corner. She didn't care. It was the thought of his gesture that counted.

This time, I removed some food items, the bedding, and a few kitchen utensils before Da transported the trunk to the hold. He showed me how to tie each utensil to the leg of the bed so it wouldn't slide away during a storm or rough seas. I stored my journal and pencil under the pillow with the hope that they might stay safe there.

"Let's go back on deck," Da said. "We need some air, and we can watch as the captain heads us toward America." He seemed excited, hopeful even.

"We're going to be fine, Johanna," he told Mother as the two of them climbed back up to the deck. He slid his arm across her shoulder, then had her stand next to the railing for extra support.

"In no time, we'll be in our new home," he added, his eyes locked in his distant dream. "When spring arrives, I'll plow the land and we'll have a bountiful crop."

I detected the slightest quiver in his voice, but still I trusted him. I'd not allow myself to ask the scary questions piling up inside me. I was pretty sure he'd have no good answers for them anyway.

CHAPTER 10

A Village on the Sea

My parents went below to rest, leaving me to survey the endless stretch of sea. As night drew near, a man with heavy footsteps came from behind then faced me and said in a nasty tone, "Hey, you." Everything about him had a sinister aura—his voice, his hair that sprung from underneath his hard-billed cap, his stained and rumpled shirt, and his discolored mouth from the corners of which pooled the spittle of chewed snuff.

"Get away from there and go back into your hole. You shouldn't be up here with the first-class passengers. They need air. And you just foul it with your presence."

My temper flared in a split second and without thinking I looked him in the eye and said, "I have a name, and it's not 'hey you.' And, just so you know, I am clean. It's your ugly words that foul the air on this boat."

"Well. So ... we have a smart one here, do we? For your information, this is not a boat. It's a ship. And you are nothing but a poor girl from a classless farm family."

"No disrespect, sir," I began in a lowered tone of voice, "but I'd rather be poor than old and mean like you."

I had no understanding of where that speech came from. It had just spilled out. In anger, he leaned forward to nab me, but I ducked under his massive arms just as the stench of his pits reached my nostrils. I raced down the stairs two at a time even though my legs threatened to give out. He didn't follow.

I knew he wouldn't.

When I climbed into my bed that night, I reflected on what he'd said. He'd cast my family as worthless because we appeared poor. He couldn't see our love for each other nor our determination to follow a dream. Bit by bit, my anger faded. I remembered a time when our teacher told us how a dream gave us something to work for, to look forward to, and to strive to accomplish. "Without that," she'd said, "an emptiness grows in your heart and anger sprouts."

For the rest of that ocean voyage, I made it my purpose to greet the nasty man with politeness. Maybe he just needed a dream.

Early the next morning, I gathered together a small pot, a spoon, a pinch of salt, and the gruel then dipped water into the pot as I passed by the wooden barrel placed close to the stairs. I was determined to cook on the sand fires. Maybe some food would settle Mother's stomach that still stirred whenever the ship rocked.

When I reached the top of the staircase, others were waiting for a turn to cook on one of the three blazing fires. A woman who'd followed me tried to hustle me aside. No doubt my age was all she saw. I held firm and smiled at her.

"My mother is ill. I must cook for my family," I asserted.

By the third day, I'd gained respect from even the bossiest of the bunch. Still, the grumbling continued. I suspected that too little food and too much tension had long ago upset everyone's daily routine. The weaker ones yielded to those who shoved the hardest. At first, I tried to stop what clearly seemed wrong, but Mother convinced me I couldn't change who these women had become. I just needed to fight my own battles.

Even bigger challenges arose on both steerage levels.

Children, according to the ship rules, couldn't play on the main deck. This point of instruction was designed to prevent games of hide-and-seek or catch-the-ball from causing chaos in the already overcrowded steerage area. One day, a rag ball landed on a grandmother's head and her husband chased the boys until he fell, hitting his knee on the corner of a bed. He hobbled back alone to sit beside his wife. Both seemed older than my grandpa.

Quiet time became a luxury no one could find. Privacy didn't exist. I learned things about people that a girl my age wasn't ready to know. One night when I had a chance to ask Mother about what I'd seen, she seemed embarrassed and said, "Not now, Kristi."

I decided to give the belly of this metal beast a dragon name: Falkor. He groaned most at night as the wind picked up and the ocean slapped against his sides. He smelled too, as would a creature long dead, because this certainly was no fairytale.

In addition to my mother, several other people on our level suffered from sea sickness. It made for horrible odors that drove me to spend more and more time on deck. The crew members prepared buckets of an equally smelly solution so we could clean the areas where people had soiled the floor.

A woman whose family bedded close to the front commode room suffered greatly from its odors. She suggested we all take a turn to bring the full bucket up the steps to pour its contents over the side of the railing. I found it hard to climb the stairs while I held the lid on the bucket and tried not to trip on the hem of my skirt. Some of the other women lifted the ends of their skirts and tied them in a fashion that made it look as if they wore boy's pants. Mother would not have approved, but she was too sick to notice. So, I followed the example of the women.

Seldom did Mother venture up on deck. Motion, no matter how slight, brought on spates of nausea and she'd be miserable for hours. When she rested, I often sat beside her and told stories. I spoke of the sea mist and how it dried to salt on my skin; the porpoise and how they played diving games beside the ship; the fish that lit up the water at night and how they all made me feel as if I lived in a crystal ball.

Da, a man known back in Norway as one who'd start a conversation with anyone, grew quiet once we lost sight of land. In the faraway look on his face, I could see that he'd sacrificed his pride and his love of farming when he went to work on the trawler. This seafaring journey, with no sight of land, was hard on him too.

By the fourth day at sea, several of the boys had persuaded their fathers to allow them to break the ship rules and play ball on deck. I too saw it as a harmless way to wear down some of their pent-up energy and, surprisingly, even the crew looked the other way.

The day had started off perfect—sunny and cloudless with a slight breeze. The players lined up after lunch and started their game. No one appeared to notice that the sky had begun to darken dramatically. The parents just continued cheering on the boys as the game became more and more intense.

I had chosen to stand close to the stairwell. There I could watch the boys and still lose myself in the cloud formations that rose in the distance. They looked like they came from the ocean bottom. When the rain first started, its droplets felt refreshing, especially after a morning of hot sun in a clear sky. No one told the players to stop the game. And they had no fear of a few drops of rain.

My own attention soon focused on a boy whom I judged to be no more than seven. The older boys had told him to catch any balls that came his way. We were all watching when a toss from the tallest of the boys sailed over everyone's heads and kept going, toward the boy. He jumped up, raised his arm as high as he could, and made a perfect catch, one for the record books.

But the wind was growing stronger, bringing with it even

blacker clouds that whipped across the sky. Temperatures suddenly dropped. What only moments before had been gentle swells took on the shape of giant claws rising from the depths. One of them rose and smacked the bow head on, enough to jar the youngster off balance. He fell back hard onto the deck. Still, and with great pride, he maintained his tight hold on the ball as a drenching rain poured down like a faucet.

A second wave hit just when he tried to stand. Sea water sloshed across the deck. Parents screamed, but their voices got lost in the fury of the ocean. The boy, still off balance and unable to find his footing on the slippery deck, was sucked with the retreating water under the bottom rung of the railing. In vain, his da had reached for his small, outstretched arm. Other parents corralled their children and headed to the stairwell. Horrified, I watched as the boy bobbed in the choppy seas, his arms flailing for something that wasn't there.

Still, he clutched the ball.

A crew member tossed a life preserver, but it fell short. The father hollered to the captain to stop the engines and rescue his son. I couldn't take my eyes off the boy as the restless tide pulled him back toward England while the ship forged ahead.

His da grabbed another life preserver and started to mount the railing to throw it. But he was yanked back by a crew member. I couldn't hear exactly what he said, but the father tried to fight the man off. Eventually, he sank onto the deck like a limp rag, great sobs heaving from his chest.

That raging storm had come out of nowhere. Its thunder, crashing waves, and bolts of lightning that lit up the dark undersides of the clouds did nothing to drown out the wails of the boy's father who cried deep into the night. His wife, heavy with child, had beat upon his chest and cursed him. By morning her sobs had stopped, and she called out, "I bleed."

CHAPTER 11

More Time at Sea

The relentless waves lashed against "Falkor," who lamented the battering with distressing groans and creaks. I held tight to the sides of my bunk. Many passengers screamed, "We're going to die!"

That first night inside the rage of the storm, Da crawled across the floor to find the barrel of herring. When he came back, he encouraged Mother and me to first suck on one, then slowly chew. The oily fish stayed down—but by the time the storm had passed I vowed never to eat it again.

Three days later, it was finally calm and I, along with many others, made my way up to the deck. The air smelled as fresh as sheets hanging on a clothesline, but more than anything I wanted to get off that ship. I shaded my eyes against the sun's reflection coming off the water and searched everywhere for land. We were like Noah on his ark. Water still surrounded us, and no birds hovered in the sky. I shivered when a breeze passed through the thin threads of my coat.

A man wearing a sweater with stains and moth tracks asked a crew member if the storm had added any extra days to our voyage. With a grim expression and a weary look in his eyes, the crewman replied, "Ja, more time at sea."

"How much more?" the person wanted to know.

"We won't know until we see land," he replied. "There's always the chance we might run into another storm."

I refused to think that could happen. We'd already been at sea for more than a week. My birthday had passed, unnoticed, and I wanted this piece of our dream quest to end.

Putrid air lingered in our cave-like accommodations. Some passengers, like Mother, were sickened with the constant rolling motion, no matter how gentle. Others coughed until their strength left them. One of those people was a pretty lady who often walked on deck with her husband. I pointed her out to Mother because I feared the worst. Mother, despite her own churning stomach, insisted on making a poultice by using our last onion. She instructed a crew member to heat water and give it to the husband. He would need to soak rags, wring them out, and place them on his wife's chest. The woman's pain eased, and she quieted. Her husband, sure of recovery, thanked everyone. But in the middle of the night, he woke all of us with his cry, "No, don't leave me!"

He sobbed when she did.

I leaned over the side of my bed to whisper to Da, "How will they bury her?" Before he could answer, a man from somewhere in a far corner began to sing a hymn.

> On a hill far away,
> stood an Old Rugged Cross.

Other men, including my da, joined in. But it was the man who'd lost his son at sea who made my tears flow. He was first to stand by the husband, first to place his hand on the man's shoulder, and first to cry with him.

After the song had stopped, a crew member made his way down the steps carrying a large piece of white cloth. Mother saw him and immediately went to speak to him, after which the worker headed back up on deck. When he returned with the requested supplies, Mother took charge. In her firm but reassuring voice she called on the other women to encircle the bunk as she began to wash the body. Da accompanied the husband to a spot where the men waited. At the completion of the ritual, the woman's enshrouded body was carried to the main deck by a tall, muscular crewman. There she was placed in a pine coffin, its lid tilted off to one side. I was puzzled by the double bottom of that final bed and wondered about the grains of sand that had spilled out.

The husband covered his wife with the tattered blanket from their bed. "I want her to be warm," he explained.

Our silence ended when nails were hammered in place to lock the lid. Crew members stepped forward to lift the casket, but Da held up his palm for them to stop. That's when six men from our steerage area came forward to lift her final bed to the top railing. We all joined in the Lord's Prayer as the box hit the water. I shuddered at the splash it made.

Most of the people slowly wandered back to the hold, but I stopped to face my da. I had to know. "How did they make the coffin so fast?"

"They always have a few made ahead of time," he said. "The sand in the double bottom is to weigh it down. The holes they drill into the bottom allow the sea to seep in, so the coffin won't float on the surface." He paused a moment, then continued. "It's bad enough to bury your loved one at sea. It's worse if the coffin won't sink."

Tears dripped onto the page of my journal that night and I wondered if Miss Robinson had known that some would die before reaching America. I had not imagined it.

Within the next twenty-four hours, a baby was born too early. This time, the tiny child would be lowered into the water without a coffin, just swathed and tied in a small white cloth, the mother too sick to say goodbye and the da needing help to stand at the rail.

When I came back to our quarters, an elderly couple started the deep watery cough that came with the grippe, and I feared for them. More than anything, though, I worried about my parents and what would happen if I lost them.

Throughout the nights of our journey, we were disturbed by a constant racket of snores, grunts, squeaks, babies crying, and whispers, most of them indiscernible. From among them, I heard my mother's voice.

"Ole, what will we do? I am with child."

"We'll manage," he replied without hesitation. "You just rest."

I pretended not to hear because the idea of having a sibling brought a combination of joy and fear. I'd always wanted a brother or sister. But I knew how much food remained in our trunk and how Mother would need extra to stay healthy. Da and I could cut back, at least until we had money to buy more.

The next morning, while Mother washed her face, I had to ask. "I overheard you and Da last night. Is it true about the baby?"

"Yes, and I'll need your help when it's time for the delivery. No need to worry, though. I'll teach you what to do."

Da and I went up on deck that next morning. There a bank of fog hung so low it made everything damp to the touch. Small water droplets fell from my hair onto my face, and I thought about the captain trying to steer the ship. How did he know he wouldn't run into something?

Finally, the fog thinned, and a shaft of light shown in the distance.

"Da, over there," I said as I pointed in the direction of the now absent light. "I thought I saw something."

Moments passed and it appeared again.

"Now do you see it?"

Again, it hid.

"It might be from a lighthouse," he said. Just then, the ship's bell rang along with three deep mournful blows from the horn. The fog, as if swiped by a giant eraser, began to lift.

"Look," I said. "Over there. Is that a strip of land? Could it be America?"

"That be the port of New York," a seaman said as he bustled past. "We'll dock in an hour or two. Best get yourselves ready. They'll process you through Ellis Island over there, off to the left."

I looked at Da, expecting him to show the same excitement I felt. Instead, the corners of his mouth curved down and the skin between his eyebrows looked pinched. It made me worry. There was no going back, and we could only go forward if we were to find Da's land, like the brochure promised. Could it be that he had lost his faith in his dream? I dared not ask. I stayed on deck as he turned his back to me and made his way down to our quarters.

CHAPTER 12

Ellis Island

The closer we got to land, the more I could see that this city had grown too big for a farmer. Tall buildings nestled against smaller ones, all of them lined up in rows. In the distance, smokestacks jutted above factories and belched their black clouds. Steadily, as if guided by some giant hand, the plumes moved in concert with the wind. I quivered anxiously as I searched for forests and mountains and found none.

When the captain steered the vessel around the tip of land, it became clear that New York City rested on an island and that the Statue of Liberty was its own, much smaller island just offshore. Everything looked like we had entered a book from school. I gazed up as we sailed under her giant outstretched arm that held a torch to light our way.

The engine's pitch and rhythm changed, and our ship moved nearer to the dock where men stood waiting. Other passengers had begun to crowd the deck to get a first glimpse of the promised land, their muffled conversations fading into something of a hum.

"My Henry has a fever."

The tense voice of a copper-haired woman cut through all others. She was standing close to me with a worried look on her face.

"You know, they send sick people back," she said to no one in particular. "What will I do if he can't stay? We have no home if we return."

Her lament stirred a pot of worries in my own mind. Mother had been sick since leaving Norway. Would they send her back?

The blare of the ship's horn rerouted my attention. The captain brought the vessel up against the dock in front of a single building on yet another small island. All engines went silent. The hemp ropes were tossed down to dockhands who caught them and circled their thickness around the pylons. My parents still had not come topside, and I worried.

I hurried back toward our bunks and there stood Mother holding on to the edge of the bed frame as she tried to walk a few steps.

"I'm strengthening my legs," she said with a big smile. "They're a bit unsure of themselves at the moment."

"Then I'll carry you off the ship," Da teased.

She narrowed her eyes and trained them on Da, letting him know in no uncertain terms that that would not happen. With a wink and an impish half-smile, he let the subject drop. I had to turn away so Mother wouldn't see my grin.

"Kristi," Da said. "I would like you to take the suitcases and wait for us on the starboard side."

With mounting excitement, I lifted the cases and for the final time counted the steps from our bunks to the now crowded stairway. It took some time, but I did locate a space to set the cases down. That's when I spied a young boy standing beside his mother.

I'd seen him once before as we crossed the ocean. That time he'd sat off in a corner by himself with a pad of paper, concentrating on drawing. I remembered telling him what a good artist he was, and he'd given me a big smile. This time, his body slumped. He had no interest in looking around.

Maybe it had something to do with the yellow tinge I noticed under his right eye.

When the boy's da came and stood behind him, he and his mother stiffened like soldiers standing at attention. I noted the absence of his pad of drawing paper and his pencil. I was hoping he'd packed them in his case. Somehow, I knew he hadn't.

Like before, the walkway from the ship was lowered and came to rest on the dock. This time, though, two men boarded, each wearing a crisp blue uniform. Their stern faces made me feel uneasy, but I relaxed a bit as my parents came to stand behind me. Gradually, everyone grew silent as the older of the two men walked halfway up the steps that led to the first-class cabins. There he stopped to survey the crowd, lifting his chin as I imagined a king might. Then, in a voice heard by all, he proceeded to deliver instructions.

"Attention, everyone! Attention! Listen closely! At the base of the walkway is a man who will ask you several questions. The answers must match up with the information you gave when first boarding the ship. In addition, each family will be asked to state the amount of money they've brought for living in America."

He paused, pointed a finger, and said in a snarly voice, "Don't think you're going to live off the government in this country. There'll be no handouts here."

A colony of seagulls circled overhead, their insistent cries forcing the man to wait until they flew off. He then continued. "When all questions have been answered to our satisfaction, you will be directed to the large brick building over there."

He swung his arm to point off to our right. The building before us was nothing short of grand. Above its entrance, a sign had ELLIS ISLAND carved into a lighter-colored stone. The few trees that existed, now naked of leaves, lined the many walkways around flower beds that held the last of the season's blossoms. Behind it ran a channel where ferry boats had started to make their way toward a dock.

"Inside the building," he continued, "you will be given a medical examination before being allowed in this country. Those who are ill may be sent to the hospital attached to the building or, if the doctors suspect an incurable disease, that person will be sent back to their home country."

The lady who had been worried about her Henry gasped, and I noticed her man had still not appeared on deck. She covered her mouth while tears spilled down her cheeks. The man who'd recited all the rules glanced her way as he walked off the ship. I was intent on telling my parents something that I quickly forgot once I noticed how perfectly straight and expressionless they had become. In some small way, it caused a sense of foreboding to grow in me where none had been before.

Next came the nurses, in perfectly starched white hats, uniforms without a crease, and maroon capes to cover their shoulders. They walked among the various family groups, looking at people but seldom speaking. The older nurse came to one group where she stopped and placed a chalk mark on the back of the woman's coat. The large C reminded me of the time the boys at school had attached a sign to the back of my friend's dress. It had read KICK ME, and they had laughed when she frantically ripped it off and chased them all the way back to the village. But now, because I liked to ask questions, I learned that the letter on the woman's coat meant that the person may have an infectious eye disease.

When that same nurse approached my mother, I truly thought my heart would stop beating. I gave a prayer of thanksgiving as she merely helped Mother arrange the sweater to better cover her shoulders. They smiled at each other, and the nurse moved on to the next person.

The younger nurse tilted up a little boy's face and peered into his tired eyes. She asked him how old he was and if he felt excited to get off the ship. Not a bashful sort, the boy bab-bled excitedly as the nurse reached deep inside her pocket to retrieve a gumdrop for him. The grateful parents thanked her with a slight bow and used a language that I surmised the nurse would not understand.

The next two passengers occupied the same steerage level as we did. I always thought they had trouble with motion sickness, but I must have been wrong. Whatever that nurse noticed in them prompted a flood of desperate pleading. The nurse did have a kindness about her, though, and she gently guided them off to one side before placing an E and a X on the lapel of each of their coats.

"Wait here," she said. "Someone will come to get you."

I couldn't determine why they needed to wait or what the letters stood for, and my parents wouldn't allow me to bother the nurse again.

"But Mother," I pleaded, "not knowing can unleash real monsters in a person's head—and that's what is happening in mine!" She would not relent.

When the nurses left the ship, the first-class passengers began to exit. Not one of them went into the red brick build-ing. Instead, a smartly dressed man escorted them around the back to two ferries that took them directly to the city.

"Why do they get special treatment?" I asked without looking at my parents.

"Shhh," Mother said in the sharp manner you'd employ with a small child.

"First-class passengers," Da whispered in my ear, "are con-sidered cleaner and less likely to bring in diseases. They also have plenty of money so no one would dare lecture them on that subject."

When our turn came to walk down the ramp, we stopped at the bottom in front of a scar-faced man. He sat in a large chair with fibers poking through its cracked leather.

"*Navn?*" he began.

"Ole Monger," Da responded.

In his oversized ledger with the light-blue lines that kept everything going straight, the man wrote all our names.

"Mr. Monger," the man said, "you will be asked to explain your financial situation when you have your examination."

Da did not flinch. And while he only nodded and thanked the man, the simple posing of that important question punctured my spirit like a pin to a balloon. Matters involving money had always excluded children; nothing could change that. But I couldn't remember any talk of sending people home for lack of money. Still, the question grew like a weed in my mind. Fantasy had shaped my perspectives for so long and now as I pushed against the adult door, it felt like leaping to the next grade level. In school, Miss Robinson had allowed all questions to be asked. "It's how we learn," she told us. In a way, I was like Alice falling through the imaginary looking glass and tumbling into another existence.

"Women and children to the right! Men to the left!" shouted the blank-faced man, his arms extended like a scarecrow. "Doctors will check you over once you're inside the building."

Mother reached over to slide the top suitcase from under my arm. She placed it in her left hand, grasped the railing, and started to climb the stairs. A lady dressed in a drab-green uniform waited at the top. The woman nodded but didn't smile as Mother approached. She was, after all, a soldier trained to do a job exactly as instructed.

Side-by-side doors built directly under the Ellis Island sign were guarded by yet another woman. She wore an apron of white, a scarf tied in the back under her hair, and a huge smile that felt almost as good as the smell of food that surrounded us when she opened the door.

Inside, a girl about my age took Mother and me to the center of the room where long tables had been set in rows and covered with white clothes. Three separate platters sat atop the table, each stacked high with sandwiches of white bread slathered in butter. Once we found a place to sit, workers brought cups of steaming soup. Neither of us ate much.

"You may each have an extra sandwich," the lady who seated us said. "We know it's hard to eat much on a ship and you may get hungry before you settle in for the evening."

Mother only allowed us to take one half-sandwich. Many other people, though, filled their pockets. No one stopped them. The workers merely continued to fill the plates with more.

When we finished eating, we were told to wait in queue at the bottom of yet another staircase that led to a second level. One person at a time was required to climb twenty steps to the top.

"It's a test, Mother. Will you be able to make it?"

She studied the challenge. When she got to the first riser, she raised her eyes and looked at the goal. I counted as she took one step at a time without holding the rail. I felt pride and relief when her foot finally came to rest on the floor of the second level. A nurse tried to move Mother on to the next room. Mother ignored the woman. Only when I came to stand beside her did we progress.

"Hurry along now," another lady said. She opened a door that led to a large room with no interior walls. A multitude of voices blended into a soft murmur. Small tables had been set up throughout the room and at each sat a doctor in his white coat. No privacy existed for anyone as these men performed their examinations. Women lowered their heads in embarrassment at having to unbutton their dresses to allow a listening device to be placed on their chests. Mother and I waited against the wall, taking in the scene before us.

A sob came from a lady on the other side of the room. She was holding the hand of a small child, and a nurse was leading them through another door. I winced at the groan of the hinges as it shut them in.

I trusted no one. So, when Mother's name was called, I stayed with her and stood behind the chair while she sat in front of the doctor's table. He indicated that I should back off, but I remained in place.

"What are you planning to do to my mother?" I demanded, speaking as if I held some position in life far above his. "Do not hurt her."

This man had a grandfatherly face and hair of snow white. I held my ground and refused to blink. My hands clenched into fists.

"I will not harm her," he said, his low-register voice gentling me in the way of calming frantic livestock. "I plan to ask some questions, check her heart and lungs, and look for lice."

Before he could finish, I boldly said, "There aren't any." I'd grown up with the belief that only those who cared nothing for cleanliness ever had lice. I'd not allow my mother to suffer that insult.

"I'm sure you're right, but it's my job to check. You wouldn't want me to lose my job, would you?"

I said nothing but my lips pursed, and my eyes locked on his. Mother squeezed my hand, letting me know that I had no need to worry.

Heart, lungs, skin, and hair all passed the doctor's tests. Questions came next, lots of them. She answered each with confidence. When she mentioned the baby, he offered his congratulations but said no more.

Throat, ears, and nose were next for inspection. In the meantime, the nurse removed a nasty-looking instrument from a jar filled with an unknown liquid and handed it to the doctor. It made my heart skip a beat.

"Please take a deep breath, Mrs. Monger," the doctor said just before he flipped her eyelid inside out. Mother remained stoic, even when he did the same to the other eye. For me, the sight was more than I could bear. I looked away.

"You're pale, but otherwise in good health," the doctor

said. "I'm sure you'll start to feel better now that you're off the ship. I don't much like tossing upon the sea either."

Mother kindly thanked the doctor and exchanged places with me. The routine repeated and after each test he wrote his summary down on the page where my name appeared at the top. When he reached for the eye instrument, I had to ask, "Why do you do that awful thing to our eyes?"

I must have surprised him, but he maintained his kind demeanor and asked, "How old are you?"

"I turned thirteen as we neared New York."

Mother did a sharp intake of breath. She didn't speak, but this time she'd clearly forgotten the day all together, not just the cake.

"To answer your question, there is a disease of the eye that is very contagious. It hides under the lid and can make a person go blind."

I thanked him and clenched my fists as the procedure began. When he finished, I quickly swiped a wetness from the corner of my eye. I wanted no one to notice.

According to the large clock on the wall, four hours had passed since getting off the ship. The doctor stamped our exit papers and pointed to a door at the back of the room. "That's the door where you go to catch the ferry. And Kristi, your mother is very blessed to have you to watch over her. Good luck to you both."

Before leaving the room, Mother and I embraced. Outside, Da stood waiting for us with a big smile on his face, something I hadn't seen in a long time. We both rushed into his arms and started to talk at once.

When the ferry pulled up to the dock, we hurried to board. The sun had hidden behind the clouds, but it didn't matter. This ride would take us to New York, one step closer to Da's dream of a farm.

CHAPTER 13

Entering New York

A gust of wind ruffled my skirt as I climbed aboard and found seats for us in the enclosed area. The ferry's engine grew louder as the captain headed straight across New York harbor. I tried to look out the window by our seats, but seawater had splashed on it, leaving behind a smeary film.

It took but a few minutes to reach the dock. There, a man with a patch on his eye and a filthy handkerchief tied around his neck caught the rope and secured it to the pylon. With a loud clank, a walkway locked in place.

Those most anxious to exit the ferry got up and pressed toward the walkway. Da motioned for us to remain seated while he went to an area where he could scan the dock for someone or something.

"Do you see that crate over there?" he asked when he returned. "I'm going to stand on it so I can look for Hjelmer."

I'd overheard when Da told a man behind a desk that he had a friend who'd help us. But I hadn't known that it was Hjelmer, himself a farmer who left Norway a year before us. I felt left out, especially because Mother didn't seem surprised by this news.

Da rushed off to find Hjelmer and left me to help Mother. As we exited the ferry, I said, "Look at those people bobbing up and down like a jack-in-the-box. I think Da had a better idea to climb atop the crates."

"I didn't see Hjelmer anywhere," he informed us as he jumped down from the crate. "But I did see an area that has some trees and grass. The two of you should rest there while I search through the crowd one more time."

It sounded easy. Just go find the grass. But the many folks engrossed in their own quest had come to a standstill. They paid no attention to those trying to pass by. Mother kept repeating *unnskylde meg* each time she bumped into someone. Da, on the other hand, had a goal. He muscled his way wordlessly through the crowd. I tagged along behind them, all the while questioning the truth of the railroad brochures about land.

Green grass and fields everywhere
Farmland for the taking

We came to the area where Da wanted us to wait. It was ugly and dirty. The few trees stood bare limbed, their red and gold leaves fallen and crushed. Da set our trunk down under a scrawny tree and took out the blanket for Mother to sit on.

"The two of you should be safe here, but don't leave this area. I'll go back into the crowd. Hjelmer must be in there somewhere."

"What if he didn't come?" I blurted out before I could stop myself. But Da had already disappeared into the swarm of bodies.

Softly, but firmly, Mother said, "Don't add your worry to your da's. He carries enough of that on his own."

Mother's admonition held the sting of a whip. My face flushed and my breathing came in starts and stops as I scoured the crowd. Time stopped when I lost sight of Da—at least that's the way it felt.

When he returned, worry lines etched his face more deeply than I'd ever noticed before. "We can't wait any longer for Hjelmer," he said. "It's getting too late. I've decided to go into the city and find somewhere for us to stay the night. I'll come back as soon as I can."

Mother had resigned herself to waiting, her eyes lowered. But I couldn't hold back.

"Da, you shouldn't go alone. Let's all go together."

He looked over his shoulder toward the city's innards. My eyes stayed wide open and focused on him in fear that a mere blink could make him disappear from our lives forever.

"I'm trusting you to watch over your mother," he said as he placed his hand on my shoulder. "Don't leave this spot. I will come back."

I nodded. But, like the worms that had ruined our crops, a thought wiggled inside my head. *If Da doesn't come back, everything is lost. We have no family here, no friends, no language, and no way to go back home.*

It was nearly dusk by the time Da made his way into the city. In the distance, a lamplighter started his evening rounds, leaving halos of yellow from the light poles to mark the way.

"I think I'll just rest here until your da returns," Mother said, trying her best to sound calm.

Pin pricks, the kind like when you've left your hand bent too long, started in my fingers and made their way up my arm. My head pounded. Da had assigned me a heavy task. Watch over Mother. I had to believe that he would come back.

I needed to take my mind off everything, so I looked back toward the crowd. I saw a man jump down off his wagon and greet a young couple from our steerage level. He helped them load their cases into the back hold and showed them where to sit. With a click of his tongue, the man urged his mule forward and into the city. I wondered if they were looking for a farm, too. Nothing like that existed on this island, or at least none I'd seen from the ship.

"They had sponsors." Mother said. Her words startled me.

"We don't have anyone, do we, Mother?"

My question went unanswered.

The night air was getting cooler by the time Da reached us. He caught me off guard with his report.

"I didn't find Hjelmer, but I came across a man who spoke Norwegian. He took me to a building with rooms for rent. It's not like home, but we'll be warm and dry for the night. Tomorrow I'll go look for work."

Exhaustion, fear, the unfamiliar surroundings—they all mixed to erase my normally sensible behavior. Back home, I would never have spoken rudely to my da nor questioned any plan he had. But something bigger had taken hold.

"I thought we came to find a farm for you and a school for me. How long do we have to stay in this city? There's no farmland here."

I'd spat out that last statement, and for an instant Da went silent.

"The truth is, there isn't enough money left for the train fare to take us out West to the farmland. I'll have to work for a short time. I'm hoping we can get there before winter sets in. Remember how we had a can above the stove at home and I'd drop money into it? We'll find one like that here and every bit of money in it will be for our fare."

Suddenly, my dream had an enemy. I had trusted my parents, but I could see that Da's farm plan had missing parts. I looked away from him and there sat Mother with the trunk already open. She, in her perfectionist mode, was folding the blanket.

I stayed a distance behind my parents as they silently made their way down street after street. A tunnel, that's what it looked like to me. Three-story buildings loomed on either side of us. Between them ropes were strung with even the most personal laundry items attached.

Men with cigarettes dangling from their lips and blue smoke rings rising to sting their half-closed eyes stood in doorways while some women sat idly on stoops. Children in ragged clothing huddled around the grates at corners of buildings, rising steam offering a moist warmth. I did wonder, though, where their parents had gone.

Da stopped in front of a building with the number 4581 painted on the doorpost, the cracks of its weathered façade blackened with soot. On the front stoop sat two boys, neither of them past the age of ten. One of them drew deeply on the last of a lit cigarette. He passed it to the other boy, who mimicked his friend then tossed the tiny stub into a puddle by my foot. That's when I noticed it had a ring of red on the end.

"It's only for a short time," Da said as he glanced back at me. "I'll work hard and soon we'll leave."

Does he even know where this land is? I thought peevishly. *All Da has is a flier and a promise, but not a plan and not a sponsor.*

Inside, a small side light cast shadows down the hallway. Greasy, child-sized fingerprints shone on every inch of reachable wall surface. Garbage lay scattered on the risers. I felt bad for Mother who treasured cleanliness and order.

"Our room is on the third floor," Da said more like an apology than a statement. "Watch your step."

Mother released her hold on Da's arm and lifted her skirt. Without thinking, she reached out to take hold of the railing but quickly withdrew it. Because I carried all three suitcases, I could only move my skirt up and away from the floor by raising my shoulders.

At the entrance to our room, Da reached into his pocket and pulled out a key. The door clicked at the release of the lock.

"Stay here for a moment while I find the kerosene lamp," he said.

While we waited, I spied a mouse squeezing into a hole that led to our neighbor's apartment. I mentioned it to no one.

Hopeless is how I felt as I surveyed the room, so dirty, so small, so dismal, so absent of ... hope. Mother said nothing but continued to hold her skirt above the floor. In front of us, a metal chair leaned against the sink while two bed frames, each topped with a straw mattress, sat sideways in the area I presumed to be the kitchen. Nothing smelled right. A constant *drip, drip, drip* came from the faucet at the kitchen sink.

I expected Mother to cry, but instead she said, "I'm so tired. Could you make up a bed for me, Kristi?"

Grateful for something to do, I removed the sheets and a pillow from the trunk while Da shoved the larger of the two beds to the other side of the half wall by the stove. I imagined bugs crawling in the bed's straw mattress but decided to worry about that in the morning. When I'd finished adding a blanket on top of the sheet, Mother lay down without changing into her nightgown.

A damp, penetrating cold chilled us to the bone. I looked around for a fireplace but saw none. The coal burning stove would have to heat the room, but the bin held only scraps, no good chunks of coal in its bottom. They'd have to do for now. Hopefully, Da could buy more in the morning or give me money to find a vendor. I didn't bring the subject up. Instead, I went to the trunk and dug through it to find the box of matches.

Da slumped into the chair and let his chin fall onto his chest. He looked like the loneliest man I'd ever seen. I'd been frustrated and angry, but the sight of him gave me a dose of determination. I would find a school, even if it had to be in this dingy city. I would find a way to be a teacher. But for the moment, I had to work off my anxious energy by cleaning something.

There was a knock at the door just as I finished moving my bed back into the corner of the kitchen.

"Da," I said as I shook his shoulder. "Someone is at the door."

Cautiously, he stood and asked who was there before he turned the knob.

"Hjelmer! Come in. Come in. How did you find us?"

"I'm so sorry about not meeting you at the dock. My boss wanted an extra job done and wouldn't let me go. I had to ask all over this area until I found you."

Hjelmer gave two small bags to Da and said, "I brought these for you. This one has enough coal for making breakfast and the other has grain to make gruel. Around eight o'clock each morning, a man comes down this street to sell his coal. His price is reasonable. Tomorrow you can buy more from him."

I wasn't sure we could.

"*Mange takk*," Da said, turning to hand the bags to me.

"I'll come by in the morning," Hjelmer continued. "You can get a job at the factory where I work. Positions are always open. People leave. People die. Marta and I plan to head west to Nebraska in a month or so. I have a cousin there. He sent us money to help with the train fare. We'll stay with him for the winter and find land in the spring. You're coming west, too, aren't you?"

"Ja. Ja. Soon. I just need a little more money for the train fare."

Train fare. But who did we know out West? Where could we stay for the winter? We're alone with no one to help us. I wanted to scream it. Didn't Da see he'd come here without a plan?

I tried to remain calm after Hjelmer left and Da, like a limp rag, collapsed back into the chair without saying anything to me. His rhythmic snore became a background to the chaos inside my head. I yearned for the familiar night smells and sounds that came through our kitchen window in Norway—a wolf howling for his pack, a moose breaking the crust of an early snow as he ambled along, the hoot of an owl, and the smell of the last embers in the fireplace. I'd not seen nor heard them since that day when Da shut our front door.

I found a rag and some cleanser in the trunk and began to scrub the black ring from the sink. The work felt good though my arms ached by the time I finished. A glance at the stove told me I couldn't leave it until morning when Mother would see the mouse droppings. She'd never cook gruel with those staring at her.

CHAPTER 14

The Cage of Repetition (1901)

The bedsprings squeaked when Da got up that first morning in America. The room had chilled even further and I dreaded getting out from under the covers. The night's darkness had not yet lifted, so Da lit the lantern and threw a couple pieces of coal into the stove. When he noticed my open eyes, he came close to my bed and said, "I want you to take the money on the counter and buy what you can from the coal man."

I nodded, swinging my legs off the side of the bed as he retrieved the coffee pot from the trunk. He sprinkled a few grounds into the bottom but added no water until he'd flushed away any staleness in the pump line by the kitchen sink.

"If we had an egg to mix with the grounds, it would taste just the way you like it," I said in my sleepy voice.

"Oh, that will come soon enough," he replied.

"Then pretend, Da. It'll make the dream come true faster."

He smiled as the water began to boil. Soon, I would hear the familiar slurp as he drank the dusty-colored liquid and chewed on a scrap of dried fish.

The first morning light soon peeked over the top of the only building we could see outside our soot-streaked kitchen window. I hated to have Da leave with Hjelmer. I believed that factory work, like fishing, wouldn't suit him at all. Long ago, in the dead of the night, I'd listened to him tell Mother, "Once a man owns land, there is no going back. It's in his blood."

I prayed. *Please, God, if he must work in a factory, give him money for the train so he can find land.*

I fell back asleep until the *clop, clop, clop* of a horse's hooves woke me. "Whoa," the driver said. Within seconds, I heard some clinking followed by the repeat of horse hooves. Later, when I waited downstairs for the coal man, I noticed six bottles of milk on the top step all lined up in a metal holder.

"Don't you touch that!" a woman shouted in a voice like the screech of a hen being robbed of her eggs.

She stood behind me, her finger pointing and her face as intent as a warrior preparing for battle. Though skinny like my mother, this woman had clearly failed to bathe before coming out where she could be seen by others. Her dress had stains, her face had an unhealthy ruddiness, and I noticed that her hands had the look of longtime neglect. An odor reached my nose when she bent down to retrieve the bottles. I'd learned from helping Mother care for Mrs. Ellefson that this woman needed a doctor, not bottles of milk. Perhaps she had been doctoring herself with an onion poultice because it cost less than medicine.

Da came back to us two hours after sunset. Coal dust smudged his fair-skinned face and highlighted his wrinkles in solid black. Too tired to eat more than a few bites, he collapsed on the bed that I'd worked so hard to free of bugs. Mother helped him remove his work clothes and rubbed his feet and legs. I scrubbed the fabric of his clothes that would forever after carry a gray tinge.

Hjelmer's wife Marta came with him the next morning.

"You now live in a new country," she said the minute she entered. "You must learn the language and the ways, so you fit in."

The men tried not to laugh. I felt excited and couldn't wait to get started. Mother, who had risen early to make a pot of coffee for Da, apologized to Marta as she poured a cup for her guest. "It's not strong. I would have used more grounds if I'd known you would come today."

Marta paid no mind to the weakness of the brew. She bent over to withdraw several squares of paper from her satchel.

"Here," she said. "You must memorize these. It's the English alphabet. Once you learn it, I will teach you to read whole words. A friend taught me and when I leave you must pass the knowledge on to others."

Marta went home that evening having taught both Mother and me several phrases in English. By the next morning, I had memorized all the letters, could write them in order, and knew most of their sounds.

"Marta," I said when she arrived. "You would make a great teacher."

"For this, maybe, but no one would hire me because I'm married." She had spoken the truth of a broken system, thereby reminding me of my goals. I vowed to fight to be a teacher even after I had married. And I didn't just think it. I wrote it in my journal because Miss Robinson had told me that words, once written, can change a life.

Our new friend proved a strict teacher, leaving us with no doubt that our very survival depended on mastering these subjects. Her routine gave me a feeling of self-assurance as I read, wrote, and spoke this new language. When Marta brought up the subject of mastering more practical things as well, Mother said I should be the one who learned those. She had a caution about venturing outside the confines of our apartment which she scrubbed down every day.

The game of shopping, as Marta called it, came first. "Shyness will make the vendor want to charge you too much. You must speak up. Don't accept their first offer when you want something." She repeated these instructions time and time again and she insisted that I speak English as we prac-ticed.

When the coal man came onto our street, she hailed him and started to bargain. The exchange soon ended, and he moved on.

"Too much. This man charges too much and is bad at giving back the right change. Wait until the other one comes by. He can be trusted."

It wasn't long before we saw that vendor moving steadily toward us, only stopping as women ran out to barter with him. His well-used cart held less of the scraps and more of the firm chunks that burned longer. His son, maybe sixteen at most, hopped down from the seat, filled my bag, and took the coins I held out to him. He smiled, bowed, and jumped back onto the seat beside his father. The best part came when Marta made me do this all on my own. I'd even gotten a few extra pieces because of my bargaining.

The more time I spent with Marta, the more I realized that the girl I had been back in Norway was fading away. Marta's view of the world and the battles I'd need to fight became clearer on one exceptionally cold day when she took me to the train yard. There we observed children of many ages come to fight over broken chunks of coal that had fallen when workers loaded the car.

"There'll come a day when you too will do battle for those scraps," she'd told me, her eyes surveying the ruckus in front of us. "Every one of those ruffians, no matter their age, is hungry and cold. Just like you, they'll stop at nothing to stay alive."

I looked at her in disbelief. I vowed internally not to mention to my parents what I had seen nor what she'd told me. They would judge it an act of thievery. I considered it survival.

When we returned from the train yard, it immediately became obvious that the chamber pot needed attention. Marta must have noticed the closing of my eyes, the wrinkled nose, and the squaring of my shoulders. I hated going behind our building to dump it.

"Here, I'll help," she said, reading my fear.

Rats. I dreaded them running across my feet before I could empty and rinse the pot.

"Don't worry. I'll kick those rats out of the way." The strength in her voice made me think of her as the bravest person I'd ever met.

In the short time we had together, Marta, though ten years older than me, became the sister I needed. On wash days, the two of us hauled water from the outside pump because the one in the kitchen ran so slow. And it was she who taught me not to ever pass by an alley without looking for discarded treasures.

"Sometimes people leave things there that they don't want anymore or can't take when they head west," she said, as we dug through a pile of broken furniture.

Early one morning, before the sun came up and after Da and Hjelmer had gone off to work, Marta took my hand and the two of us roamed up and down the neighboring streets.

"What are we doing?" I asked.

"People sometimes put things out during the night. They don't want to be seen by the landlord because they plan to go away without paying the rent. That's when you can find the best items."

Sure enough. Not that first time but on the next we found a baby bed, some rags for washing, a dress for Mother whose belly had grown too big for hers, and a pram with a sign attached.

Our baby died, so take it.

Though Mother expressed her excitement over what we'd found, she spent hours and hours using her Lava soap to destroy anything that could make us or the baby sick.

On our last afternoon together, Marta looked up from her quilting and met my eyes. Calmly and matter-of-factly, she said, "Children don't survive here. Only warriors do."

The next day they left for Nebraska.

I cried.

Though we'd been in New York for a whole month, the can on the kitchen windowsill remained empty. Not even a nickel could be set aside after we paid the rent and bought some food and coal. I begged Da to let me find a job, but he refused.

"Your mother needs you here," he said as I helped carry home the grocery purchases. "And when you dish up the food, make sure she gets the largest portion."

In December, the rent went up by ten cents. After that, our coffee grounds had to be used even more times and the soup held only the memory of meat. Fresh vegetables seldom floated in the water that continuously simmered on the stove. Neither of my parents complained. But Mother's normally rosy cheeks became pale and sunken as the winter winds found their way in through the cracks of the poorly sealed building. All day we wore sweaters or coats even though I stuffed rags around the windows and crammed scavenged newspapers in the openings between the boards.

Not once did I mention school to my parents. The boys who sat on the steam grate had told me I could go and that it would be free. In fact, the law said I should be in school. But no one enforced it, and Da wanted me with Mother.

"Teaching girls is a waste of time," the oldest of the raggedy boys said while making fun of my Norwegian way of speaking English. I didn't respond. I'd figured out that he couldn't read and when I tried to teach him, he got upset. I think it embarrassed him that a foreign girl knew more than he did.

CHAPTER 15

Exchanging Innocence for Strength

"The only way to save money for the train is to share your rooms with others," Marta had blurted out one day before they left. "We live with seven other people and have no more space than you. It's too expensive to stay alone. Everyone must work if you want to save the money to escape the city and find a farm."

Marta's parting advice echoed inside my head. Mother heard it too, but she had either chosen not to share it with Da or else Da had refused to listen.

Da stopped talking about the farm after Marta and Hjelmer left for theirs. Maybe he'd lost faith. The perfectionist inside of Mother attacked the walls and floor with her scrub brush, exchanging everything she couldn't control for something she could. Paint came off the walls and the wooden floors warped as they soaked up the soap and water. I came close to mentioning school but couldn't figure out how I'd study the lessons at night and still do the things Mother couldn't or wouldn't do.

And, just like Marta had said to me, the day came when only dust remained at the bottom of the coal bin and Da wouldn't get paid for two more days. Mother dressed herself in every garment she had and paced a path around the room, but still she shivered. I had to go to the tracks.

"I'll be back soon," I said after putting on the winter coat I'd grown out of since leaving Norway. I purposefully didn't tell Mother where I planned to go. Maybe she guessed, though, as I put on the hat and mittens she'd made by unraveling a moth-eaten sweater I found in an alley.

Outside, the wind had the spirit of an evil witch. It whistled and sent tiny flakes of snow whirling around the corner of every building. I bent my head into its icy breath and trudged toward the train yard. The much-used yarn in my mittens no longer held back the cold and an ache that began in my fingers moved up my arms.

When I approached the yard, two men had already begun to scoop chunks of coal into a truck they'd backed up to the tracks. Each time they forced the shovel into the cubes, some of the pieces fell to the ground and bounced under the train car. At least half a dozen boys fought for the precious fuel in a windmill of elbows and fists. Without hesitation, I dove into the battle where each of us fought to protect what we had touched. Several times a blow hit my arm. One landed on my shin and yet another found its mark in the corner of my eye. No one cared that I was a girl. These coal scraps meant life and warmth to all of us.

When my bag finally held enough for another day, I left the yard and hurried back to warm the stove for Mother. I assumed she'd comment on my appearance, but she only glanced up and returned to her knitting ball, which came from yet another found item unraveled.

When Da got home that eve, he immediately noticed the warmth in the room, the coal in the bin, and my black and blue tinged eye. He knew we had no money, but I stood my ground and confessed how I'd gotten the coal. His lips formed a thin, tight line while listening. He then spoke sternly.

"Never go there again. Those boys could have done much more than give you a black eye." I will admit, I thought he meant a worse beating, but he knew things I'd not yet dreamt could happen.

"I must go," I insisted. "It's too cold in here for Mother and, besides, I can't cook our food without it."

The words flew from my mouth before I could stop them. Speaking back to my da like that could not be excused. Still, I knew I'd have to go back even though my heart felt broken for Da. He'd come to America sure of finding his dream, but now his face looked more like a defeated soldier in a prison camp. I would have cried had Marta not convinced me that I needed to be a fighter, a survivor—I'd not give up my dream, nor Da's.

Even on the nicest of winter days, I couldn't coax Mother to go outside. Something had changed inside her. Back in Norway, she loved the outdoors, and we often went for a hike in the woods. We'd take turns identifying the tracks in new fallen snow or stand perfectly still to listen for signs of life in the sanctuary of the forest.

I came to believe that New York contained no peace and no silence. There were beautiful names for ugly streets. And its nighttime noises were of men returning from work. Some ran up the steps while others dragged their feet across them in total exhaustion. A man who lived on the second floor directly below us always tumbled and cursed.

Mother couldn't relax until Da arrived back home. He said little about his day and she had nothing to tell him about hers. Nothing, that is, that wouldn't worry him. I alone knew of her frenzy if a mouse crossed the floor, or a cockroach climbed the wall.

"Disease can spread like wildfire," she always said as she preached the evils of filth. The longer she stayed in that apartment, the more her anxiety grew.

My only friends came from among the children who huddled at the corner of our building. None of them had proper clothing. All wore faces smudged with dirt and caps pocked with moth holes. One of the older boys sold morning papers and earned a dime or two depending on the edition. He'd buy a quart of milk and share it with the others. I guessed that he'd taken on the role of parent to the younger ones.

"You need to drink milk so your teeth don't rot out and the gang on 32nd Street can't beat on you anymore," he said to the others as I stood on the front stoop early one morning. I wondered then if girls could sell those papers too, because our family couldn't afford any milk.

Most people stayed away from the boys, didn't want to touch them or even look their way. Men often hollered, "Get out of here, you waif," or "They're nothing more than rats the way they scrounge about for food."

One mid-weekday, a well-dressed man bumped into a boy of no more than three. The little one started to cry as the man said, "Don't touch me, you good-for-nothing urchin." The anger inside me shot to the boiling point. I jumped from the stoop where I'd been sitting and rushed at the man. I shouted and probably swore. I stamped my foot in the puddle next to him, then reached to pick up the crying child. Before I moved away, I looked at that man and spat out, "He's just a little boy! You, sir, are an ogre of the ugliest kind." The man glared at me, cursed me for dirtying his trousers, and raised his arm to strike me. He must have thought better of it, though, because he spun around and departed in a huff. At least I'd dirtied his pant legs and spats and that felt good to me.

At supper that night, I shared my story of the man—leaving out the part about the puddle. Da said, "The street children are orphans with nowhere to go and no one to care for them."

I was familiar with what an orphan was, but I hadn't associated it with these boys. "Are there any girls orphaned?" I asked my parents. Again, Da filled in the blanks. "Yes, there are, but they don't mix with the boys. They find their own way to survive." I wanted to ask more but I couldn't imagine there would be an answer I'd want to know.

The next day, I asked one of the boys where he and his brother slept at night.

"Me and him, we don't live nowhere. We got no folks, so we sleep where we can."

Suddenly, Da's explanation became real, and my mind tried to make sense of it. These children had done no wrong. Still, they had ended up alone and it made me shudder. Another boy with ears that stood away from his head kicked at a loose rock.

"My folks had too many kids, so they threw me out," he said, the morning sun shining through the tips of those ears. I felt as if someone had punched me.

That night, tears stained my pillow after I entered what the children had said into my journal. My childhood belief that monsters swam in our fjord paled in comparison to here, where they threw children away like broken chairs.

· · · · ⟊ · · · ·

On the fifteenth of March 1901, Mother's birthing pains began. Da had already left for work and would know nothing of the events to follow that day.

"He'd be no help," Mother said when I asked why she hadn't told him. "Besides, he must bring home a full week's salary if we are to pay the rent."

Mother had coached me on the details for delivery of this baby. I'd tried several times to locate a midwife and found one. But that lady didn't look like she'd ever washed her body or combed a hair on her head. Mother had instilled in me all the reasons for cleanliness, so I simply declined to mention this woman to her.

Mother paced about that morning as I made some coffee and gruel, neither of which would she take. And, for the first time, I realized how she must have missed the women at home. They'd all meet to assemble a quilt, make meals for a church event, or just sit and reminisce. She could take the reductions in food and warmth but, after Marta left, a deep loneliness had descended on her. To have even one of those women in our lives now would mean so much to both of us.

Hour by hour, the contractions grew worse and closer together. I covered the bed with layers of old newspapers and topped them with the thin blanket. I told her we had very little coal left and that I should run and get some. She shook her head and put on a second sweater. She forbade me to leave. By late afternoon, she took to her bed, where I wiped her brow and held her hand, which tightened around mine each time the pain gripped her body.

My brother came out of his warm haven waving his little fists at the chilly air and screaming for all of New York to hear. His hair, the color of good coffee with lots of cream, was unlike mine. His eyes were the clearest blue I'd ever seen.

"He's so skinny," I said as I swaddled him in the ragged towel I'd put aside for this purpose.

"He'll fill out," Mother responded as I handed him to her. "That's what Mother's milk is for. And you should know that his name is Peder, after my grandfather."

Once Mother had checked him over from head to toe, she gave him back to me to clean up while she rested. Peder didn't fuss amid all the attention. He immediately fell asleep when I placed him in the found cradle that Mother had obsessively cleaned many, many times.

Within the hour, he began to cry. I tried to comfort him, but Mother woke and said, "Bring him to me. He's hungry."

Peder had barely begun to suckle when the door to our home opened and there stood Da. His eyes grew wide as he took in the scene before him.

"Our Peder has arrived, and he is perfect," Mother announced.

Da approached their bed and leaned over to view his son. He gently ran his fingers through Peder's hair and onto his cheek before leaning in to kiss Mother's brow. Later that night, he sang to Peder while gazing, transfixed, into his son's angelic face.

Every muscle in my body hurt after I finished cleaning their bed and the kitchen. I could barely move when I crawled into my own bed that night. Morning came too soon, with the sun's rays poking through our kitchen window and Peder crying for his milk. The truth of our circumstances still stared us in the face. We were stuck outside our dreams. Only three coins sat in the can on the window ledge. Payday had not yet arrived. And I had to find more coal.

CHAPTER 16

The Fragility of Hope

By early May, my patience had come to an end. There was no way to deny that unless I found work, our dreams would dry up and fly away.

"I must find a job," I insisted as I faced my da one morning at breakfast.

He took a sip of coffee that looked more like worried water to me. The beat of my heart drummed in my ears while I tried to wait for his reply. When that didn't come fast enough, I spoke up again.

"Please, Da. I'm thirteen and children younger than me are already working in the factories. I know how to sew. The extra money would help buy food and we could save some for the train fare."

A pulley squealed outside our kitchen window as someone moved their laundry across the wash line strung between the buildings. Time crawled slower than a turtle. When his answer finally came, I almost missed it. He hadn't looked at me. He hadn't spoken. He just gave a slight nod, stood up, and left for work.

I slept little that night. In truth, I had no idea what people did in a factory nor how much money I would make. Mother warned me that women didn't receive the same pay as men, a concept that she accepted but I couldn't.

The next morning as we all gathered around the table for

breakfast, Mother reached over and took Da's face in her hands before softly kissing his cheek, a gesture that surprised me.

"Neither of you should worry," she began. "Peder and I will be fine. Hurry along now or you'll be late, Ole. And Kristi, have faith. You will find work today."

I hugged Mother, then followed Da into the hallway and down the three flights of stairs. In the dim light cast by the lamps on each landing, I noticed his shoulders were off kilter. They no longer squared with his body but curved into his chest. On his head, strands of silver grew where brown had once been. How could I have missed this?

Outside, the street teemed with men, women, and children—some even younger than me. They all walked with eyes forward, like our neighbor's blinkered horse in Norway. We passed by a man who appeared as old as my Grandpa Carl. His eyes were rheumy, and he walked in a dejected manner.

I lost myself in daydreams about the people we passed. Every one of them was silent as they traversed the roads and sidewalks that led to a place called somewhere. A few carried a lunch pail. But most, like Da and me, brought nothing.

"Follow those women," Da said, indicating the street where they veered off to the right. "You should be able to find a job in that district because most of those factories make garments. Just look for Help Wanted signs in the windows."

"I can do this," I said confidently, placing my hand on Da's arm for emphasis. "You'll see."

"I know you can." He never looked back after that, just faded from sight as more women crowded the street and tried to pass by me.

"Move out of the way," said one angry woman who'd bumped hard against my elbow.

"*Unnskylde meg*," I said, having slipped back into my Norwegian tongue.

The woman took no notice of me. She tilted her head down like the others and continued to shuffle across the hard-packed roadbed. I followed until I spied a hopeful sign:

Fuller Shirt Factory
Help Wanted

"May I help you?" the lady behind the desk called out.

"I've come to apply for a job."

No doubt my voice quivered, but my eyes had latched onto her hair. Short and in the latest style, neat golden rows had been crimped to perfection down each side of her head. A circle of ruby red rouge had been applied on her cheekbones. It made me think of the time when Mother had crushed some dried red leaves and rubbed their soft color against her cheeks. The difference was Mother made it look natural, but this woman looked like a clown.

"You'll need to speak to Mrs. Ostenberg, over there, at the last desk."

I thanked her and moved on to stand in front of a rather severe-looking woman, her posture rigid, her dress like no other I'd ever seen. Mother had taught me that when it came to dress material, certain colors and patterns should match a woman's age. This woman had clearly gone outside the rules and, to add to the mistake, she had adorned the bodice of her dress with mismatched, oversized, multicolored buttons.

"Excuse me. I'm here to apply for a job."

She raised her head self-consciously, stretched her neck to its full length, and looked up at me with a less-than-friendly expression. Her voice reminded me of a lady in our village who always spoke like she had found fault in you and that punishment would surely follow. The problem came in that you never knew what, if anything, you could have done wrong.

"Do *you* know how to sew?" She practically jeered.

I bristled internally, but sweetly replied, "Yes, my mother taught me years ago."

"But do *you* know how to use a sewing machine?"

Her accusatory tone rubbed me like sandpaper, so I took a moment before replying, "Yes, we had one in Norway." In truth, the machine belonged to my aunt, and I'd only used it twice.

From a carefully organized bin on her desk, the woman took out a piece of paper and slid it toward me. "So. Can you write?"

I was being insulted, but I smiled anyway before responding. "I read and write all the time."

"Then put your name and address here." She indicated a specific line on the paper.

My age never came into question. After I proudly wrote the information in the precise manner taught by Miss Robinson, I looked up at the lady. Her lips and the corners of her eyes had tightened. She glanced at my name, but she didn't bother to use it. She merely said a terse, "Follow me."

Taller than most women, her rigid stance made her look like one of Da's leveling devices had fused into her spine and I almost laughed. She lifted her chin slightly in the direction of the solid mahogany-stained door and started to walk. A black painted sign beside the door read *Factory Entrance.*

CHAPTER 17

Factory Life

My rigid overseer yanked open the beat-up door. Inside, row after row of women were bent forward over sewing machines, trying to guide their fabrics in lines both straight and curved. *Clicks* and *clunks* issued from the needles jabbing material and the women working foot pedals. Body odors mingled with those of machine oil. The room I'd first viewed as large now seemed much smaller because I had the sense that its walls were closing in on me. I must have stopped walking because the woman hollered at me.

"Well. Come on! Don't dawdle!"

"I'm sorry," I said, running to catch up.

Tin soldiers. That's how I'd describe the machines if I could write a story for my students. One after another, they were lined up in rows facing each other with just enough space between them for one person to pass. Another lady, this one dressed in a drab green uniform, walked halfway down the aisle and passed in front of us. I could only see her back. But her soldier-like way of walking made me think she'd like to find women to holler at.

I kept up with the tall woman in the strange dress until she stopped and pointed to a machine without an operator.

"Here. Use this one. Your job will be to sew the side seams on the shirts."

Stiffly, she walked back toward the door that led to her

desk. I half expected her to click her heels together and march. I didn't know if I should laugh or cry, so I just sat down.

At first no one around me lifted their head or spoke. I had no idea where or how to start. This machine bore no semblance to my aunt's. And besides, she hadn't taught me to thread the bobbin.

I glanced at the woman on my left. Her hair style brought back memories of Marta, lending me the idea that I might ask her for help. Instead, I gasped when she stopped her work, looked at me, and smiled. Her finger went to her lips to indicate I should remain silent. After a quick look to determine the whereabouts of the supervisor, she whispered, "Watch me."

I made a few mistakes in the beginning but soon enough I learned to thread the machine, stitch the seams in the proper manner, and pile the finished work on the table in front of me. From time to time, another worker came, took my pile of shirts, and carried them over to other workers who added sleeves, cuffs, collars, or buttons. When complete, the shirts ended up on a table next to two machines that billowed steam whenever the operator pulled down the lid. The older women, scarves tied around their heads, maneuvered those open-jawed hulks in a precise rhythm. "They're called mangles," explained my work neighbor who had dared to help me. I'd never seen anything like them and instantly sensed danger.

My attention must have strayed too long because from behind me came a deep voice that startled me.

"You must finish all the work in front of you before your shift ends. We tolerate no slackers."

Her criticism felt like a slap. I quickly leaned toward the machine while placing my foot against the ornate metal pedal with "Singer" stamped in the middle. The smell of her body occupied the space behind me long after she departed. I only relaxed a bit when she moved on to berate others. I fantasized about her falling into a vat of starch that made her walk like a wooden doll until she learned to be more pleasant. The vision forced me to cover my mouth so I wouldn't laugh out loud.

Our first break came a full six hours after I'd arrived, and I urgently needed to find the commode room. Fifteen minutes, that's all we were allowed—not nearly enough time to navigate a room crammed with workers and only four commodes.

I concentrated on the sounds around me as I made my way back to the machine: the shuffle of feet along the floors, the scraping of chairs dragged back and forth, the hum of machines operated twelve hours a day, and the swoosh of mangles opened and shut like menacing beasts. To the owners it probably sounded like money. To me it sounded like a dragon's roar.

In midafternoon, a scream that could have curdled milk echoed off the walls and brought all work to a stop. The lid on one of the mangles had slipped from the hand of the woman operating it. It fell on her arm, smashing the bone between its plates and sending the smell of burning flesh into the already rancid air.

"Get back to work!" shouted the supervisor as two other workers rushed to lift the cover.

"How could you be so careless?" the drab-green clothed lady shouted in the injured woman's face. "You. Yes, you." She signaled to a worker sewing buttons on shirts who was trying not to be noticed. "Get over here and operate this mangle. We have quotas to meet."

"And you, you're finished here. Get out," the supervisor said to the injured woman whose gray hair was wrapped in a purple head scarf. "And there'll be no pay for you this week."

From behind me came a lady who looked as if she'd worked on a farm all her life. Her large hands, patchy with raw skin, carried a cloth dripping with cold water. She wove her way past the supervisor and gently wound the cloth around the burnt arm. With one arm resting on the injured woman's shoulder and the other keeping the cloth in place, the farm lady walked the sobbing woman out the back door.

"I don't want to see either of you back here ever again."

The supervisor's cruel words used up every bit of air in the room. But no one missed seeing the bright red as it moved up the neck of that drab-dressed matron. Again, she started to bark out orders to others as if her life depended on it. Maybe her job did. But I no longer feared her. I vowed to survive despite her actions.

By the time I returned home that night, I was nearly limp. Mother insisted I eat, though to do so took my last drop of energy. She asked how my day had gone. I gave her the minimum and spared her the details. "Fine." Disappointment appeared in her eyes, but I knew the truth would make her insist that I not go back. I had to go. For me, the desire to escape the city pulled like a magnet. Da needed his farm. I needed my school. Nothing would make me quit.

I didn't hear Da come home from work that night and hardly recognized his voice the next morning as he stood over me. "Time to get up, Kristi."

Mother had boiled an egg and made gruel. I still wasn't hungry, but I'd seen the problems working a twelve-hour shift without food could bring.

On my way to the factory, I caught up with the woman who sat next to me. The night before, she'd explained that the back door was for workers to enter or leave. "You'll be fired for sure if you ever go out the front one," she warned.

At six o'clock on Saturday evening, the whistle blew to mark my first full week at the job.

"Come on. I'll show you where to get your pay," said my new friend. She led me to a queue that inched toward a small room with a window. Only a half dozen or so others were lined up in front of me when I finally saw the man and the money he disbursed. Those who were considered grown women received a bigger pile of paper money than the children, and I certainly did not consider myself to be one of them. Besides, none of the money piles equaled what I figured Da would bring home if he worked in this factory.

By the time I came up to the window, I had worked myself into a frenzy and an angry protest spilled out.

"Why is it that we all worked the same number of hours and yet don't receive the same pay?"

The man standing behind the glass skillfully took aim at the spittoon in the corner, spewing a thread of brown liquid. He looked back with a sneer that exposed holes where teeth had gone missing.

"If you want to keep this job, little girl, I suggest you take the money and be quiet."

"I'm not a little girl," I said as I plucked the dollar bills from him. I counted only half the pay awarded to the woman who sat next to me. I glared at the man and walked away.

This time I told Mother, who scolded me. "You must keep your thoughts to yourself, or no one will hire you."

I did keep quiet after that, though I soon noticed the friends I'd made the first week no longer talked to me.

I felt proud to drop a coin in the can, and even Da put one in. Mother smiled as if the act had sprinkled fairy dust on her and lit the fire of hope once more. The money I earned, though small, allowed Mother to add an occasional slice of meat to our meals. One week she even purchased a block of cheese and two oranges. The sweetest change, though, was the lilt of her humming while she set the table.

I soon concluded that the women and children at the factory only worked to survive. No one was chasing a dream. Their spirits had shriveled and died.

I'd not let that happen to me.

CHAPTER 18

Life Changes

Summer arrived with a heat that continually sapped our energy. For days, no breeze came through the kitchen window nor down the city streets. Nights never cooled. Some people slept on their fire escape landings. I wanted to, but my parents refused to allow it even though all I wanted to do was see the stars come out at night.

"The lights of the city will hide the stars," Da said in a downcast manner. "Anyway, the factory smoke hides everything."

Inside the factory, our bodies dripped with sweat and the gears of our machines grew hot to the touch. The trapped air smelled worse than ever, but no one dared ask the supervisor to open the windows or turn on the fans. The lady sitting next to me said that everyone feared losing their jobs if they spoke up. "Best to keep quiet," she said.

But the day came when I could no longer be silent. I just needed to be kind when I did speak up, like Mother had told me. "If you oversee others," she said, "it's a lonely job, and no one wants to be your friend."

So, on the hottest day I'd ever experienced, I waited until the stiff-necked lady walked behind my chair. "Excuse me," I said. "Could you please have someone open the windows or turn on the fans?"

It took a moment for her reply. When it came, I listened intently.

"Soot will come in if the windows are opened and that will ruin the fabric," she said before wiping the sweat off her brow. "And the fans are broken—there is no one to fix them."

"Thank you," I said, adding, "that makes sense, and no doubt you must be as miserable as we are."

She hesitated just long enough for me to catch a fleeting sadness in her eyes. Still, even after my question, her reprimands continued. And though we all tried our best to keep sweat off the material, when it did fall, she was right there to criticize. Mother had explained to me that this woman should be pitied. Most likely, her pay depended on how many shirts we successfully finished. Nonetheless, I could see that many hated her. Others took her meanness to heart and cringed when she spoke. I managed by thinking of myself as a princess in a castle. Words couldn't climb walls, so only my lack of concentration could hurt me.

CHAPTER 19

Clouds of Sickness Descend

Mother had regained her joy-filled nature after Peder arrived. Da carried the pram down for her and set it by the stoop so she and Peder could "get some air." Despite the heat, they took long walks every day—that is, until I came home with rumors. The women at the factory told of a disease called scarlet fever. Many knew people who had died from it. And on the way home that day, I came across a sign in a window that read:

Quarantine
Keep Away

From the look on Mother's face, I almost wished I hadn't told her. Her cleaning frenzies returned that very evening and all her walks came to a stop. Da and I were told to wash with lava soap and its pumice made our hands bleed. Every night, she boiled our clothes and scrubbed them so hard that the fabric soon wore even thinner than before. Streaks appeared on the walls where repeated scrubbing had begun to destroy the surface. She insisted that our kitchen window remain shut. When Da and I closed the door on our way out, she had us stuff rags under it. Fear had started a personal war within her.

The orphan boys, who had become my friends, told me they knew of the sickness but had no fear of dying. Their worry came from the thought of being buried in Potter's Field, a place I knew nothing about.

"At Potter's, you're no more than a bag of bones left to rot in a common grave. No coffin for you," one of them offered.

"Yaaah," another spoke up. "They toss you in a deep hole, cover you with some dirt, then add more bodies until you sink so low even God can't find you."

I didn't know if I should believe them. When I asked someone at work, they told me it was all true. If you had no money, the undertakers didn't waste time making a coffin or adding a marker so your grave could be found. The thought made me so sad I almost cried.

Six-year-old Daniel died on a Sunday morning. Truth be told, he'd been my favorite with his red hair, steel-blue eyes, and a happy disposition that broke into a gap-toothed smile whenever I came around. About a week earlier, spits of blood had started showing up when he coughed. I gave him my handkerchief. He didn't seem to mind that it had a flower embroidered on the corner. At the end, his friends carefully placed him in a sling made from a yellowing sheet stolen off someone's line.

"Where will you take him?" I asked as an older boy was placing a small raggedy blanket under Daniel's arm.

"We'll keep him hidden here until after dark," another of the boys said. "Can't let the police find him. Later tonight, we'll bury him in a grassy area where we can put a marker."

"Just a minute," I said. I ran back into the building to rescue the toy rabbit some other child had thrown onto the first riser.

"Here, he needs this," I said as I gave it to the leader. "He's afraid of the dark and the rabbit will keep him company."

Days came and went in a blur. Each morning, Da and I went to work spotlessly clean. By nightfall, we'd come back smelling of sweat and streaked with factory grime. Mother no longer sang to Peder. She asked no questions about our days. Da took on a look of defeat. His muscles, once tight in his shirt sleeve, began to wither. I made up stories during the day and told them to Peder at night as he giggled and cooed.

Finally, an evening came when a welcome breeze skimmed my face while walking home. Everything ached from leaning over the machine and the factory's heat had sapped all my energy. Sluggishly, I mounted the five steps leading to the front door of our building and when I opened it there could be no doubt that nothing had changed inside. The odors of people, their food, and commodes that needed dumping truly made me want to just stay outside. At the very least, I hoped to persuade Mother to open the window.

Up the stairs I trudged to the third-floor landing. Bending over to remove the rags from beneath the door, I heard a deep moan from inside the apartment that sent shivers up my arms. I swung the door open, and there stood Mother with Peder lying limp against her shoulder, her eyes two blanks. She babbled nonsense, and I feared she would collapse. My brother was dressed only in a nappy, his rosy cheeks chapped and his little mouth slack. I touched his back and found it burning with fever.

"Mother, give him to me."

I struggled to untangle him from her arms. Peder was inert, like a wilted plant in need of water. He didn't move when I placed him atop my bed and no sound came from his parched lips.

You know what to do. Just concentrate.

The words circulated in my brain like a chant as I filled the basin with cool water, grabbed a clean rag, and began to sponge his body. I wanted Vaseline for his chapped lips, but we'd not brought any when we left Norway. My hands shook and for an instant panic took over. Between moments of sponging his body, something told me to drip water into his mouth, so I did, hoping he'd swallow. Most ran out, but I kept trying.

Mother paced, mumbled, scratched at her arms. One of the times she passed by me, I reached out to touch her hand. She had no fever, but she seemed to be addressing her own mother who had died years before.

When Da arrived home, his face quickly drained of color as he took in the scene before him. I allowed no time for questions, just gave orders.

"Get Mother settled in the other bed and keep this basin filled with cool water."

With a calm I'd not witnessed in a long time, my da took hold of Mother's hands and laid them against his chest. He brushed his beard against her cheek and kissed her forehead before encircling her in his arms. Softly, he sang the first verse of a familiar lullaby and Mother's agitation stilled.

> *Hush my baby,*
> *Be still,*
> *No tears,*
> *Sweet smiling you have no fears.*

He continued with the second stanza as he led her to their bed. He eased her down onto the mattress and held her in his arms, resting beside her until the two fell asleep. I cracked open the window and took the blanket from my bed to place over them. Its scattered moth holes made me think of all our lost dreams, some set aside, others gone forever. I didn't know for sure which was which, so my tears escaped for both. *I should pray,* I thought to myself. Somehow it seemed beyond my strength, though, and I hoped God would understand.

A sound like flapping wings startled me and I turned toward the window. There, on the outside sill, an owl had come to perch. Never had I seen nor heard of one in this tree-less city of soot. My skin prickled. I raised the window even higher and shooed him away. Back home, owls meant death—and I could not let that happen.

Maybe an hour or so later, Da awoke and came to check on Peder. I showed him the faint red patches that had begun to appear on my brother's back and front. Da's face grew tense.

"What is it?" I whispered so Mother wouldn't wake.

"He's got the fever. Scarlet fever."

It felt like a mountain had dropped on me and I could hardly breathe.

"We need something to write on," Da said as he hurried into their room. When he returned, he offered me the only paper he could find: their precious marriage certificate.

"*Skrive det,*" he demanded.

"But Da, I have some blank pages in my journal. We could use those."

"No, you must forever protect your journal and the story of our road to a new farm."

I struggled to recall even one time when he had mentioned my gift from Miss Robinson. So, with great care, I turned over the certificate and wrote in both languages.

Karantene — Hold Deg Unna
Quarantine — Stay Away

Da's hammer slammed against a nail to secure the paper to the outside of our door, and our home became a temporary prison. I resumed the sponging of my brother and willed him to get better. I told him stories and showed him the toys Da had made, but still his usual smile didn't appear. Da went back to hold Mother.

Peder opened his eyes to the first rays of dawn streaming through the windowpane. I smiled down at him and leaned in to kiss his cheek before placing the rag back in the cool water and wringing it out to start all over again. But by then his eyes had gone gray and death stared back at me. My sweet brother had taken his final breath.

I'm not sure how to account for my next actions. Maybe the lack of sleep had gone on too long because I never called out to Da or Mother. Instead, I carefully lowered myself onto the bed and fell asleep next to my brother. Dreams came in jumbled masses of confusion. Nothing made sense. I screamed when a ghost touched me.

"Kristi. Kristi. Wake up."

Groggy and gasping for breath, I found my way back from the nightmare, though I felt chilled, even wet, and someone had a hold of my arms. Again, the voice called my name, but this time I calmed. Da had come to save me.

"Oh, Da," I sobbed. "Peder is gone."

Da's eyes were puffy, and his hands had a shakiness to them as he spoke. "Mother can't prepare Peder's body. You ..." He couldn't finish, so I said, "I'll need the washing bag from under your bed."

Mother had once told me that the hardest assignment she ever had was to prepare her own mother. "I had to reach deep inside myself," she said. "The sacred task needed doing. I could cry later when no one else was around."

Da sat by the table, his head bent in prayer while I gently cleansed little Peder. When I finished, he placed his only son in the blanket Mother had made from well-used scraps. Gently, he lifted Peder into his arms and started toward the door.

"Where are you taking him?" I asked.

After all, rules for handling the dead had been posted on every street corner. And no one could leave a house that had the quarantine sign.

For just a moment he stopped and looked back at me. "The undertaker will not have my son to throw in some nameless grave."

He left no doubt that he would rather be thrown in jail or even die than have that happen to Peder.

"But Da, what will the police do if they find him with you?"

He gave me no answer, just walked out the door. I stood locked in place. Dumbfounded. That's how I felt. The weight of what had happened stabbed my heart and grew heavier with each minute that passed. When Da returned, he came to the table, sat down on the chair with the uneven leg, and took hold of the warm cup of coffee I'd made for him. He didn't drink it, though. He fixed his gaze on the only thing he could see outside our kitchen window, a brick wall dotted with soot, a twin to ours.

Later, Mother came into the kitchen. Without asking about Peder, she just sat down on the chair next to Da and peered into her own cup of weak coffee. Maybe she knew but couldn't form the words.

My entire body felt numb. I should have gone to work, but I knew I couldn't.

Shouldn't I cry?

My eyes stayed dry while the only feeling I had left in me was to care for my parents. I couldn't lose them too.

CHAPTER 20

Locked in Loneliness

The law required the quarantine sign to stay on the door for two weeks. Our food wouldn't last that long. I checked the flour bag and it only had enough for one more piece of fried bread for each of us. No vegetables. We only had reused coffee grounds and a pot with a small helping of leftover soup. No one would knock on our door. No one would bring food. Back at home in Norway, someone would have done these things for us.

Two days after Peder died, Mother sat on the edge of the bed and looked at the empty corner his crib had occupied. She turned to face Da.

"Have we lost Peder?"

"Yes," he said, a tear choking his voice.

Mother slid back under the blanket. Da handed her the scrap of material Peder always clung to at night. She pressed it to her nose and drew in his scent. When the shadows of that night began to deepen, Da took his Bible from the suitcase and held it out to me.

"I'd like you to read to us," he said. "Start at Psalm 91. It's your mother's favorite."

I leafed through the thin pages in the center of the Bible until I came to the Psalm. *He who dwells in the shelter of the Most High, will rest in the shadow of the Almighty.*

My parents fell asleep before I'd spoken the final verse. I

placed the old family Bible back on the table before going to my own bed. Layers of heat remained trapped in our rooms, but still I shivered and crawled under the only blanket I had.

Saturday morning brought with it the hard reality that our cupboard crumbs had been cleared away by the night bugs or a stray mouse. Da and I should have been in line for our pay. Instead, we sat at the table, cradling cups of water with a hint of brown meant to pass for coffee.

"We need food," he said, then added, "I'm going to get some."

"But it's nine more days before we can leave the house."

"I have a plan. Just trust me."

"But Da, I'm afraid for you."

"You mustn't worry. I'll be careful."

The pink of dawn had barely crested when Da placed a chair over by the kitchen window, raised it all the way open, and climbed out onto the fire escape. Down the skinny ladder rungs he went as more and more street noises filled the air. Vendors had come to display their wares. Horse hooves clopped on the dirt-packed road. From time to time, the milkman would stop, descend from his cart, leave full bottles of milk on someone's front step, then collect the empty ones that clinked against the metal container as he carried them. None of the new full bottles would ever be for us.

I waved when Da reached the bottom. He placed a rock on the last step of the ladder so it wouldn't retract. Rats came out of nowhere to scurry across his feet. He kicked them aside, their squeals echoing off the building walls.

Watching him disappear around the corner, I worried how he planned to pay for the food. I hadn't asked and he'd not said. I was sure he'd never steal. However, the thought crossed my mind that he might have taken our train fare money. Though it made me feel guilty, I rushed to check. Every penny remained.

Another cup of boiled water entered my aching belly as

I waited. Time seemed to be moving slower. When I heard a *clank clank*, I rushed to the window. Da had started to climb the ladder, his coat pockets bulging, and a loaf of bread tucked under one arm. When he reached our landing, he passed me the food treasures: flour, some carrots, turnips, potatoes, a small bag of coffee, and the still-warm bread.

"The bread has raisins inside," he said with a rascally-like smile as he swung his last leg inside. "And I didn't steal any of this. I had some money left from last payday because I didn't pay all our rent. The man told me I could catch up this week, but with our sign on the door he won't throw us out."

I couldn't look him in the eye. I felt deep regret that I had doubted, questioned, or suspected for one minute that my da would use our train money.

"On Monday," he continued, "with or without the sign on the door, I must find a new job while you care for Mother."

"You can also pick up your missed pay at the factory when you go back to work."

"They'll just keep it. I wasn't there to get it," he said. "And the same goes for you. Factory owners won't save a job or a missed paycheck. I've seen it happen many times."

My stomach felt like a rock had dropped in it. How could this be true?

In the middle of the night, Da woke to find Mother's nightgown soaked in sweat. The few good teeth she still had rattled and her whole body shivered.

"Kristi," he hollered to me. "Get some rags and cool water from the pump. Your mother has a fever."

For the rest of the night, we took turns sponging her body. Still the fever raged. Eventually it burned a hole in her sense of reality. She began to talk to Peder as if he lay curled in her arms. She sang to him in nonsensical syllables. As the first light of morning came through our window, faint spots of red appeared on her chest and back. By noon, the color had spread across wide areas of her body, arms, and legs.

Neither Da nor I aired our fears as the day wore on. His special loaf of bread continued to rest on the table untouched, though I noticed a corner had been chewed by some hungry creature. I'd made new coffee to keep us awake, but I didn't get to start the stew I'd planned. By suppertime, Mother's breathing came in short spurts and with great effort.

Da and I stopped our sponging and took hold of her hands. Her slender fingers should have had a piano to play—I wondered why she had always been ashamed of them. Yes, they had a roughness from scrubbing our clothes and cleaning the house. They even cracked and bled some days. But love is what I saw in them. I was gently stroking her wrist with my fingers when a gurgle escaped from her chest. After a sharp gasp, the last of her air released. My mother had died.

Everything stopped. I sensed an absence so deep that it locked me in place. I gulped for air as if I had just risen above the water and found nothing to hold onto. Da softly sobbed, his once strong shoulders heaving with the effort. Again, I couldn't find the strength to cry.

Once he finally quieted, my da reached over to close her eyelids. I knew he should, but it felt as if he'd lowered the top of the coffin before I could say goodbye.

I thought back to the hours she and I had spent talking since coming to New York. Without farm chores to do, she'd decided to continue my education, but in a different way. Childhood had been set aside and lessons a woman should know were discussed. When I went to work in the factory, she guided my thinking about others, especially those who often proved unkind. *They have sorrows you can't imagine,* she'd said, though at the time I hadn't totally accepted that explanation. When Marta came into our life, Mother stepped back to give her time to teach me what Mother didn't know—how to survive in this strange city.

How can I ever go on without you? My very spirit cried out.

I felt something touch my shoulder, and a voice like that

of Da's said, "I want to lay beside her." Trance-like, I rose and moved over to my own bed. I got in under the thin blanket and soon fell asleep. Nightmares came and went. In them, the air lay heavy on my chest like a thousand stacks of lumber. I couldn't escape. I struggled to bat away tangled vines. I ran through a dark, dark forest. A voice called out to me. *It's you who must be strong now. Your tears can wait.*

I awoke to sweat running down my brow and my heart pounding. I sat up, panting like a runner who'd just finished a race.

The rusty bed springs creaked as Da was getting out of bed. Shuffling around the corner and into the kitchen, he looked like a walking skeleton, his trousers held in place only by his belt and his shirt meant for someone many sizes bigger.

"I'll heat up the coffee," I said as if it were the most normal of tasks at a time like this.

"No, not this morning," he said. He laid his head upon the table.

Sunbeams shone through the window and landed on the floor where a cockroach scurried to find the darkness again. I stood, but my legs barely held me. A whip-like sound caught my attention. I looked outside the window. Someone's sheets hung on the clotheslines. No longer white, the squares flapped like the sails of a ship. To myself more than to Da, I said, "I must prepare Mother."

I have no memory of gathering the supplies or even the act of washing. A haze fogged my mind. Da may have told me he needed to leave and get the undertaker, but I didn't know he had gone until he returned. I'd just finished adjusting Mother's best dress against her skeletal frame. The undertaker followed him into the bedroom, looked down at Mother, and immediately demanded payment for his services. The only coins we had lay at the bottom of the coffee can. I could hardly breathe when Da poured them into the man's outstretched hands. That stranger didn't know nor care about Mother. He didn't ask about her story. He only wanted to escape our realm of disease and death. I couldn't blame him, but ...

Two men bundled Mother in a shroud and carried her out the door. In my head I counted each step as they descended the staircase. At the bottom, the wind caught the front door and slammed it shut.

Da collapsed on their bed and sobbed as if his grief would never stop. He kept saying, "I wanted her to be with Peder, but I couldn't carry her."

CHAPTER 21

New Jobs Needed

The fantasies of childhood went away the day my da first tacked up that quarantine sign. And although it should have stayed on the door for another two weeks when Mother died, I took it down after only one. We'd have to go out for food well before then. And this time, I had to be strong. Da had gone into himself. I wanted to survive—but I couldn't be sure he did.

"We need jobs," I said in a manner not to be questioned.

Da fell into a nothingness as he took the last swallow of pale coffee from his cracked cup. He nodded, stood, and walked out the door. Before the end of the day, he'd found a job at Lackawanna Steel. There he flung shovel after shovel of coal into a furnace.

He came home covered in coal dust; his back bent in pain. I told him, "That work is too hard for you." But he refused to discuss it. He just crawled into bed and rose before the sun to do it all over again.

I went back to the sewing factory, confident that they'd have an opening. The same straight-backed lady rehired me, but not before she'd made it clear that I couldn't fuss nor demand the pay of a grown woman.

"Alright, but I do want the money owed to me for the week I worked before we had to quarantine."

The woman glared at me; her face frozen in a permanent

frown. "You didn't come to get it, so it stays here."

I pictured Mother standing beside me saying, "Stay calm. Don't speak back to your supervisor."

I must have faced her for too long because she shooed me toward the factory door. When I pulled it open, the noise rushed at me, and the smell of machine oil soaked back into my clothes and skin. Row upon row of women sat bent over their machines. This was their existence. They didn't bother to raise their heads. My stomach grumbled and I remembered the crumbs I'd forgotten to rescue from the bottom shelf in the cupboard. No doubt a trail of ants would take them away before I came home.

In my prayers that eve, I asked forgiveness for the vegetables I'd stolen on the way home when a vendor turned his back, but I knew I'd steal again. My da needed food and maybe it would repair his will to survive. Besides, payday wouldn't come for another five days.

Every chance I got after that, I talked to him about our dreams, his land, and my schooling. Sometimes I'd point to the empty coffee can, saying, "Mother and Peder would want us to go."

The days wore on, and I worried that the strong man I once knew was shrinking even further inside his clothes. I told him to eat, but he only nibbled and picked at the food, none of which could have added muscle to his frame anyway.

My own state was revealed from a cracked mirror leaning against the backside of the building. It reflected a pale-faced girl wearing a ragged dress that not only draped from her shoulders but hid the fact that she had become a woman. I tried to give her a name. It was then I realized I'd once known her as a princess in stories she'd made up. But her dress looked more like a bedraggled Cinderella, and the light of hope barely flickered in her eyes. The reflection frightened me, and I ran back inside.

With Mother gone and Da in a fragile state of mind, I took

on the chores of laundry, shopping, meals, and cleaning. Even then, our life slipped into disarray most days. Tired is the only way I could describe my life. Each day, I'd glance into the coffee can that held a couple of coins. They weren't enough for a loaf of bread and certainly not a ticket on the train. I knew because I'd gotten a copy of the train schedule. On one hand it told me how much we needed. But without help or sharing the cost of an apartment like Marta and Hjelmer had done, it would take years to get enough. I missed Marta and her big-sister type of guidance.

As fall became winter, Da's slender body shivered while drinking his morning coffee. We needed more coal, so I went to fight with the others for the lumps that fell by the tracks. I certainly couldn't pay what the coal man wanted for a bag when we could barely afford food.

In April of the following year, my fourteenth, I came home to find Da collapsed in the stairwell. He had a cut on his head and at first, he didn't recognize me. I banged on the door next to the staircase and asked the man who answered to help me get Da upstairs and into bed. I thanked him and offered some carrots as payment. We had nothing else because rent had taken all our money the week before.

That evening, Da's body shook all over. His teeth clicked rapidly though I had covered him with both of our blankets. Sweat rolled off his forehead. His fever raged and his mind wandered.

We needed food, so I had to work. Da couldn't anymore. On payday, I went to my factory and his. My money was given, but the owners at the steel factory refused to give Da's to me.

"He didn't complete the week," they told me. I called them evil scoundrels.

On Sunday, I used my pay for vegetables to make a thick stew which I encouraged Da to eat. His fever had gone down a bit, but his eyes remained glazed and the handkerchief he held to cover his cough was spattered in blood stains.

During the night, I made an onion poultice to put on his chest. His cough had grown deep and painful. The arrival of a troubling rumble reminded me of when he used salt water to ease a sore throat. Not long after, my da took his final breath. I held his hand and looked down at his sunken chest with sadness, but no tears.

I reminisced about when we lived in Norway such a short time ago. Da had loved to work in the fields, chop wood for winter, make a piece of furniture for Mother, and help those in need. He laughed a lot too. He never failed to say *I love you* or give a big bear hug. The truth was, he'd not laughed since the day he closed the door to our house on the hillside.

I reached over to close my da's eyes and said, "I promise to find the land you came to farm. And when I'm a teacher, I'll tell my students to follow their dreams, no matter what comes their way."

CHAPTER 22

Moving On (1902)

I dropped into the chair by the table and contemplated the empty cup before me. I calculated that if I poured water over the used grounds, I could make something that passed as coffee. But thinking used up energy and left none for the doing.

Only the older women wash a man when he dies. This adage traveled across a great ocean. The only response I had was, *But you don't understand. There are no older women here, just me.* The sun retreated and the smell of promised rain drifted in through the open window. *You are the older woman now. Fill the basin and prepare your da for his maker.*

I felt a touch on my elbow, but when I rose from the table, no one appeared. I heated water to wipe away the coal dust. I soaked his hands, washed his face and arms, and combed his thin hair. I covered his see-through skin in clean clothes. I noticed that he'd left the Bible open to Chapter 37 in Psalms. I read it to him.

"Fret not yourself because of evildoers; be not envious of wrongdoers! For they will soon fade like the grass and wither like the green herb. Trust in the Lord and do good."

These tasks numbed my spirit. I don't remember making coffee, but soon found myself sitting at the table with my own shallow cup.

My mind wandered back to the years when I wrote magical stories where time had stopped. Pretending. That's what

I wanted to do now, and for a time, I allowed myself to linger in that world.

But all too soon, reality became the beast that rampaged in my mind. The authorities here would consider me a child. If they knew my family had died, they'd take me away—somewhere—and that frightened me. I could still hear Marta's voice: *Children don't survive here. Only warriors do.*

I have no idea how much time passed before I went to retrieve my suitcase from under the bed. Just like Mother had done when we planned to leave Norway, I placed it on the table and began a damp-wash. Once it dried, I added into its hungry-like opening one spare dress, two pairs of recently mended undergarments, some threadbare socks, a few rags for my monthly time, my hairbrush, Da's Bible, my journal, and the last of the pencils Da had sharpened before he fell. Like when we'd left home for America, I'd have to wear my coat since there was no more room in the small case. Our quilts would have to stay behind. *Maybe the downstairs neighbor will like them*, I reasoned. *I'll add that suggestion to the note I slide under his door.*

Only a few coins remained from Da's last payday. We had planned to add them to the amount owed for rent, but I divided them out instead. The undertaker would want a dollar's worth. I hid the rest in the side pocket of my case. The last things I packed were two slices of fried bread.

Click. To my relief, the lock held. My brain flooded. I didn't know where I should go. *Exactly how does a young girl plan for something like this?* I couldn't be sure if I'd spoken that out loud or not. I only knew I had to leave by the next day because that's when the rent came due. And if the authorities found me alone, I might discover that the orphan boys had been telling the truth all along and I'd go to jail. I couldn't risk that. "Run away. Live on the streets like us," they'd told me many times.

But I'd never seen a girl in their midst. The older ones

walked the street at night and talked to men. Mother had always said to stay away from them and their ways.

I'll just have to make my own path. Maybe I can find a new job and at night sleep in an alleyway. That way I can save up for the train fare before winter sets in.

Morning arrived. I gathered my things, said goodbye to Da, and left our room for the final time. I slipped my note under the door of the man who'd helped me get Da into bed. The quilts would serve as thanks for his assistance.

That morning, sunbeams tried to force their way through clouds emitting a slow drizzle of rain. There I stood, a girl of fourteen, all alone, holding a suitcase, and not knowing where to go. I shook off my thick fog and vowed: *Mother. Da. I won't let you down. You'll see. I'll make you proud of me.*

Coming onto the walkway, I decided to first find where the passengers boarded at the train station. Surely, if I could just get there, I could somehow catch a ride west—even if it meant sneaking on a railcar like Da once told me he'd seen others do.

I can't say why I decided to head north onto Church Street, but that's what I did. By midmorning, I'd weaved on and off Thomas Street, West Broadway, and Leonard Street in my effort to avoid the officers that patrolled the neighborhoods looking for troublemakers and wayward or orphaned children. Those men wore blue uniforms and had a night stick attached to their belt. To me, they looked like they rarely missed a meal.

My coat grew heavy as it soaked up the fine rain instead of shedding it. When the sun came out, its sour and sweaty odor caused people to give me a wide berth as I walked. One child even said loudly, "You stink." I knew he spoke truth.

Sharp hunger pains shot through me as I smelled someone cooking a meal other than soup and fried bread. I'd not eaten since the day before, but I needed to keep going. Besides, I'd lost confidence in my sense of direction. The city had no trees with their north-facing moss to guide me, and the sun was often invisible behind block after block of tall buildings. Occasionally, I spotted a black column rising from a factory smokestack. It made me wonder if I should go back and find the one where I had worked instead of trying to hop a train.

Walking on, I encountered some men idling the day away in front of a building. Even though I was trying to look respectable, one of them gave me a wolf whistle—at least that is what Da had called it. I understood what that meant. Mother had explained it. So I kept my head down and walked faster.

I could only guess at the time of day. When the newsies called out the evening paper headlines, I knew I'd better find a spot to make a bed before the darkness came. My legs ached. My feet had blisters.

I looked down each alleyway as I passed by. Most had been claimed by garbage and rats. The one that finally caught my eye had small piles of left-behind furniture stacked along the wall of the building. It looked familiar. That's when I realized I'd passed it before. I wanted to cry—I'd walked in circles.

The alley smelled bad, like all the others. But I found an opening amongst the furniture that had just enough room for me to crawl inside. Sleep. Oh, how I wanted to find refuge in it. But I knew I should eat something first. I took a half slice of bread from my case and carefully chewed each bite. *This may need to last several days*, I thought. I was shaking, though, and a small crumb fell to the ground. A gray mouse ran out from his hole in the wall to make off with the morsel. I made no sound, just kept my eye on him. I'd grown too tired to care.

Night came on. I'd always thought it hid many things, but it didn't hide the girls. Some were my age. All were alone with no suitcase. When men called out to them, they went willingly. I recalled from Mother's talks that danger lurked everywhere, and it made me sad for them.

I woke at the first sign of dawn with an ache in every muscle in my body. Hunger consumed me like a roaring lion, making me realize I needed something other than fried bread. Carefully, I reached into my case, took out a dollar's worth of coins, and tucked the money deep into the bottom of my dress pocket. *It's all I have until I find work and even then, I'll have to wait a full week to get paid.* At this rate, I wouldn't soon be stowing away on any train.

After I found a safe spot to store my case out of view, I went to look in front of the building. Rough-looking boys roamed around the vendor carts. Some tried to snatch a carrot, an apple, or a whole loaf of bread from any cart that didn't have two people watching over it. Others headed for the milk wagon where I heard a driver holler, "I'll beat you when I get you." Those boys knew how to steal. And I couldn't take a chance on losing my money. So I waited for them to get chased away from the man who sold cheese and dried meats. The man's eyes narrowed as I approached. I knew I needed a bath and my dress had taken on the filth of street living even though only a day had passed. Before he could speak, I politely showed him twenty-five cents and asked for some meat and cheese worth that amount.

"Well, miss," he said, tilting his head a bit as if he couldn't quite figure me out. "You're an odd one for sure."

When he passed the food over to me, he tucked in an extra chunk of cheese. It wasn't big, but it meant a lot. "That's for not stealing," he said. Back in the furniture pile, I nibbled on the cheese, chewed a small piece of dried meat, and placed the rest in my case.

The night's rest and morning nourishment had revived my spirit, so I headed down a side street hoping to find a way out of New York. The city felt like a vise squeezing the life out of me.

I walked several blocks before I found a public water fountain. There I washed my face and hands before taking a long drink of water. A few feet away stood a lady raising her voice to a boy who appeared to be her son. He staggered backward, turned his head to one side, and held his palm to his cheek.

"Excuse me," I said to the lady who still wore an angry look. "I'd like to find work in a sewing factory. Do you know where one might be?"

"How should I know?" she said before wrenching the arm of the boy who was beginning to cry.

At the next intersection sat a newsie with his unsold morning papers. "Can you direct me to a sewing factory?" I asked.

"Sure, though I don't know why you'd ever go there. They don't hire no orphans."

"What makes you think I'm an orphan?"

"Because you smell like one," he said without apology. "Go left on this street. It's a long way, but you'll find it. The building is taller than all the others. I think they call it the Triangle Shirt Factory or something like that."

Thanking him, I walked and walked and walked all the way to the corner of Washington Street. There it stood, just like he said, taller than all the others. I studied the building for a time and wondered if they ever opened their windows.

The walk had made me sweat, and I needed to wash again. Across from the factory entrance, a small park had been built with swings, a bench, and, in one corner, a water fountain. There, I tried to wash, but I'd forgotten to bring soap, so the desired result proved hopeless. I tucked my coat under the park bench for safe keeping and headed to the factory, sure of being hired. The lady at the front desk looked directly at me and made her ruling before I even had a chance to tell her why I'd come in the door.

"You look like an orphan."

"I'm a skilled seamstress and I wish to apply for a job."

"Then why are you carrying a suitcase?"

"Because I don't trust people. Too many like to steal when

you're not at home."

Frowning at me, she called a rather large man over to her desk.

"Usher this orphan out. Now!"

"And don't think you can come back," the man added as he shoved me out onto the sidewalk.

I couldn't argue. I was an orphan, and I was dirty. The newsie had been right. I'd not get a job. But I felt confused. *Why could I work if I had parents, but not if they died?*

CHAPTER 23

How Long Can I Wander?

The wind picked up. A newspaper page blew across the street and stuck against the base of a tenement building. Someone had once desired it and now its value had been reduced to garbage. I understood. I sympathized with it as if it too held feelings. But underneath my dirty dress, my skinny frame, and my orphan title, I hadn't stopped being Kristi. I still believed in school, and I still wanted to be a teacher. The only thing I knew for sure was that I didn't feel much like a warrior. Loneliness came, went, and came again. I didn't know where to go or how to find my way, so I just walked.

By late afternoon, dark clouds skimmed across the sky and with them came drops of rain that hit the ground like a wad of *snus* projected into a spittoon. I'd forgotten my coat back at the park. Wet, my dress would become see-through if I didn't find shelter.

Within a block, I spied an alleyway that had a large cardboard box atop a wooden pallet. There I found a degree of shelter, enough for a time anyway. After crawling inside, I maneuvered myself so I could look more closely at what surrounded me. Almost immediately, I spotted a small boy huddled between two boxes on the other side of the alley. *He can't be more than three*, I mused. I wondered who could ever banish a child so young. I gestured for him to join me, but instead he pressed himself more firmly against the wall of the building, all the while holding tight to a raggedy blanket.

Sing him a song. The inspiration came on quickly and almost left before I recognized that singing to him might work to ease his fear and draw him to my side.

"Baa, baa, black sheep, have you any wool? Yes, sir, yes, sir, three bags full." I began.

By the time I'd finished, the youngster had come to join me. His body shook from the cold rain. I had no blanket or coat to cover him, so I simply held him close and rubbed his back.

"Wake up. Wake up. It's time to go home," Da said, as he shook my arm. "Bring the little one, too. You'll be warmer inside and there's hot food for you. Wake up."

I bolted up to a sitting position before I'd even rubbed the sleep from my eyes.

"Da. You're alive," I said, panicking once I realized where I had slept.

"Calm down, Miss. Calm down," the voice said.

I tried to look up, but the sun shone in my eyes. I could only make out a russet-colored beard. Da's beard had turned gray. I screamed. I kicked at the arms trying to latch on to me. My instincts told me to protect the boy. But there were two of them, men dressed in robes, like Jesus wore. I felt the boy slipping through my arms and I screamed again. I reached out to pull him back. That only made him cry more, and he started to beat his arms against the robed man who held him.

"Leave him alone!" I shouted. "Don't hurt him!"

The man closest to me took a step back and stood to his full height before beginning to speak.

"I'm Brother Andrew from the Children's Home Society. Is this young man your brother?"

The man seemed tall enough to touch the sky. But his

voice had a gentle and familiar tone to it. While he calmly waited for my reply, I studied his well-trimmed beard and deep blue eyes.

Skeptical at first, I finally said, "No. I found him last night in this alley. He was alone and crying."

"I wasn't crying," the boy quickly corrected. "I'm a big boy. I just had the hiccups."

"What's your name, son?" asked the man who held him.

"Charles, and I'm this many," he said. He held up three fingers and smiled broadly.

The tension around us released and everyone laughed.

"Well, Charles, I'm Brother Mark," the older man said. "And where are your parents?"

"They got tired, and I couldn't wake them. They coughed a lot, too. One day a man came to take me away, but I escaped and ran fast. He was too fat to catch me."

Long-held tears ran down Charles's cheeks. When he reached to brush them away, he choked out, "I just want my mommy."

"Charles, I promise to try to check on your parents. But in the meantime, I think we should all go to a warmer place and have some breakfast. How does that sound?"

The boy nodded enthusiastically and threw his arms around the neck of his new white-haired friend. Gracefully as I could, I climbed out of the wet box and offered my name.

"I'm Kristi. Kristi Monger."

My hands had grown clammy and prickly. The men seemed nice, but I hadn't trusted anyone since losing my parents. The muscles in my face tightened, and I asked, "Where are you taking us? Will we go to jail?"

Brother Andrew was quick to reassure me. "No, Kristi. We won't be taking you to any jail."

"Nay, nay," the other man added. "We want to bring you to a house, a house with lots of children who also lost their parents. It's called an orphanage."

Orphanage. I imagined the sign: *Orphan-age.* No one I'd ever heard of treated orphans as family. How could I believe this place would be any different? Besides, no one had asked me about my parents. Neither had I offered that information. And now I wasn't sure that I would ever tell. What if this was one of those evil places the street boys always told me about?

"I don't think we want to go," I said. I reached out to take Charles from the man who held him.

"Why not?" Brother Andrew quickly asked, a puzzled look on his face.

"Because you'll lock us in there and we won't be able to leave. I know. That's what the newsies told me. And besides, I need to find a school again and the land my da always wanted. If I'm in an orphanage, I won't ever be able to find them."

For the longest time, we stood looking at each other. Finally, he broke the silence.

"My parents died as we crossed the ocean. When the ship reached New York, I tried to get a job. But factory owners didn't want me because I was tall and skinny for a seventeen-year-old. They told me I wouldn't be strong enough to work alongside the men. One day as I walked the streets, I saw some children laughing and playing outside a building. They let me join them in a game of hopscotch—that is, until a stout lady in an apron chased me away."

The man fell silent. The distracted look on his face reminded me of Miss Robinson, who would sometimes lose her place in a story. I wanted to hear the rest of his.

"I couldn't blame the lady," he continued. "She didn't know me. And by then, my clothes were hopelessly filthy and I'd gotten even skinnier. Bathing hadn't happened since my family left home in Sweden. More than anything, I must have looked scary, and she was intent on protecting the children.

"The next day, I came back and knocked on the door. The same lady answered. I explained that I needed a job. She looked at me up and down, then pulled me inside by the arm. I didn't know until later that I'd come to an orphanage. I wanted to impress her, so I did every job she gave me, not once complaining."

"Did she give you this robe and is your name really Brother Andrew?"

"My name is truly Andrew, but I'm not a priest or a Brother," he confessed. "I'm just an orphan who likes to help other orphans."

Every part of me wanted to believe him, but I had to ask one more question. "Then why do you wear the robe?"

"Because children seem less afraid when I wear it."

It hadn't made me less afraid. I was still mulling over his answer when a whiff of lye soap set me to thinking of my own filth. I'd not bathed in so long. What must these men think of me? While neither of them had mentioned it, I still felt intense shame.

Meanwhile, Charles had put one hand on each side of Brother Mark's face to make sure the man listened to his earnest babble. I remained anxious and unsure. But maybe, just maybe, the orphanage people could help me find a way back to school.

"We do need food, but I for sure need to find a school so I can become a teacher."

For some reason, I didn't wait for a reply. I merely picked up and passed on Charles's scrap of a blanket while holding my suitcase in front of my dress. I didn't want the men to see through the thin fabric, still damp from last night's rain.

"What's for breakfast?" Charles asked. "I'm hungry."

"How about you, Kristi? Could I interest you in a hot breakfast?"

The question had come from Brother Andrew. I nodded while never letting my eyes stop searching his. "Come along then," he said cheerfully as he beckoned us to follow. We walked what seemed a long way, stopping only when we came to the base of a brick building, set well back from the corner of Twenty-third Street.

"At one time, this building housed workers who made fancy clothes for women. But a few years back, the Society asked the City of New York for permission to convert it into a home for orphaned children."

Clay pots dotted the side of the stairway leading to a large double-door entrance. Each pot contained multicolored flowers with a delicate perfume that didn't quite mask the city's odor. The windows facing the street had been thoroughly cleaned—not a fleck of soot remained. And I noticed that the sidewalk had been swept all the way from the building to the corner trolley stop.

My awareness of my own filth made me ask, "Is there somewhere I can wash up before I go inside?"

"Oh, there's a special room in the hallway where you can. And besides, our cook Hilda is a stickler for cleanliness. Clean hands, clean hearts. That's her motto—especially for the boys, who don't like to take baths."

"I don't want a bath," Charles adamantly inserted as he looked Brother Mark directly in the eye. Lightning fast, Brother Mark began tickling Charles's sides and tummy. Peals of laughter rang out as the little boy tried unsuccessfully to escape.

"Shall we go inside?" Brother Andrew asked, indicating that I should follow him.

When the door opened, the warm scent of oven-fresh bread filtered into my nose and made my mouth water. Before I could completely enjoy its aroma, I heard a crash and the laughter of children. I looked off to the left where a rather rotund woman, wearing a full-length apron, juggled two plates of food as she entered the dining room.

"James, that mishap means you'll be doing extra dishes today," the woman said without raising her voice.

"That's Hilda," Brother Andrew said. "You'll meet her later. For now, let's go this way."

With long strides, he walked down a side hallway, occasionally angling his head in my direction so I could hear his explanations. "Mark is taking Charles to another room to have a bath. I'll ask Nellie to bring in a fresh change of clothes and more hot water for you."

I heard every word, but still it felt like I was just floating along in a storybook. My new protector opened yet another door. There before me was a large tub that reminded me of our water trough back in Norway. The only differences between the two were that this one was white and perched atop four skinny legs.

"Excuse me." A girl of twenty or so carried two buckets of hot water, which she dumped in the tub to mix with what was already there.

"I'm Nellie," she said. Brother Andrew slipped past us and out the door. "Here's a new bar of soap. I love this kind. It has lavender blossoms mixed inside it. Gives a sweet smell and makes a girl feel special, if you know what I mean."

She placed the soap in a holder on the tub's edge. Then, she reached into her pocket and took out another.

"This one will kill any lice that may have nested in your hair. I'd advise you to wash it at least two times."

Lice. Mother would have been so ashamed. I didn't think I had any, but my head started itching at the thought.

By the time I walked out of the room, I had a dress that no one could see through, newly made underwear that I later discovered had been a gift for each child from some local church ladies, shoes and socks that fit, and, best of all, hope—a feeling that reignited once I looked and felt decent. Nellie took everything I wore when I came in and burned them all in the barrel out back. I carefully wiped off my journal and Da's Bible—but the suitcase went in the fire.

"You'll find a new suitcase under your bed," Nellie told

me. "And I'll take those books to your room so you can go and eat."

By this time, the dining room had emptied of most children. Dishes had been cleared away; crumbs brushed from the table. Clean white cloths, each crowned with a bud vase holding a single flower, lay atop every table.

"I think the flowers make it seem more like home," Hilda said when she saw me touching the blue vase. "I'm Hilda. You must be Kristi."

Her voice had a deeper tone than most women. But my attention was drawn to the look of her hands—muscular with red, raw skin, they reminded me of Mother's on wash days.

"Follow me," she said. "There's someone I want you to meet."

I had missed seeing the young girl when I walked in, but there she sat near the back of the room, all by herself.

"Inga, this is Kristi and she has just arrived. Maybe you could share a little about yourself while I fetch a plate of food for her."

I could tell that Inga was shy because her eyes wouldn't meet mine at first. When I sat and said hello, she spoke up.

"I'm ten," she said hesitantly. "My family came here a couple of years ago from Stavanger, Norway. My mother is dead and my da, well, I don't know exactly where he went. I've been here for about a month now, but I hope to find new parents soon."

I wanted to hear more, so I tilted my head toward her and asked, "How do you find new parents?" It hadn't crossed my mind to hope that another family might take me in.

"Brother Mark told me that from time to time, he or Brother Andrew take a group of orphans and head west on the train. There are people out there who will give us a home, especially farmers. Some need boys to work with them and others want a girl to keep the wife company. I'm big enough to help with children, too, so maybe I'll get a brother or sister, something I haven't had before."

She sounded so confident. Our conversation came to an end when Hilda returned carrying a plate with small portions of fried potatoes, bacon, eggs, and toast. My stomach growled but Hilda dismissed my apology.

"Make sure you eat slowly and only take small bites. Your stomach has shrunk. It'll take a few days before it can come back to normal."

Inga excused herself just as Charles entered riding on the shoulders of Brother Mark. I complimented him on his new clothes and clean hair. "You look so handsome."

"Can you tell Kristi about your bath and what was in the tub with you?"

"A boat, I had a boat—and lots of bugs!" he said as if it was the greatest thing ever.

Later, Clara, one of the older women who worked at the Home (as everyone called it), showed me to a room on the second floor. There she announced, "This will be the bedroom you'll share with three other girls. Your bed is the one by the window. If you need more blankets, just find me and I'll get them for you. I also put a nightgown under the pillow. I guessed at your size, so let me know if it doesn't fit."

Overwhelmed and still thinking this had to be a dream, I neglected to thank her. But, in no time, she came back and said, "I forgot to tell you that I put your new suitcase under the bed. Your books are inside along with the pencils. And, whenever you're ready, you can explore the rest of the building."

After she left, I glanced out the window next to my bed and realized it overlooked the street that brought us to this place. It was clear that the orphan boys I'd met didn't have to live outside. They could come here. But I also realized they had all grown frightened and distrustful. People had treated them badly, called them names. They hid whenever they suspected someone wanted to take them away. *Maybe I could go back and tell them*, I thought.

It wasn't long before curiosity took over and I decided to explore. Down the hallway and on the other side of the second floor, I found the boys' section where Charles had a bedroom. He sat on the bottom of the stacked beds and chatted with his new friends. The room next to his had a wall of windows. Brother Andrew sat crossed legged in one corner and was reading a story to a group of children.

Someone had constructed shelves for books. Other areas had baskets with wooden toys and handmade dolls for the girls. A short stack of paper sat next to a cup of pencils. It had the appearance of a miniature school—I imagined myself as the teacher.

As the days passed, I, like all the others, had my name added to the list for work assignments. One day, I was to read to the younger children after our lunch break. I could hardly contain myself as I hurried down the hall and into the room. There, standing off to one side, I witnessed a worker, nicknamed Punk, gripping the arm of Michael, who had just turned four. It was easy to tell from the wet stain on Michael's pants that he had waited too long and ended up having an accident. His head hung in humiliation as the worker said nasty things to him and raised an arm to strike the boy.

"No!" I hollered. "Don't you dare touch him!"

Just in time, Brother Andrew rushed into the room, seized the man, and ushered him out the back door. Punk never did return. I dried Michael's tears and surrendered him to Brother Andrew, who found another pair of pants for him to wear. When he brought him back, I let Michael pick out a book. The story was about a brave boy who slayed a dragon. I told Michael that he was just like that boy.

I came to understand that the goal at the Home had always been to find families for orphans. But I worried. After all, by the end of summer I'd turn fifteen, much older than any of the others. So, when Brother Andrew came to sit with me on the back porch one morning, I had to ask.

"The other girls in my room have told me that some of the children are taken on a train ride to find new homes. How can that be? Will I ever find a family that will take me in? After all, I'll be fifteen in late summer."

My voice had cracked a bit, and I almost cried, expecting him to say I'd gotten too old. But instead, he continued to rock in the chair at his steady pace until he put down his pipe, leaned forward, and answered.

"Many people have gone out West to find land and settle down. It's the hardest work they'll ever do, but it has rewards. The land is prairie, and few trees ever grow there. Most build a sod home first, then break ground and plant their seed. If they last on the land for five years, it can be theirs—and that's the goal."

He took a sip of his tea. "Farmers hope to find a boy to help them. Others want a baby, or maybe a girl to help with the children they already have. These folks meet us at the train station and sometimes choose a child. That child becomes an indentured servant. Often, folks adopt them. In the meantime, that family is required to provide room and board in exchange for the help."

I hesitated for a moment before saying, "I'm a good worker, but I need to go to school so I can become a teacher."

"The families are required to allow you time for schooling, but nothing past the eighth grade. The rest is up to you."

Shortly after the official start of summer, Brother Andrew came into our room and told Inga that a nun from another orphanage had planned a trip west and it would start in two weeks. The nun had room for one more child and Brother Andrew wondered if Inga wanted to join them.

Inga hadn't shared her family history with me, so I listened in surprise to her reply: "After my mother died, my da signed away my brother, sister, and me. I don't know where they are or who took them. But I'm the oldest and I promised to find them."

Inga's subdued tone made me think she'd traveled back in time and pulled up a weed of sadness.

"Not all agencies keep good records," Brother Andrew replied, "but I will try to help you when you are finished being an indentured servant."

"But I don't understand what that is," Inga said.

"In a way, it's like taking a job without pay. The people you live with will provide your food and lodging in exchange for your work up to the age of eighteen."

Inga took him up on his offer. I envied her opportunity and felt the ache of loneliness set in when she left. Thank goodness for Hilda who, like a favorite aunt, often listened to me as I shared my dream of finding a place where black smoke didn't sully the air, a place with farmland so I could think of Da, and, most important, a place where children went to school so I could learn to teach.

Sometime in the second week of August, I was scrubbing the front entrance floor on my hands and knees when Brother Andrew approached with a serious look on his face. "In a few days, I plan to take a group of children west on the train. It'll be my last trip this year. Would you consider joining us?"

I rocked back on my heels and looked up at him. "I want to go. But would anyone really take me at my age?"

"I won't lie to you, Kristi. You may get to the end of the journey and have no success. All I can say is we'd come back here and try again in the spring."

I shuddered and placed the rag back in the wash water. Finally, I stood and looked directly at him.

"My dream is out there. Somewhere. And if I don't try, I won't ever find it. So yes, yes, I will go with you."

CHAPTER 24

The Train Heads West

My thoughts raced like squirrels chasing in and out of the tree branches. My legs wouldn't lie still. Toward morning on the day we were leaving, I gave up my effort to sleep, deciding instead to go spend some time alone on the back porch. It had become my personal hideaway soon after I arrived. Hilda trusted me, but she wouldn't allow the younger children to go there for fear they might knock over the kerosene lamp and burn the house down.

Someone had left a window partially open, and I could feel the air's cool freshness and the absence of bitter factory odor that would surely arrive as soon as the boilers had been stoked. Our janitor was the one who found the porch chair in a trash heap, fixed its cracked spindles, and stained the wood a mahogany color. Hilda had woven a round cushion to cover the broken and cracked reeds in the middle. Her addition added multiple colors and a pillowy feel.

Agnes, our stray cat, pounced on my lap as soon as I sat down. She purred when I stroked her back. I mulled over which of the other children would come with us on this search. Brother Andrew had confided in me that he wanted to bring Johanna and Jon, siblings that had come to live at the Home shortly after Charles and I. On the night they'd arrived, I'd gone off to read in my room and looked out the window when I heard someone knock at the front door. One of the workers opened it and there stood a family. The father looked down at his shoes while the mother kissed each child before giving them over to the worker.

"There isn't any food to give them," the father had told the worker. "We'll come for them when things improve."

Brother Andrew told me that the parents had signed the children over to the orphanage. They would not return, though Johanna, the older of the two, held onto the belief that they would.

Charles would also come with us. Brother Mark had searched for his parents, just as he promised. Eventually, he confirmed that they, like so many others, had died of consumption. Charles became a true orphan with that report.

Hans, a boy of ten, made me worry. He walked with a limp and was often teased by the other boys. While their teasing could not make him cry, I was aware that if you were different every careless word would hurt in your heart. He often went to a corner and read to the youngest ones, who had not yet learned to point fingers at him.

The cooing of a mourning dove brought me back to the present. The sky had turned pink, and I needed to hurry. Up the back stairs I ran. I grabbed my suitcase and went down to the dining area. Nellie, the first worker I met when I arrived, instantly brought a bowl of hot cereal with brown sugar and cream on top. It was offered as a treat, so I knew I must eat it—but worry had stolen my appetite.

"Do the best you can," she counseled. "This day is scary for everyone."

The noise level escalated as excitement filtered throughout the Home. At one point, I noticed Hilda going into the hallway to place a sandwich in each suitcase.

"Don't dawdle," Nellie called out. "Hurry and finish eating. In five minutes, you must all be lined up by the front door."

I suspected I'd be hungry later, but I just couldn't eat any more. So off I went to get my suitcase. Nellie and the other workers had already started to give hugs by the time I came to stand in line. Repeatedly, they did a final check for smudges on the younger ones' faces. When Nellie came to me, she held me tight and whispered, "You can do this. I just know you can. And you will find your dream."

I wanted to believe her. I smiled, inhaled deeply, and drew back my shoulders. She went to retrieve the last of the boys who pretended they wanted nothing to do with displays of affection. Katie, Johanna, and Minnie, however, reveled in the attention.

Hilda, last in the line of staff, took hold of my shoulders and looked me in the eye. "Now don't you worry a mite about a new family. They are out there waiting for you. When you find them, I want you to write to me." Her eyes welled up as she placed a coin in my hand. "For postage," she said.

I wanted to remember everything about her. She had mothered all of us in so many ways. But when she stopped at the door to the kitchen, she turned around to look at me one more time. She raised her arm in farewell and we both seemed to know we wouldn't be seeing each other again.

. . . . ⚬❀⚬ . . . .

"Everyone. Listen closely!" Brother Andrew called out. "Each of you has been assigned a partner. Now take that person's hand and follow me."

Katie, her red hair bouncing, joined up with Minnie and the two of them headed toward the front of the line.

"Hey! Girls shouldn't be first," one of the boys called out.

Katie didn't like to take a back seat to anyone. "Yes, they should, and you better move over." This made me laugh and calm down at the same time.

Johanna, as expected, took responsibility for her brother. She'd become a mother to him since their parents had abandoned them. Jon protested when she brushed away a piece of cereal from his shirt collar. "I'm not a baby!" He raised his chin and stood as tall as any three-year-old could—but still held fast to her hand. They needed each other.

The other boys paired up but refused any physical connection.

"Listen," I said, coming up from behind them, "if you won't hold hands, then you will walk like gentlemen."

The look that came from Brother Andrew confirmed that I commanded as much authority as he did. Without a fuss, they fell in line behind the others. I brought up the rear.

The twelve of us orphans stood together along with Brother Andrew at the end of the block to wait for the streetcar. No more than ten minutes passed before one stopped under the sign and the door opened to expose a jovial driver.

"Come on in," he cheerfully called out. "Find a seat in my fine car. It's going to be a wonderful day."

While I waited my turn, I studied the exterior of our conveyance. Its red sides with black trim had not an ounce of dirt. Inside, the first seat behind the driver was occupied by a lady with a large black hat. Her pursed lips told me it perturbed her that we had entered her domain. My assumption was confirmed when she said to the driver, "Why do you let these dirty orphans ride?"

It was a rude comment, especially considering everyone had bathed the night before and our clothes, though not new, were spotlessly clean. Her words angered me, and I thought I might say something when I passed by—but the driver did it first.

"Ma'am, there are plenty of seats in the back if you'd rather sit there."

Her face took on a bright shade of scarlet. By the time I finally entered the streetcar, I had decided to follow the polite example of the driver.

"Good morning, ma'am," I said. "I hope you have a pleasant day."

From the corner of my eye, I could see the driver turn aside, cover his mouth, and let a big smile grow on his face.

Brother Andrew boarded behind me and held out the money for our fare.

"There's no charge for these youngsters," the driver said, refusing the offer.

Brother Andrew drew back a bit, looking puzzled.

"I'm an orphan, too," the driver continued. "And there's no shame in that. Besides, everyone needs help sometimes."

Brother Andrew nodded thanks and, right on cue, the lady said, "Well, I never!"

At the stop on the west side of Seventh Street, Brother Andrew stood, thanked the driver, and instructed each of us to do the same as we exited. Directly in front of us was a building with a sign announcing The Pennsylvania Railroad Ticket Office. I thought we'd go in, but instead Brother Andrew led us down a side street and onto another trolley car. This time, the driver accepted our money. We had to cram three to a seat since none of the other riders wanted to share with an orphan.

Several stops later, our conveyance halted by a dock, and we boarded a ferry to cross over to the state of New Jersey. When we left the ferry, we walked the few blocks to the train station. With so much to see, everyone slowed down, and I had to urge the stragglers along. It reminded me of when I got lost trying to find the right train car back in England. The memory made my heart race.

"The Chicago Special," Brother Andrew said, stopping to point it out. "That's the one, on the first track. That's our train."

The station area had a dirty smell to it. Soot floated in the air and grease coated the thick wooden planks under the track line.

"Stay with your partner and line up behind me," Brother Andrew said, loudly enough to be heard over the noise around us. "Our car is number twenty-five. That'll be a long walk, so we need to hurry."

The *crunch, crunch* of gravel under our feet echoed off the walls of the station. And though I really didn't like this place, I had to admit it had a mythical aura to it. The black engine could have been a creature emerging from the slime of a bog. Steam shot from under the wheels and curled around passengers' legs as if to pull them under.

No one teased ten-year-old Nathanial when he jumped aside to avoid red-hot cinders that rose from the smokestack and fell all around us. We all knew that sparks had set his parents' home ablaze.

Quite far down the line, I noticed the conductor signaling us to hurry. I stopped and looked at the car beside me. It didn't hold passengers. We'd already gone by all of those. These cars carried coal or grain, and some had animals. We kept walking and by the time we reached number twenty-five, I could see that it had no steps. It was truly nothing but a box made of horizontal wooden planks on the side with large openings between each board. The door to the car slid off to one side, reminding me of the one on Grandpa's barn.

"Move along," the conductor said. "The train must depart on time."

That's when Brother Andrew placed himself directly in front of the man. "Sir, why aren't you seating us in one of the forward cars?"

Even from where I stood, I could see Brother Andrew's face muscles tighten and fists clench. Thrusting his finger into the lapel of the man's blue-tailored suit, he said, "I know there are seats in the passenger cars."

The man harrumphed, straightened his back, and marched away without answering. The younger children looked like they might cry. To his credit, Brother Andrew put on a smile, ruffled the hair on some of the boys, and rubbed the cheeks of a few girls. His gentle voice resumed and one-by-one he assisted everyone up and into the barn-like shell.

Inside, hay had been scattered across the floor. In one corner, bales were arranged to make a small commode area. In the center of the car, a dipper hung from the rim of a wooden barrel containing water. Sometime past, animals traveled in this car. Dung and urine had soaked into the floorboards and now they gave off a stench that made the girls hold their noses.

"I know this isn't what we hoped for, but it is adequate," Brother Andrew said to smooth over the situation. "Before the train starts moving, I want everyone to find a comfortable spot to sit. There are only twelve of you, so everyone will have plenty of room."

I led the girls to a corner where two bales formed an L. Katie climbed on top of one so she could look out between the slats while the other two girls sat on the floor. The boys dropped their cases where they wanted to sit and went to peer through the openings in the closed door. Though Brother Andrew had individually spoken to us about this trip, he called us all over to sit in a circle and listen.

"We're all on an adventure—and good adventurers must know as much as possible about their journey. Don't you agree?"

Everyone nodded. "While we're on the train, there'll be times when it slows but doesn't stop. That usually means they want to grab a mail bag hanging from a pole by the track. Other times, the engineer will bring the train to a full stop because they either need to pick up passengers or refill the supply of water and coal. Those are times when we can get off for a bit and stretch our legs. And if there are people on the station platform, we'll find out if anyone is interested in taking one of you home."

"What if no one wants us?" eleven-year-old Bernard asked.

"I don't want any of you to worry about that. There will be lots of stops before we arrive at our destination in Minnesota. And along the way, we will be switching to other trains with much better cars."

Shouts rose from the boys and the girls covered their ears

to muffle two long and loud toots. As the giant iron wheels began to roll, our car lurched forward, and everyone stood to watch the city fade from view. Once we entered the countryside, I finally relaxed. The smell of factories was replaced by that of fresh cut hay. This felt one degree closer to seeing a farm like Da had wanted. And if I found a home, they had to allow me to go to school. On that, I would not bend.

CHAPTER 25

The Train Moves On

The train's wheels traversed the joiners, the *clickety-clack* rhythm lulling me into a half-sleep while the others talked quietly or played Old Maid. My mind wouldn't let go of what my heart felt—the toll from being alone, the guilt of being safe when others had died, the voice that said *it's all up to you now and if you fail all is lost.*

I could see each of them in the distance—Mother, Da, and Peder. They stood in the middle of a cornfield that had no worms. I ran toward them but slammed into an invisible wall. I couldn't cross over. I beat on it. I cried and hollered at them. I promised to be a better daughter. But no one noticed me, and I sank to the ground sobbing.

I must have slept for some time because the background noise around me had changed. I recognized Jon's voice. "Why are we stopping?" he whispered to his sister, who now sat next to me.

Brother Andrew, as if he'd heard Jon's soft query from across the train car, said, "This is Bloomsburg, Pennsylvania, the first stop on our adventure. We'll usually see people standing on the station platform waiting for us."

No one made a peep. I lifted myself into a sitting position, alert and alarmed. Whatever we'd find on the other side of that door scared me more than I'd ever admit.

"It's important to look your best," he continued. "Brush

off any hay that's clinging to your clothes or hair. And have someone check your face for smudges. They need to be wiped off, too."

Escaping steam made its way up the side of our car as far as the first slat opening, sending a shiver along my arms. The train had stopped. Strangers could be seen on the platform waiting to choose one of us. How many stops would there be before the end came? Brother Andrew hadn't said.

"Make sure your tags are properly pinned to your clothes," he counseled before reaching over to help one of the boys. "People must be able to read them."

I was the one who'd made the tags at his request. Each contained the child's name, age, nationality, Catholic or Protestant, and baptized or not. On the day I returned the twelve completed tags, I asked why those items meant so much to people.

"It can make the difference between a new family and a rejection," he said. "Taking on a child, especially one too young to work in the fields, can pose a great financial strain on the family. Not knowing the child's language only makes it worse. And ..."

Here he hesitated and looked off to the side. "And no good Catholic will take on a Protestant child. So, religion matters."

Metal scraping against metal brought on a long squeak as Brother Andrew pushed the door of our car open. Light burst into the open space and I sensed my pretend courage start to wither away. I had no one to talk to who'd understand my feelings. The children all considered me like a big sister, afraid of nothing. And Brother Andrew counted on me to act as an adult. I wondered if Marta had ever felt afraid.

I decided to act like a brave character in one of my stories. I smiled as I gently encouraged Minnie to stop chewing on her lip before moving over to Johanna, who had wound a lock of hair around her index finger. Only Katie looked like she could take on the world. The boys, however, appeared to puff out their chests as they went to stand by the open door. Once they noticed the people, though, they stopped as if glued to the floor. No one moved until Brother Andrew jumped from the car onto the platform.

Several of the townspeople had come to greet passengers. Three men had their eyes trained on us, while their wives stood closer to the station wall. *This must be how cattle feel when they go to the market*, I thought. Hopping down from the smelly car, I hoped the aroma had not seeped into my clothes.

Brother Andrew led the way through the crowd, past the men and on to the shade of the overhang. When we lined up, Jon stayed by his sister while the rest of the boys stood as a group. I, being the oldest, stood on the end by the girls and wondered if they felt as anxious as I did.

"Not chosen." I could see the sign hanging above my head. I just couldn't bear the rejection, so I started to make up stories in my head that fit the people who'd come to look us over.

I started with the man in the gray three-piece suit. His big belly pushed against the buttons on his vest. I pictured how funny it would be if they all popped off and flew across the platform. Jowls sagged below his chin, and his head appeared to sit directly on his body, as if God had forgotten to give him a neck. Sweat rings spread from under his armpits, suggesting a melting snowman.

Next to the snowman stood a tall, slender man who kept looking at his timepiece. He paced across the platform in his neatly creased trousers and fancy vest that matched the lining of his coat. I figured he must have wealth, but his clothes couldn't hide the worry trails marked on his cheeks nor the deep furrows in his brow. Maybe, like the White Rabbit, he was always apprehensive about being late.

The last man wore faded jeans held in place by red suspenders that crisscrossed the back of his blue plaid shirt. He chewed lazily on a piece of straw. His collar-length blonde hair was like that of the prince in the Sleeping Beauty story.

Though it was impolite, I couldn't take my eyes off him—at least not until a rather high-pitched voice broke the spell.

"Oh, Georgie! Isn't he just darling?"

No doubt this woman was the wife of the snowman. Her size easily matched his. She had stopped in front of Nathanial. Hopelessly shy, the boy couldn't look at her. Red blotches began to show around his neck and on his cheeks as the woman lifted his tag. She drew her face closer and proceeded to loudly recite the words on Nathanial's tag to her husband, who stood some distance away.

"My name is Nathanial. I am ten years old. I am of German descent. I was baptized in the Lutheran Church."

A slight breeze brushed across the platform, sending the odor of mothballs into my nostrils. *She must have forgotten to air out her dress after keeping it in storage*, I thought.

"Let's take him," she said with neither a look back at the snowman nor a single word to Nate.

I winced. Nathanial had always been a sensitive boy. And though I wanted to believe the woman and her husband would be kind, she'd still not spoken to him. She seemed to consider him more like a number attached to an article owned by another family and now lost to the highest bidder. Without any discussion or so much as a glance at the boy, the snowman signed the papers and Nathanial became an indentured servant to these people. No one had asked if he wanted to go with them.

Obviously, I'd not thought this whole process through when Brother Andrew explained it to me. Now it all seemed wrong. We should have a say in our futures. Marta had taught me to be strong in this new country, to reason for myself, to make my own choices. But now I could see that for every one of us with the titles of orphan and child, the choice just didn't exist.

"*Sprichst du Deutsch?*" the woman asked as she tilted his chin to examine him. Nathanial looked over at me with his questioning eyes. This woman had never carried on a conversation with him. She didn't know he'd been born in New York and that his parents never allowed him to speak German. When he remained silent, she cleared her throat as if to erase the question and start over.

She waited a short time, then slowly reached out and took hold of his hand. He looked ready to cry despite his desire to be brave in front of the others. Everything had happened too fast. Reassurance, that's what he needed, and none of the other children understood. So, before his new mother could walk away with him, I reached out, knelt in front of him, and looked up at the watery eyes he tried so hard to hide.

"We'll miss you, Nate. But now you'll have a good home."

That's all it took. The others came in behind me and each of them offered encouragement. Nate smiled, even laughed as some of the boys clapped him on the back. We all waved as he walked away with his new family.

After we returned to our places, the watchman's wife came forward. A petite woman, she wore a flat straw hat with dried flowers stuck here and there on the brim. Unlike the first lady, this one only approached the three younger girls. She read their tags before having a short conversation to help each of them feel more at ease. She lingered in front of five-year-old Katie.

"Katie. What a pretty name. And look at your hair," she said as she reached to touch the red locks. "I always wanted red hair just like yours."

The attention made Katie beam and I prayed she'd go home with this lady. I remembered the night Brother Andrew told me how hard it could be to place someone with red hair.

"I brush it faithfully every day," Katie said with great pride.

"Esther. Come along." The sound of the husband's words cut like a sword. "There's nothing here of interest to me."

Without a backward look, the watch man descended the side stairs and headed toward the town's main street. The woman reached out to caress Katie's cheek. Both had puddles of tears sparkling and ready to spill from their eyes.

"I would sign the papers if I could," the woman said, "but my husband has told me that women aren't allowed to sign the legal papers."

Like a dog called to heel, the pretty woman started to leave. When she reached the stairs, though, she stopped and hurried back to Katie. From her dainty purse she took a handkerchief to dab at Katie's tears.

"Be brave, beautiful girl," she whispered in Katie's ear, before she went to follow the man. She walked back toward the town, her head lowered, and tears falling.

The third man still stood in the shadow of the overhang. His wife placed her arm into the crook of his and together they moved toward Charles. Without glancing at his tag, they both bent down to the boy's eye level and struck up a conversation. Whenever they got around to reading it, they'd find that he was three. However, no one knew his nationality and he'd been baptized in an unnamed denomination. I remembered the Sunday when Brother Andrew took him to church to have the sacrament performed just in case it hadn't been done. *Most people want to know that the child was raised a Christian,* I clearly recalled him telling me.

Charles wasn't shy. He introduced himself to the man and started up a line of jabber that made all of us laugh.

"I'm a big boy and I want to be a cowboy someday."

"Well, then, if you would like to be our son, we'd sure be proud to take you home with us."

"I git a new Mudder and Da!" Charles said, jumping up and down as if he had springs in his feet.

"Yes, and if you want to be a cowboy, you should let your mother take you to meet Robbie. That's the name of our horse. And when we get home, I'll unhitch him so you can ride around a bit. He's very gentle, especially with children. But Robbie can't see, so you mustn't guide him where he will get hurt."

We all applauded the happiness that bounced off Charles as he shouted, "I git to wide Wobbie!" His new mother walked him over to the horse. Charles, shorter than the length of Robbie's legs, spread his arms as far up and wide as they would go on the horse's chest. His mother felt under the buggy's seat until she found a carrot then gave it to Charles.

"Will he bite me?"

"Oh, no. Robbie is very careful."

We watched Robbie cautiously approach the extended carrot. Delicately, he used his lips to feel down the side of the orange treat until he came to the boy's fingers, then backed off a bit before taking a bite.

After the papers had been signed, the children all wished Charles well in his new home. The man lifted him onto the buggy seat and placed him by his new mother. At that very moment, my stomach let out a loud growl, and everyone laughed.

"It is time for lunch, you know," I said, glancing at the station clock. "Maybe we should all eat the sandwiches Hilda put in our cases."

"Hold off on that idea for a moment," Brother Andrew said. "I want you to watch the children while I talk to that man over there."

I guided the children to the edge of the platform where they could sit and swing their legs while looking at the horizon.

James teased Minnie. "Do you think we'll fall off the earth when we get to the end of the track?" She looked frightened but only until Katie punched his arm and told him to behave.

"Children," Brother Andrew called out as he came up behind us. "The pastor told me that his wife is preparing fresh sandwiches for everyone. We can have Hilda's later as a snack. For now, I think it would be good for you to use the outhouse on the other side of the church."

Almost before he'd finished speaking, the boys headed out

at a dead run. The girls, ever ladylike, walked across the last of the brittle grass stubble, each obediently holding another's hand.

"There's a water pump on the side of the building," Brother Andrew said to me, "so go wash up. I'll straighten everything in the rail car and empty the chamber pot. We haven't got much time, so don't let anyone lallygag."

The boys hurried in and out of the outhouse. Washing up was barely attempted—even though a bar of soap lay in a dish right next to the pump. I didn't call them on it. We'd all had enough excitement for one morning.

As I exited the outhouse, Emil shouted for everyone to come over to him. There, slightly hidden amongst the last leaves of summer, lay a yellow dog with newly born pups snuggled against her belly and hungrily nursing. The mother seemed curious about the children and not overly upset to have them gently touch the babies. This simple discovery felt good on a not-so-normal day.

Abruptly, the conductor shouted, "All *aboooard!*"

Brother Andrew hastily thanked the pastor as I made a game of racing the children to the train. The promised sandwiches would be left behind, or so I assumed. But when the final whistle blew and our car jerked forward, the pastor's wife reached up to hand Brother Andrew a bag.

"Goodbye," she called out, her arm raised high in a hearty wave. "I hope you enjoy your lunch."

She blew kisses to us and walked with the train the full length of the platform. Once we were at the end, she stood waving and yelling, "Good luck!"

Everyone except Brother Andrew went to sit by their suitcases. The car weaved a bit, its wheels crossing faster and faster over the joiners. After he offered up a prayer of thanks, Brother Andrew asked me to pass out the sandwiches. The first one, and all that followed, had a thickness to them. Each had been wrapped in waxed paper held in place by a piece of tape. In the very bottom of the bag were apples—perfect ones, without worm holes.

Some of the children had already begun to eat when I opened my sandwich and realized she'd put fried chicken between the bread slices. It reminded me of when Mother would make the same sandwich. But that was before the bugs, before the oldest chicken became soup, and before the other two had had to be sold or given away as payment.

A couple of hours later, having passed into the state of Ohio, the train arrived at a station where the sign read Windham and from what I could see, the town couldn't have been more than half the size of the last one. Only two men stood on the platform. Once we'd formed our line, which now had ten instead of twelve, the men walked past each of us, mumbling to themselves. With a shrug of their shoulders, they simply left with no explanation. My mind, still partially lost in the befuddlement of leftover sleep, was glad to see them go. Both would have fit better at an animal auction. They had a smell about them that reeked of too much tobacco and too little bathing. I think they wanted a trail hand for labor, not a child to love.

Back in the train car, Brother Andrew announced there'd be one more stop when we reached the middle of Ohio. That place happened to have a man's name, Elmore, and we arrived just as the sun had started to settle lower in the afternoon sky. By the time we left, I was showing my anger at the process of home finding.

Bernard, a rather self-conscious boy whose eleventh birthday we'd all celebrated back at the Home, went to live with a man and his wife who looked like farmers. Older than anyone else who had come to see us in the other towns, neither of them bothered to speak to Bernard. They just squeezed his upper arms and checked his teeth. They hadn't even read his tag before telling Brother Andrew they wanted "that boy."

I felt sick inside. Bernard's face had turned pale. And when another of the boys tried to congratulate him, Bernard nudged him aside in anger.

Horrible thoughts gnawed inside my head. *What if they only use Bernard as a hired hand and don't think of him as a son? What if they make him sleep in the barn all year and refuse to feed him much?*

Bernard had always loved animals, had a gentle way with them, and he refused to kill even a mosquito. I couldn't believe he would ever find love from these people, so I shared my fear with Brother Andrew and pleaded that he not allow Bernard to go with these people.

"Someone will check on him in a few weeks. They'll for sure use him on the farm, but that's not unusual," he said to reassure me.

But a lot could happen in a few weeks, and I didn't want to be right. Winter was coming on, and he'd be so cold if they made him stay in the barn.

The couple gestured for him to sit in the bed of their wagon, not inviting him to ride on the empty seat up front. None of us showed happiness as dust rose from behind the wagon and Bernard went on, all alone, to a farm somewhere in the woods.

CHAPTER 26

Mabel and Henry

I dreaded getting back on the train. Each subtraction from our group wrought a change in me. Surely, we'd not be asked to parade again on this day. The thought of spending the night in the stink of that train car buzzed in my head like an angry bee.

In no more than an hour, we arrived at a covered area beside a platform with no station building but many lines of tracks for storing train cars, especially ones carrying coal and grain.

Brother Andrew slid the door aside and said, "Tonight will be a special treat. Just on the other side of this field is the home of my friends Mabel and Henry. The last time I came here, they had bunnies, chickens, cats, and an old dog named Trofust. Before we leave this car, though, look around and make sure you've got everything. Get your suitcases—this car won't be here in the morning."

The boys, all five of them, jumped onto the platform and hurried to wait by the field on the other side of the train car. Katie, Johanna, and Minnie allowed Brother Andrew to carefully lift each of them out of the car while I made a final inspection.

The field that edged the train tracks had tall grass dotted with wildflowers. Someone had cut a path down the middle and at its end stood a rather tall woman wearing a full-length apron. Brother Andrew raised his arm high and waved with all his might. The woman returned the gesture and waited as our leader spoke to us without taking his eyes off her.

"That's Mabel," he said, and he ran off to meet her.

"My Andrew," she called out with arms open wide.

By the time I made it across the field, the two of them were standing in an embrace. Some of the boys started to snigger, but our opinionated Katie hushed them with a scornful look. I studied this woman whose apron was adorned with ruffles on the bottom. Some strands of her gray hair, twisted and pinned atop her head, hung loose and curly, like a broken spring.

"I've missed you so much," she said, looking tenderly into his eyes. "Your room is waiting for you, and I sewed on the missing buttons from the shirt you forgot last time."

He gently kissed her cheek and smiled. Then, as if remembering us for the first time, he took a moment for introductions.

"These wonderful children are ..."

"Oh, I can figure that out. Just let me give them a proper welcome."

Three-year-old Jon, first in line, quickly said his name and age—but ducked out from under Mabel's welcome hug to avoid the kiss she tried to plant on his head. A loud *yeuuuw* instantly issued forth from the other boys. The second they were free, they ran off to the porch to meet Henry, who clutched a bat in one hand and a ball in the other, ready to play a game. Mabel directed the girls to the new kittens in the barn and to Trofust, who generously provided dog kisses.

That left only Mabel and me at the edge of the field.

"You must be Kristi. Andrew told me he hoped to bring an older girl, but he didn't tell me how beautiful you are."

My face felt hot, but she seemed not to notice my blushing.

"Since you're the oldest, I'm hoping you'll help me set the table and finish preparing the meal."

"I'd love to," I said, glad to have something to distract me from the events of the day.

"Follow me," she said then turned toward the house. I tried to keep up as each step of her long stride covered a lot of ground.

At the back porch, she stopped to say, "Just set your suit-case by the banister when we get inside. We have a small com-mode room here where you can wash up and be first to try out this new bar of soap. It's the craziest thing I've ever seen. It floats in the water."

In the washroom, I watched her put the stopper in the sink, run the water, and drop in the *Ivory* soap—its name stamped right on top. It truly did float, and we both laughed.

As I entered the kitchen, Mabel began to speak as if we were in the middle of a conversation. "Dishes, silverware, and glasses are in this cabinet. None of them match, but that's the fun of it. You can set the table for, let's see, I guess I forgot to count how many children Andrew brought."

"There are nine of us left," I offered.

"Well, then, with Andrew, Henry, and me, that makes twelve."

Mabel had no fanciness about her. While I folded the napkins in the manner taught by Hilda, Mabel mashed the potatoes and stirred the gravy. The tune she hummed as she worked had a familiar pattern to it.

"What's the name of that song?" I asked.

"Oleanna. It's about a lazy young man's desire to leave Norway for something better." She started singing the first verse.

> *Oh, to be in Oleanna!*
> *That's where I'd like to be,*
> *Than be bound in Norway,*
> *And drag the chains of slavery.*

In Oleanna land is free,
The wheat and corn just plant themselves,
Then grow a good four feet a day,
While on your bed you rest yourself.

I teared up.

"I'm sorry, child. I've made you cry."

"That song reminded me of my da. He wanted to find land where his corn would grow without being killed by bugs or starved of rain. I miss him so much."

Mabel looked sympathetic. "When my da died, it felt like I'd plunged through the floorboards into the cellar."

Behind us, the screen door screeched then slammed against its frame as someone entered.

"When should I ..." Brother Andrew stopped himself, having caught us before we could dry our tears.

"In a few minutes," Mabel responded without a glance his way. "I'll call you in when all is ready." Back he went to tell the others to end their games, return the kittens to their mother, and pay a visit to the trough by the barn.

At supper that evening, conversations flowed, and laughter erupted. It felt like hope was back. And, when the last of the dishes were done, Henry went to retrieve a round metal tub from the back porch. Mabel set a kettle on the stove to heat. "You've all had a long day. Everyone needs a bath."

"Girls first," she told Henry as he snuggled up behind her.

"Okay, everyone, do you all see that box in the corner?" Henry said. "Inside are pajamas of all sizes—my Mabel made every one of them. Before your bath, you must each choose something that fits you. They'll be yours to keep."

Henry went over and planted a big smacker on Mabel's cheek, eliciting another round of *yeuuuws* from the boys. He laughed so hard at those boys I thought his sides would split. Without delay, he chased them out of the kitchen and into the living room so Brother Andrew could read a story while we girls bathed. When the youngest girl had finished, Mabel ushered them upstairs to bed, leaving me to my privacy.

When he was sure I'd finished, Henry brought the boys in. He and Brother Andrew emptied the tub of its sweet-smelling water—the boys wanted none of that. Their time for bathing proved much noisier than ours. Someone worked the pump handle as water splashed into a container. The kettle gave out a whistle and the boys protested loudly. "I don't need a bath!"

Mabel and I ventured to the porch. She had me take a blanket from the sofa as she retrieved a shawl from the corner chair for herself. Crickets began to sing and lightning bugs floated on tiny drafts of air just above the grass. I hadn't felt so peaceful in a long time.

"Did you ever have something you wanted more than anything in the world and it became all you could think of night and day?" I asked.

"Do you have such a thing, Kristi?"

"More than anything, I want to go back to school and study to be a teacher. I've wanted that since Mother first taught me to read. But now, here in America, I wonder if my dream can ever happen. Besides, all my family's plans fell away one by one. Somehow, I don't think dreams come true in America."

"What would cause your dream to fail?"

"Well, what if no family wants me and I'm sent back to New York? I'm older—and a girl. Boys are wanted to help on the farm. In truth, I can work hard. But going back to school is really the only thing I want in my life. And I've heard that some men don't want their daughters educated. They say it's a waste of time and money. I can't go into a family like that."

"What you say is true. I do think if you want this badly enough, you'll find a way to get it done—even if it takes longer than you'd planned. Don't give up on it. It's a wonderful goal."

The silence between us seemed to last forever. Finally, Mabel spoke up. "Henry and I had dreams, too, but we needed to rethink them after a few years."

"What did you want?"

"We wanted children. Lots of them. And, in a way, we got them. Just not how we planned. Though it's hard to see now in the dark, out on that knoll are several kinds of flowers. Our Odin is resting under the peony bush. He loved to climb trees. He fell from the highest branch of the oak." After a pause, she added, "Five days he lingered before passing on."

"And our Gertie, she's under the lilac bush. Her hair was raven colored." Mable's voice grew faint. "But no one could make her breathe."

"Winifred got the croup and died before her first birthday. The daisies line her bed."

"Then Lars. He came that next year in the dead of winter. My milk wouldn't come in. Our cow ..." I waited for the next part. "Well, she got frightened by a winter thunderstorm, kicked down the fence, and ran off into the night. Henry didn't find her until spring because the snow had fallen so deep. By then, she had died. And so had Lars."

"Now," she concluded, "we have the children Andrew brings to us. We love you all and try to provide some joy while you're here."

After that story, I don't remember anything else we talked about. Eventually, Mabel got up and asked me to follow her into the bedroom. There, at the foot of the bed, a cedar trunk with brass clamps rested upon a rag rug. Digging through its contents, Mabel heaped sheets, pillowcases, and a well-used quilt to one side.

"Here it is," she said. She held a leather-bound book, its cover rubbed thin from much use. She handed it to me, and I gasped. My fingers trembled as they traced the title.

"*Little Women!* What a treasure. And it's just like the one my mother used to have."

"What happened to your mother's book? Did she have to leave it in Norway?"

"No, she brought it in her suitcase. When our ship docked

in New York, she accidentally left it on the bed in steerage. She didn't discover the loss until our first night in the apartment Da rented for us. I offered to go back and get it, but by then it was dark out and Da wouldn't hear of it."

Mabel listened carefully. "This one belonged to my mother. I always thought someday I'd pass it on to my own daughter. Now, I'd like to give it to you, so you'll keep the dream of teaching in your heart."

I shook my head. "I couldn't take your book."

"Well, then, maybe you'd like to sit and read it for a while."

"That would be wonderful."

Mabel escorted me back to the living room. After placing a beautifully crocheted throw on my lap, she said, "Read as long as you want. No one will disturb you."

I must have fallen asleep because I woke to the laughter of children and the sizzle of bacon frying in a cast iron pan. The book, Mabel's precious book, lay resting on my lap and open to page twenty. Hurriedly, I folded the throw, placed the book on the side table, and ran upstairs to get dressed. When I came down, there stood Henry at the stove scrambling some eggs.

"Come sit and eat," he said as soon as he saw me. "Mabel went to get some more eggs." Not realizing I'd grown up on a farm, he added, "They'll be the freshest ones you've ever eaten."

Minnie motioned for me to sit by her. I eased myself onto the bench, unable to stop looking at the platters of bacon, eggs, fried potatoes, and bread toasted on the open flame of the stove. The food seemed endless. Strawberry and rhubarb jams, each in their own fancy serving dishes, made me think of the time long ago when Mother had all she needed to make these same treats.

"Take more of everything," Henry told everyone as he replenished the platter of eggs. "You never know how long it might be before lunch."

"Train's coming," someone yelled after its three long toots. I gulped the last of my milk.

"Hurry and get your suitcases—and be sure to thank Mabel and Henry," Brother Andrew said as he ducked his head around the corner of the kitchen, and I noticed he'd changed into regular men's clothes.

Henry raced the boys to the porch, where he shook hands with each of them, saying with a broad smile, "Nice knowing you, men. Come again when you can and maybe we'll have a chaw."

The boys, who knew what that meant, assumed proud postures, and snickered at the girls, as each of them got hugs. Though the boys tried to dodge Mabel at the edge of the field, no one made it. They all got both hugs and cheek kisses, which they immediately rubbed off. The fondest goodbye, though, was saved for Brother Andrew, whom Mabel held for an extra-long time. She made him promise to come back soon.

When I reached the train, I glanced back for one last look. Henry had his back to us. I could see that his sadness at our departure had spilled over because he took out a large handkerchief from his back pocket and rubbed it across his face. I took another look at the knoll and its garden of flowers. I vowed to make one just like it for my own family. It could overlook fields of corn and wheat and they would look down with a smile. I wanted to be like Mabel and Henry—givers of gifts like rest and love, things that can't be wrapped.

We still had bales of hay in the new railcar, but no one complained. Like before, the metal wheels screeched as the car moved down the track, and our journey continued westward.

CHAPTER 27

The Journey Continues

Before Brother Andrew took a seat, he told us, "Today, there'll be several stops plus a change in trains as we move toward the end of the line. None of the stops will last very long, so you'll need to pay attention and line up without delay."

I chuckled to myself as I thought of the White Rabbit, always unsure of where he needed to go and always glancing at his watch. "Oh dear, oh dear," he kept saying before he fell down the hole and into the clutches of the Red Queen. I had a quick daydream of sledding down a mountainside with no way to stop. Next thing I knew, I'd have to go back up to do it all over again, like Sisyphus.

That's when I heard, "Tell uth a thtory, Krithti."

Emil stood before me with an impish grin on his face, his tongue peeking out from the hole where two teeth had once been. He lisped, but only since the teeth fell out. Many times, while I lived at the Home, I'd overheard this same boy weave tales of dragons, ghosts, and goblins. He was a gifted story-teller, far beyond someone his age—much better than I, if I were to be honest.

"We want a thcary thtory," he said, droplets of spit escaping through the gap.

"Alright," I agreed with a smile.

"From the time I could walk, my mother had warned me about the forest and the fjord. The one held trolls and the other had no bottom to it. But it would soon be Mother's birthday and the only gift I could think to give her was a bouquet of flowers.

"On the hillside behind our barn, I picked a few arctic willows, bluebells, and mountain avens before starting back down the hill. I thought I heard someone talking, which made me stop and look back toward the forest. I called out, 'Is anyone there?' No one answered. I got scared and took off running toward the fjord."

"What happened next? Were there any monsters?" James asked.

"When I got close to the edge overlooking the fjord, I stopped a moment to pick more flowers. But the ground had grown soft after a heavy rain, and it gave way. I slid into the water. Its icy cold took my breath away. My eyes froze open. All around me swam huge fish, some with long stingers for whiskers. Others showed their sharp teeth. A snake that looked big enough to swallow me in one gulp slithered by!"

The children's eyes grew wide as they waited for me to go on.

"Finally, a giant-sized hand reached down and lifted me above the water and back onto the cliff ..."

"Your story will have to wait," interrupted Brother Andrew. "We'll soon arrive at the first stop of the day."

"Ahhh," Emil sighed. "We want to hear more."

"Maybe later. For now, everyone should use the commode. And like before, check for hay in your hair or on your clothes. And smudges on your face. You want to look your best."

In no time at all, a slight breeze delivered the steely odor of brakes gripping hold of giant wheels, drawing everything to a halt. When Brother Andrew opened the door, we saw that we had been left to disembark some distance down the track from the platform. Evidently, no one cared if we struggled to exit our car or had to walk through the weeds. Needle-sharp balls of bur stickers hung all over their stems and clung to our clothes like glue as we crossed the field. Tiny dots of blood appeared on our fingertips after we pulled them off.

Three well-dressed women stood at the top of the platform stairs. "Excuse us, please," Brother Andrew said as he came to stand in front of them. Though they moved aside, one of the ladies pressed her lips together and wrinkled her nose. Another whispered just loud enough so we could hear, "They're orphans. Don't let them touch you."

Welcome to Chicago, read the sign above the station. *I'm not so sure about that*, I thought. Indeed, Mabel had warned me about this place.

"It's got a continual busyness about it," she'd said.

She was right, and I immediately disliked it.

"Here come the orphans!"

There stood a lady with a pointy nose aiming an accusatory finger toward us. Her voice grated like a door in need of a good oiling.

"Move aside." This demand came in the same authoritative tone Miss Robinson used when she wanted no nonsense from anyone. At first, I couldn't locate the source, but seconds later a brown-haired woman appeared, pushing her way through the crowd. By the time she reached us, we had lined up facing the station with our backs to the train. Without hesitation, she walked straight to Emil.

"Hello," she said. "My name is Mrs. Pedersen. And who might you be?" She looked him straight in the eye and ignored the tag.

"I'm Emil and I'm five," he replied politely.

"Tell me about yourself, Emil. What kind of things do you like to do? What games do you play? And do you have favorite books?"

"I make up thcary thtoryth," he said. "And I'm good at my numberth. Playing cardth ith fun, but I'm no good at baythball."

"I see you've lost some teeth. Did that hurt?"

"No, but I had to thwollow blood, and I didn't like that."

"My husband and I like numbers, though we are terrible at making up stories, so we'd leave that to you. What's your favorite card game?"

"Mothtly I like Old Maid."

Just then, a man dressed in jeans and a tired old gray shirt came up to stand beside the lady. A big black dog with a tail that swung back and forth followed close behind. Emil took a step back and almost fell from the platform. Hans caught him by the arm to stop his fall.

"Well, well. Who have you found here, Clara?" the man asked, a big mischievous grin on his face.

"This is Emil and he's five."

"Hello, Emil," the man said as the boy tried again to scoot back. "I'm pleased to meet you. And this here dog is Max. He sometimes shakes hands, too."

"I'm afraid of dogs," Emil said, once again edging backwards.

"Did one scare you or bite you?"

Emil nodded. "Last year, a big brown one chased me and ripped the leg of my pants before I could get to the door."

This time, the man knelt in front of Emil and waited for their eyes to meet. "I'm sorry that happened to you," the man said softly. "But you don't ever have to worry about Max doing that."

While Mr. and Mrs. Pedersen continued to speak with Emil, the crowd surged closer to the rest of us, and my attention was drawn to the other children. There were ladies in the crowd who simply read name tags, while a man pinched Lars's arm, and a snooty woman crinkled her nose as she passed by Katie.

"Red hair," she sniffed, as if it were the plague.

But as I looked back at Emil, he stood there with such a huge grin on his face I was confident he'd found a home. His new mother helped him get acquainted with the dog while his new da went off to sign papers with Brother Andrew. It was then that I noticed the man's shaky hands and worried he might be sick.

Nearby, Hans, the only boy old enough for farm work, found himself being rejected by a couple who obviously had no understanding of how much their words had hurt him.

"He'll never do," the man said in a tone of disgust. "He's got a limp. I don't want a cripple."

He spat out these harsh judgments as if he'd swallowed kerosene instead of water. I was furious. I marched right up to the man, aimed my finger, and glared at him. But before I could speak, Brother Andrew took his arm and sent him on his way. I couldn't hear what he said. Hopefully, he gave the man a good talking to.

Poor Hans. His shoulders slumped and he swatted at James, who had tried to make him feel better.

"Boys, don't fight," I said. "By the end of the journey, the right folks will come along for each of us. You'll see."

That's when the craziest memory came back to me. In Norway, Mother had daily brushed aside a web that the same spider made anew every night. One day I said, "I think we should leave the web. It's beautiful. And every day, she works hard to make it a little stronger." After thinking about it, Mother had given in to me. "I have to admit, that spider does have persistence, a quality that I admire."

I soon found myself lost in more daydreams as people came and went from the platform. I hadn't noticed anyone coming alongside me, so I jumped back when a hand reached out and touched my face. The smell of alcohol and filth invaded my nostrils. Bloodshot eyes assessed me in a way that felt all wrong. I reared back and screamed, "Don't touch me!"

Everyone looked my way—and in what seemed no more than an instant, Brother Andrew pulled the man backwards, roughly escorting him down the platform stairs. I don't think that man's feet even found the steps. Before he knew what happened, he was lying on the ground with Brother Andrew standing over him.

"You're drunk. Leave here now—and don't let me see you ever again!"

He yanked the man to his feet and pushed him away from the platform, kicking him in the seat of his pants. I shook all over but held back my tears. People stared. When Brother Andrew returned, he put his hands on my shoulders. "Did he hurt you, Kristi?"

"No. He just really scared me."

"We'll go back to the train as soon as I ask if anyone else has an interest in a child."

As he left my side to make his final inquiries, I saw his fists tighten. I'd never seen him so upset or angry, but the fear wouldn't stop. And sure enough, when he wasn't looking, some roughnecks, maybe a few years older than me, sauntered over to face us.

"No one wants you orphans," the oldest one said.

"Yeah. Why don't you go back where you came from?" another added, spitting a wad of tobacco between the feet of James and Lars.

Brother Andrew returned rapidly to face the leader of the pack. "You boys need to move on along. There's nothing here for you, and these kids don't want trouble."

"Then get them out of here. We don't like ..."

"Where's your folks, young man?" Brother Andrew interrupted, looking right into the eyes of the youngest.

The boy looked startled at first. Then he got angry. He had opened his mouth to say something when a constable came up behind him and took hold of his ear. The officer pinched it hard as he looked over at the others.

"You boys move on, or I'll throw the lot of you in a cell."

Reluctantly, the ruffians headed away from the station, but not before one of them stuck his tongue out at the back of the officer.

"Thank you, sir." Brother Andrew offered a handshake.

"No problem. I hate seeing kids picked on, especially these orphans. If I had a missus, I'd bring this fine young man home with me," he said, reaching an arm around Hans. He gave his shoulder a quick squeeze. "Yes, you'd be a fine son indeed."

The constable took a moment to look at each of us, then grabbed the brim of his hat, gave a nod, and walked briskly into the station.

Brother Andrew gathered us around him. "Another train is coming in about an hour. It'll be much nicer—no more bales of hay, just regular passenger seats. Let's all go back now and get your suitcases."

The boys jumped up and down amidst hoots of joy, and the girls skipped together across the platform. I waited to walk with Brother Andrew and wasted no time expressing my concerns.

"What's wrong with Emil's new da? I noticed him shaking."

"He has a disease that I don't know a whole lot about, but it's nothing that others can catch. It makes the nerves in his body not work properly. One thing's for sure, though—it won't stop him from loving Emil."

After we'd gone a few more feet, he added, "I'm so sorry about what happened back there."

My assailant's behavior had made me feel ashamed, and I wasn't sure I wanted to talk about it. But Brother Andrew had stopped and the two of us stood face to face.

"That's the most scared I've ever been," I said. "What did he want? Did I do something wrong? Was he looking for a child to take home?"

My mind groped for answers that made sense in my known world. I suddenly felt like a very young child terrified by the kind of evil only found in horror stories.

"No," he began. "He didn't want a child. He came toward you because you are no longer a child."

Like an idea that has just been clearly explained, I real-ized that I knew this man. He was like the men who called out to the girls on the streets of New York. I felt queasy as the phrase "no longer a child" dangled before me. I envisioned a door with frightening things behind it, things that derailed life adventures and ruined precious dreams. What if my goal had other dangers lurking along the way? After all, even Da's plans for a farm hadn't included sickness and injury. What else would jump out at me now that perfect strangers recognized my childhood had fallen away?

"Lars."

Brother Andrew's call brought me back from the dark. "Climb up in the car. I want you to pass all the cases down to Kristi."

I veered off the sad path my mind had been racing down and took note of the others' excitement. Their only objective was to see the new, better ride we'd have on the next train. Maybe being an orphan didn't matter as much if you could ride a train with real seats.

When we entered the station, Brother Andrew told us to go sit by the window that overlooked the tracks.

"Listen carefully," he said once we'd all settled in. "Early this morning, Mabel made a lunch for each of you and placed it inside your suitcase. There's a bologna sandwich, a carrot, an apple, and a molasses cookie dipped in sugar. No other food will be provided until tonight when we come to the end of the line."

There. He'd said it. The phrase stuck in my gullet: *end of the line.* If only I could know for sure that a family would take me even though I was no longer a "child."

"Those of you who can read should watch for an engine with Chicago, Milwaukee, St. Paul, and Pacific Railroad Company written on the side. That train will take us for the next several miles. The ticket master told me we have the entire car to ourselves."

A cheer rose from everyone but me. I held back, suspicious about why we would have a car to ourselves. Didn't anyone want to sit with us?

"Where does this train take us?" I asked.

"This time we're heading for the state of Wisconsin."

I don't know why I asked. His answer meant nothing to me. I had no understanding of where each state might be on a map, and besides, I still felt shaken because the man on the platform had touched me.

I kept the others close by while Brother Andrew went to speak to the conductor. A heavy cloud of worry had crept into my mind. It was day two and only four of us had found homes. A whistle sounded and drew my attention as our train came into the station. My anxiety would have to wait.

"Our car is number five," Brother Andrew said when he came up behind me. "Johanna, would you lead the way?"

"Ahh, girls can't count that high. She'll get us lost," James teased.

Johanna gave him "the look" which she later told me meant "boys are just so childish." It felt good to watch her stride to the front of the line, square her shoulders, then look back and say, "Follow me!" I had to laugh, though I covered my mouth in time to hide it. She was our Pied Piper.

At car number five, Johanna stopped and pointed to the gold painted number. Swinging her arm in the direction of the door at the top of the stairs, she tilted her head a bit to one side and smiled as if to say, "See? Girls can do anything." The boys just shook their heads and tumbled over each other to find their own special seats.

"Don't touch it! This is my seat!" one of them said.

I had wanted the seat next to the door so I could relax alone. Thankfully, no one else asked for it. I swung my case onto the far end where it rested on a threadbare velvety material, its red cover so cracked that the stuffings of horsehair poked out. *It's not a hay bale*, I thought, *but this isn't a car for the fancy passengers, either*. The others seemed not to notice, but I tucked the information into my imaginary book of grown-up knowledge. Page one: Society has degrees of acceptance and today we've only moved up one notch.

The window by my seat had streaks of dust and soot on the outside, making it hard to see the clock on the station wall. We hadn't even reached the halfway point of the day and I had no more energy. I decided to lower my window, admitting a most awful smell.

"Ewww ..."

"Close your window," the others all called out. Brother Andrew, who sat across from me, offered an explanation.

"When the wind is just right, you can catch a whiff of the stockyards. You'll see them as we pass by on our way out of town. Cattle and hogs, all brought in on the trains, are unloaded into the pens that lead to the processing plant. The building is over there, where you see the smoke."

As we pulled out of the station, I could see the pens he'd mentioned. Cows. Pigs. They'd all been packed tight against one another. Animals' heads were pointed into the air, their eyes wild with fear—they smelled death. I'd seen that look before when Grandpa Carl got out his tools to butcher a cow on his farm. The beast had sensed what would happen and tried to run. She bellowed right up until the very end. Mother had been angry at him for allowing me to watch.

A short distance further, row after row of houses came into view. Box shaped, small, none painted, they all had raw wood for an exterior. Not a blade of grass poked through anywhere, only mud with planks of wood extending like a walkway from each house and ending at the main door of the factory. None of the planks crisscrossed to allow neighbors to visit nor children to play. That absence felt wrong. Clearly the factory owners wanted workers, not a community of people that grew into a family.

I questioned Brother Andrew as to why anyone would want to live amidst the filth and smell of blood and death. He told me that the factory owned the people, but I didn't really understand what he meant—at least not until years later, when I read *The Jungle* by Sinclair Lewis.

When we'd left the odor behind, I decided to open the bag lunch Mabel had made. As I lifted it out, I noticed that my new nightgown had something heavy inside it. It couldn't be my journal, nor Da's Bible, because they rested in the other corner where I'd placed them. Almost afraid of what I might find, I freed the contents from the gown and there lay *Liten Kvinner*, Mabel's copy of *Little Women*. Shaking, I took the note out from inside the front cover.

> *Dear Kristi,*
>
> *I've given you this book because I want it to be the first of many in your personal library. Write to me when you find your new family and I'll come to see you on the day you graduate from Normal School.*
>
> *You have the love and gift of learning. Be sure to use it for the good of others.*
>
> *Your friend,*
> *Mabel*

CHAPTER 28

More Stops to Find the End

A long trail of smoke drifted by my window. I diverted my gaze to land upon seven-year-old James, who sat alone in one of the first seats. He swung his restless legs back and forth one at a time, as if he were running. Since his hearing wasn't good, I suspected that if someone took him in, they'd need money for hearing aids. Without those, James would miss so many things in life and kids would tease him. At the Home, Brother Andrew had explained to the others that James needed their help, not the taunts or poking that made him cry. That simple explanation was all it took for the others to feel important, like teachers. They protected him and he no longer cried. But people weren't always so kind, and that made me worry. Back in Norway, I'd often observed my parents standing up for someone that others had picked on.

"The next stop is La Crosse, Wisconsin. It's only a few minutes away," Brother Andrew called out as he made his way to the front of the car. "I want each of you to straighten your area and put away any games you've taken from your cases. This time you'll need to bring your suitcase, because we'll board a different train in about an hour."

"How many more stops before we reach the end of the line?" I had to know. More stops meant more chances. When he told me there were only two after this one, I felt a panic rise. The orphan-parade game had started to wear on me. So far, not one couple had shown the slightest interest in my life story.

"Darn," Katie said, smacking the back of the seat in front of her with the flat of her palm.

"That's not a fit word for proper ladies and gentlemen," Brother Andrew said.

"But we don't like it when people stare at us."

She stood and stomped her foot twice with some of the boys nodding in agreement. I went to comfort her, kneeling to straighten her hair bow.

"Katie, Brother Andrew wouldn't bring us here if there weren't good people. I'm betting you'll soon have a new mother and da. But until that happens, it's important to show everyone how brave you are."

I'm not sure who I was trying to convince, her or me. After all, no one should have to worry about being unwanted or sent back. And yet, we all knew our chances became fewer after each stop.

Two quick whistles announced our arrival just as I noticed the wall clock, and questioned the time.

"Can that clock be right?" I asked. "It seems later than that."

"Yes, it's right. We've crossed into a different time zone and gained an hour. Back in New York, it's three o'clock."

A time zone. I knew about them. Miss Robinson had told us, but I'd always imagined that I'd feel something when it happened. And how should I spend this extra hour, I wondered?

None of the people on the station platform spoke to us or showed any interest as we exited the train and lined up under the canopy. I tried to block my disappointment by scanning the landscape. Hills—small ones, nothing like our mountains back home—had replaced the flatlands we'd come through. Some had been planted with crops that now awaited the harvesters. Others were covered in grass with cattle either grazing or resting under trees.

My wandering thoughts, along with any sense of calm, ended abruptly with the sudden approach of footsteps. I looked up to see a clean-shaven man wearing a thin plaid shirt with blue suspenders and patches on the elbows of that apparel. He headed straight for Jon. Johanna took my hand.

Behind him stood a woman with her hair tied back in a bun and wearing a simple paisley-patterned dress. Her face, though young, had the lines and texture of too many hours in the sun. Gently, the man lifted the tag that I'd pinned on Jon's shirt just that morning.

My name is Jon Magnusson. I am three. I am Norwegian. I am a Lutheran. I am baptized.

The man ruffled Jon's hair and then moved on. He read no additional tags as he made his way down the line to view the other boys. Johanna and I looked at each other. This little boy, her brother, was the only family she had. The man nodded to Brother Andrew and the two of them walked into the station. Johanna went over and drew her brother in close. A tinge of fear crawled up my spine.

Without being asked, I herded the children away from the window where they might overhear Brother Andrew and the man. A few people approached the others to read their tags. I listened to the conversation inside.

"Jon has a sister who's five. Could you find it in your heart to take them both?" Brother Andrew was pleading.

The anxiety of the moment made me look over at the backs of the couple. The man, head down, kept moving his foot in circles as if looking for an answer.

"We are poor," he began in an apologetic tone. "We only want a son, a young one, that we can raise as our own."

"His sister, Johanna, is a good girl," Brother Andrew

argued. "She could help your wife in the kitchen and with other chores around the house."

Still, they wanted only Jon.

Brother Andrew gave the man a pen and watched as he filled it from the ink well. When the paperwork had all been signed, Jon's life had forever changed. Maybe someday these people would adopt him. But, for now, the papers made him an indentured servant, not their son.

Finally, the station door opened, and the couple went to stand in front of Jon. This time the man spoke to him. "Jon, we have decided to be your new parents."

The lady smiled but avoided looking at Johanna, who stood guarding her brother. I might have liked the couple, but now all I felt was numb. Tears spilled from Jon's eyes. In desperation, he grabbed his sister's dress in his fist and held tight. Between gulps of air, he called out, "Johanna! I want Johanna!" His begging broke my heart.

"Jon," Brother Andrew said soothingly to the frightened child. "These are good folks, but they can only take one child. You'll be happy here and Johanna will find another home."

Panic showed in every corner of that little boy's face. His sister got down on her knees and brushed back his hair. She wiped his tears and kissed his cheek.

"Don't worry, Jon. You will forever be my brother, no matter where we each live."

At the Home, this sweet boy resisted all hugging and kissing in front of others. But now, as I stood biting my lips between my teeth, he surrendered to his sister.

"You must be very brave," she told him then gently guided him over to the man, his new da. We all called out our good-byes as Jon was lifted into the man's big arms and carried off to the wagon, his eyes sending an urgent message to his sister. An eeriness crept over the rest of us, interrupted only by the thud of Jon's suitcase when it landed on the floor of the wagon. I hadn't even considered the separation of a brother and sister. In my mind, it just wasn't right.

Brave Johanna kept her arm up until a cloud of dust hid the wagon and the last member of her family disappeared. Brother Andrew brought her back to stand by me, then moved off to the other side to round up the others.

I hardly noticed that other people were looking at our tags, that is until a couple came by with a son in tow. They took time to speak to everyone, including me, but four-year-old Minnie captured their attention the most. They shared stories of their life with her and told her how they owned a bakery. The boy, who I guessed to be about seven, introduced himself as Ove.

"If you become my sister," he said excitedly, "our parents will let you have a donut or cake slice every day."

Minnie's eyes widened as he added, "I was an orphan when I came here two years ago. My parents died as we crossed the ocean from our home in Sweden."

Minnie listened intently. Then, as if sensing a prayer had been answered, she looked him square in the eye and declared, "I know my ABCs."

Ove's eyebrows shot up. "When you become my sister, I can teach you how to read because I go to school. My favorite thing, though, is to draw pictures of animals. Da tells me that someday I'll be a great artist. Isn't that grand?"

The two of them chattered and laughed nonstop. It lightened our sadness—even Johanna had to smile. I didn't notice the man signing the papers because the woman had captured my attention. She couldn't stop telling Minnie how everyone in town would love her and Ove would make the most wonderful big brother.

"One day you can go to school, too," the woman added. "And maybe you'll enjoy drawing like Ove does. I've always thought it would be fun to use icing to draw on my cakes. One of you may want to help me with that task."

The woman made me think of Mabel and Henry, who'd

never met a child they didn't love. Now, I believed that Minnie would have a family where that same blanket of security could surround her.

All too soon, the time came to say goodbye. We girls gave hugs and the boys shook hands, then watched as the new siblings skipped ahead of their parents, their blonde hair lifting with the breeze, their laughter an elixir.

The crowd whittled down. Those who had no interest in a child were wandering off. Brother Andrew instructed the remaining six of us to wait on the bench closest to the track.

"This next train will be our last ride. Look again for the name Chicago, Milwaukee, St. Paul printed on the side. It's the same company, but usually these cars are newer and the seats more comfortable."

The train did look clean and brand new. The name was painted in gold letters, making it stand out against the shiny black of the engine. A thin line in a matching gold color ran along the side of the first several cars, the ones in which passengers would ride.

Johanna needed a distraction, so Brother Andrew asked her to locate our car, number seven. She'd grown up in an instant when their parents left them at the Home—even more so now that Jon had gone away. I saw in her a determination to succeed, especially now that she was alone on her journey. This time, none of the boys teased her. Though younger than all of them, she possessed an unnamable something that they wanted for themselves.

Once inside the car, it was easy to see that everything Brother Andrew had said about it proved true. The seats were plush blue velvet. Curtains adorned the windows and lines in their paisley pattern matched the seats.

"It's so soft," Katie said. She curled up on her seat and soon fell asleep. Lars and James made a game of pressing their faces against the window, then breathing on it and drawing pictures with their fingers.

"You two will now clean that window thoroughly!" Brother Andrew told them with firm conviction. "And when you're finished, remember to never again be disrespectful of another's property."

Johanna, who wanted time away from the others, went to sit alone toward the front of the car. I didn't blame her. Somehow, a brother being taken away had a different feeling than having one die.

Hans, a boy who liked numbers, was soon engrossed in the pages of arithmetic problems that Henry had made up for him.

I looked out on the busyness on the platform. People were milling about like ants, where if one of them stood still the others would. That's what I thought might be happening to a lady with a baby in her arms and a small boy holding tight to her skirt. Someone had bumped into her, and she'd lost hold of her suitcase. Like a person stuck too long in a mud pit, she started to cry. The boy pulled at her skirt, his eyes turned up in fear, and the baby flailed in her arms. I hurried out of my seat and headed toward the door.

Brother Andrew reached for my arm. "Where are you going?" he asked.

"The lady, the one with the two children, she needs help."

"I'll do it. You stay here with the others."

Even without his robe, there had always been something about this man that made people trust him. When he reached the woman, he pointed back to me and seemed to be explaining my desire to help. I nodded to her. She wiped a tear from her cheek and looked over at Brother Andrew, who already held the boy and the suitcase. She jostled the baby a bit and I saw her show Brother Andrew her tickets. I lost sight of them as they went off to find her car. When he returned, he stopped by my seat.

"That woman is alone. Her husband died recently, and she's headed west to join up with family who've offered to take her in. Not all women are that fortunate, especially when they have children. She wanted me to thank you. You saw how others just walked on by her."

As I settled back in my seat, I recalled a conversation I'd had with Mabel. We talked about my plans for school and she, like Mother back in Norway, told me how some men don't want their wives or daughters to be educated. At the time, I'd not considered the full scope of that way of thinking. After all, how would a woman support herself and her children if she had no learning? And who would care for the children if she did find employment? Like an infinity knot, every question braided into another. What would I do if faced with that challenge? I had no family to go to and no training yet to be a teacher. Suddenly, I felt like someone who'd been dropped from a mountaintop and told to grow wings to fly.

"Can I sit with you?" Lars asked Hans. Lars didn't answer, but he did slide over to make room.

Hans, like the rest of us, had a story, and it was Hilda who shared it with me. That poor boy had found the Home all by himself. But he hadn't knocked for entrance even though the night had grown cold. He just sat on the stoop and waited for the morning. Hilda found him, shivering so bad that she called for someone to carry him in. A bruise from an earlier black eye was fading to yellow, though he refused to give up who had hit him. In the first days, he lashed out at any boy who asked him about it. Once it faded, though, he became gentler and flourished in the love coming from the staff. Eventually, he told Hilda that when he was five, he broke his leg. The doctor, miles away, would cost too much. So, his da had set it himself. It hadn't healed right. Now he limped. Still, like other boys, he loved to play the rough and tumble games. No more mention of family ever escaped his lips.

In truth, we all had stories of losses. Mine was weighing heavily that day. I found myself reliving every detail of walking up the apartment stairs in New York, hearing the agony in Mother's voice as she sang to Peder, watching the scarlet patches appear, and breathing in the air from their last breaths. Did our friend Marta know I'd be alone? Could that have been why she prepared me? Did Da die because he got hurt at work? Or was it because he gave up wanting to follow a dream that didn't include Mother and Peder?

CHAPTER 29

When Will It End?

"Kristi. Time to wake up."

"Where are we?"

"In Minnesota."

"Then this is the last stop?"

"No. One more after this."

Dejected. Unwanted. Afraid. That's how I felt when Brother Andrew sat down beside me.

"I can tell you're discouraged, but please don't give up. These last two communities have always taken children."

"Great! I'm sick of parading in front of people!" The others whipped their heads around and I looked away, afraid I might cry because I'd put sound to the thoughts I carried.

Brother Andrew squeezed my hand, then stood to calm the situation I'd created. I felt ashamed. I'd let him down and acted like a child instead of the adult I wanted to be.

"Everyone. I need your attention," he called out. "We've passed into the state of Minnesota and the first town we'll stop at is called Mankato. I've been here many times, and people always seem to want a child added to their family."

We all knew the routine—check your face, your hair, and your clothes. But I'd come to believe that anyone who judged us by our looks wasn't worth knowing. And our tags had no value. They told nothing of what we'd been through.

When the train finally jerked to a stop, each of us hurried onto the dirt-packed street where a horse-drawn wagon ambled along. Maybe it was just weariness taking over, but as I looked around discouragement grew inside me. Everything seemed scraped clean of the fairy dust of hope.

Once again, we lined up by a station wall. This time, though, I leaned back against it and watched. A man came up to us chewing on a piece of straw. His mud-caked boots smelled like fresh manure. He had a scraggly beard, obviously untended for some time. *Inconsiderate.* That's how I judged him. Eventually, he walked away without speaking to anyone.

Just then, the door to the station opened. A man wearing a round hat and a gray suit escorted his wife along the line we'd formed. The woman criticized something about each of us in a high-pitched, offensive voice. *Perhaps she should look in a mirror, I thought. Maybe then she'd notice the huge stain on the back of her skirt and the drooping fragment of lace that would rip away with a simple tug.*

"So," I said to Brother Andrew, "where are all the good people?"

Meanwhile, James was striking up a conversation with an older man who wore pointy silver attachments on the heels of his boots.

"You shouldn't have those on," James told the man. "You'll hurt the horse if they bump against his side. And what are they, anyway?"

"They're called spurs," the man replied. "And I'd never be mean to my horse. He's my best friend."

"So, why wear them?"

I never heard his reply because a lady in a pale lavender dress had knelt in front of Johanna. She silently read the tag and then looked directly at the child. In the first kind voice we'd heard since arriving in this town, the woman somehow coaxed from the girl the story of losing her brother to another family. When Johanna had finished, the woman shared a story of her own.

"You know," she began, "when I was no older than you, my brother fell off a wagon and landed on his back. He lived about three days, and I stayed by his side the whole time. I still cry when I think of him because brothers are very special, aren't they?"

Johanna nodded, unable to speak, tears running down her cheeks. A tall man came up to stand behind the lady. He seemed in no hurry. Eventually, he assisted the woman to a standing position. She thanked him and proceeded with introductions.

"Johanna, this is Palmer, my husband. My name is Claire. We are known in town as Mr. and Mrs. Olesson. We own the dry goods store. I have an orange cat named Purdy, and my husband's dog is called BooBoo, because he's always getting into something he shouldn't."

Mr. Olesson casually reached into his jacket pocket and withdrew a peppermint stick. "Did you know that your name means gift of God?" he asked as he offered the treat to Johanna. Her eyes widened and she slowly shook her head. Suddenly shy, she thanked the man, but she wouldn't eat the candy. Instead, she motioned for him to lean down to hear her say something.

"Yes, I'd be happy to do that," he said without further explanation. "And you know, we've always wanted to have a daughter like you. Isn't that true, Claire?"

Again, the lady smiled before kneeling to face Johanna.

"What do you think, Johanna? Would you be willing to take us as your new parents?"

Johanna had borne so much responsibility for so long; I was hoping she'd say yes and could go back to being a little girl.

"Yeeeesss," she choked out through her happy tears.

I think the others clapped for her, but I'm not sure because I couldn't take my eyes off the couple who were smothering her with their hugs.

The husband disappeared with Brother Andrew into the

station. Only Brother Andrew came back out. But before we could say our goodbyes to Johanna, the man came running up the side stairs waving peppermint sticks overhead.

"Johanna insisted," he said, distributing one to each of us. We all thanked him.

"I was positive someone nice would want you," I said to Johanna when the time came to see her off. "You'll be fine now. Someday, after you're settled in, you can write to Jon. I'm sure that Brother Andrew will give your parents the address to use. You can tell him all about the animals at your new home. He'll be so excited to hear from you."

We watched the three of them walk hand-in-hand down the center of the street. By the time I turned my attention back to the others, I could see that Lars was talking to a man in a black shirt with a white collar. Next to him stood a woman and a boy slightly older than Lars.

"It's good to see you folks again!" said Brother Andrew. "And Gus, you've grown so much!"

"I'm the tallest boy in my class," he replied with a lift of his chin and a smile as wide as his face.

"You're so right," the man said. He ruffled the boy's hair, which appeared to make the boy shy, but only for the moment. "Andrew, today we've come to find a brother for Gus, and he's picked this young man."

Lars's eyes grew wide and his mouth gaped open. Gus immediately began to explain how he'd been on the train just the year before.

"You really want me?" Lars asked of the parents.

"Yes, Lars, we do. Would you like to live with us and have a big brother? And maybe later a sister, too?"

Thinking what to say wasn't easy for Lars. He stalled for so long that I wondered whether he was giving them time to change their minds. Finally, he responded with a simple "Yes, please."

Gus tugged on his arm and said, "Come on! Let's go play ball!"

"Goodbye, everyone! I have a brother now!" he hollered, and the two boys ran off as brothers tend to do.

"Andrew," the man said as he prepared to sign the papers. "We thought you should be first to know. We've decided to adopt Gus."

Brother Andrew shook the man's hand hard enough to make his arm fall off. Gus would no longer be an indentured servant, a term I'd come to hate.

Once our line had dwindled down to four, most people left the area, and those that remained showed no interest in us. Only one stop remained. I couldn't go back. I just couldn't.

"Wait a minute," said a man who came running at us with his camera equipment. "I need to get a picture for the paper. You kids will be on the front page of the Mankato Times."

He didn't bother to check in with Brother Andrew—he just lined us up and set his three-legged camera holder in place. When he seemed satisfied with our arrangement, he stuck his head under a black cloth, held up a stick, and *poof!* went a flash of light.

"Thank you so much," he said before reaching in a sack to pull out sugar cookies for all of us. He waved at Brother Andrew just as the conductor called out, "All aboard!" Our end-of-the-line ride was about to begin.

The conductor showed obvious displeasure as we entered the car. "You better not mess up this car with crumbs and sugar."

I caught Katie sticking her tongue out at him when he wasn't looking.

"Don't worry," Brother Andrew responded politely. "I'll see to it that everything is kept neat and clean.

"Huh!" scoffed the man.

The station clock now read six-twenty. Dark clouds were building up in the western sky. I smelled rain. The wheels of the train scratched across the rails as we headed into the oncoming darkness. The excitement I'd felt at Mabel's that morning had fallen away at each stop, one layer at a time. Now, a towering fear loomed in front of me. Another rejection for any of us meant ... I just couldn't say it.

CHAPTER 30

End of the Line

"Pipestone City. Final stop for the night," the conductor announced as he walked from car to car.

This news came at me like the point of a spear. My eyes were wide open, but the deep darkness of my dreamscape still lingered. I barely remembered leaving Mankato. Now my head had started to ache.

I drew back my window curtain, exposing the intense blackness of a night undiluted by a new moon. The lights of the station sparkled through the droplets on the windowpane. I felt like a child who just wanted someone to make it all go away.

"Are we doing another show tonight?" I asked, barely able to bear the prospect.

"No, it's been a long journey, and we all need a good night's rest. The hotel isn't far away. They'll have good food and a tub to soak in, too."

The train had once again stopped in a place where our car didn't reach the platform. I imagined us clomping through the mud while first-class passengers hurried from their cars directly into the station. We'd all be filthy, in which case for sure no one would want us.

"Gather up all your belongings," Brother Andrew said. "Katie, straighten your pinafore. And don't forget your ribbon from under the seat."

Brother Andrew had a plan I hadn't thought of. He walked us single file through car after car until we arrived at number two. From there, we descended onto the platform and into the station. I stayed by the three children while Brother Andrew spoke with a man wearing a rain slicker. He'd just come in from hitching his dapple-gray mare to the railing post.

No one inside the station paid us any heed. They all seemed content in a way that suggested they'd found the missing piece of their puzzle. We certainly hadn't found ours, and the exhaustion from the day's events had done nothing to help.

"Follow me," Brother Andrew said. "Even though the rain has stopped, I've found a man to take us to the hotel, so we won't have to walk in the mud."

The wheels on the two-seater buggy spattered the horse as he made his way through puddles. Some of it sprayed backwards onto the driver, who scolded. When we reached the hotel, lights shone from every room as our driver halted the buggy close to the front door.

A princess could live here, I marveled as I studied the structure. Its red-toned rock was carved precisely, each block expertly placed against the other until it was as high as three houses. The front door was adorned with black handles carved in the shape of mythical sirens. Painted onto its glass panels was the inn's name: *Calumet Hotel*. I was sure an evil stepmother would appear and tell us we couldn't stay.

"I want everyone to be on their best behavior," Brother Andrew emphasized as he started up the wide staircase. "Wipe your feet on the rug inside the entryway and do not sit on the furniture in the lobby."

He reached to open the first door, stopping to say, "There will be no bickering here. I'll get the room keys. The girls will be together in one room with us boys in the other."

"That's not fair," Hans said. "They don't have to share with as many."

"There'll be plenty of space for everyone. And you'll be happy to hear that each of the rooms has its own commode area complete with a big tub."

I think he added that last piece on purpose, knowing how much the boys hated baths. As if on cue, James responded, "Yuck! I hate taking a bath."

Clearly the boy had had enough for one day. I waited to hear Brother Andrew chide him. But Hans had already mounted the red rock steps, wiped his feet on the rug, and taken hold of Brother Andrew's extended hand. Together, they opened the glass-paneled doors and strode proudly into the lobby. The floor was covered in a thick red carpet topped in the middle with a smaller oval rug in another design. The rest of us followed until we all stood in front of the high-topped counter where a sour-faced man looked down at us.

"Good evening, sir," Brother Andrew said. "We have a reservation for two rooms under the name of Bjorgson, Andrew Bjorgson."

Strange. Up to that moment, I hadn't thought of Brother Andrew as having a surname. Suddenly, his change of clothes plus this new information made a difference in how I saw him.

"Yes, I do see a reservation here," the man said. He peered over the top of his glasses at our group. "Are these children ... ?" He winced as if he'd bitten into a rotten apple.

"That's correct, sir; they are orphans, come to find new homes."

"Hmmm," came his tone of dissatisfaction. The man's eyes narrowed, like the wolf in Little Red Riding Hood, ready to pounce on his prey.

"They'll have to bathe before entering the dining area, and we don't want any lice in the bedding."

James was fascinated by the small cubicles where all the skeleton keys were kept. Better to see them, he stood on tiptoe and rested his chin on the counter.

"Don't touch the counter!" the man said in a wicked snarl.

"You'll get your dirty fingerprints all over it."

Poor James moved back; fear written on his face. Brother Andrew immediately squared himself in front of the man.

"The children do not have lice, sir," he said with emphasis, yet not too unkindly. "We'd just like the room keys."

I wanted to confront the grouchy man myself, but had no energy left. So, when Brother Andrew called out for me to hurry, I rushed to the base of the stairway where Katie was determined to hold the banister with her small hand spread wide. In front of her, Hans had stopped to inspect the mirror-like patina of the sculptured rail.

"Isn't it perfect?" he said admiringly as he ran his fingers across the shiny railing. "Not a scratch or a crack anywhere. I wonder how they do that?"

James had gone on ahead of Hans. He didn't care about the woodwork. Rather, he enjoyed the creaky noises coming from certain steps. Mischievous and overtired, he stopped on the first landing and rocked back and forth on a board.

"That's enough, James," Brother Andrew said. He placed a restraining hand on the boy's shoulder.

Even a castle has its loose boards, I thought as I mounted the first riser. My foot sank into the deep red spongy carpet. When we came in, I hadn't noticed its design of inlaid roses. *Who but a princess has red carpet* went through my head—and almost out my mouth.

At the top, three floors up, Brother Andrew handed me the key to room 301. "You and Katie should settle in while I get the boys organized. I'll order sandwiches brought to our rooms because it's too late to eat downstairs."

I nodded and unlocked the door. Katie, first to enter, let out a gasp. "Look at that bed!"

"I'm not sure we should touch it," I said, picturing the grumpy man downstairs. "He must have given us the wrong key."

But Katie acted like she hadn't heard me. As if drawn by an

invisible string, the strong-willed girl made her way around the room and touched every piece of furniture as she chanted, "I love this room, I love this bed, I love this chair ..."

I found myself attracted to the walls, papered not painted, with a design containing bouquets of hydrangeas, peonies, and baby's breath.

"You can almost smell them," Katie said after I'd pointed them out to her.

"How do you like your room?"

I guess we must have failed to close our door, because Brother Andrew had entered and neither of us had even noticed.

"No wonder that nasty man didn't want us to stay here," I mumbled as I kept surveying our surroundings.

"Oh, there's no doubt that you belong here!" Brother Andrew said to dispel any idea that we weren't good enough.

"What's behind the door?" Katie asked as she rushed toward it.

With one quick twist of the faceted glass handle, Brother Andrew exposed the hidden surprise.

"A room to wash up!" Katie said gleefully, as if she'd opened another present. "And look at the pretty bathtub!"

I looked in the direction Katie pointed and there, tucked neatly into a corner, was a tub deeper and more ornate than I'd ever seen. Suspended upon slender eagle-shaped legs with talons gripping crystal spheres, its smooth white glaze sparkled.

"Look here, girls, your tub has two faucets—one for hot water and the other for cold."

With only a slight twist of the handle, water gushed out and Katie giggled.

"And what's this?" she asked, this time her finger pointing at something familiar yet different.

"It's a commode," he told us as he lifted the lid covering the seat and exposing the water below. "Just pull on this cord and everything disappears."

"But where is the catalogue paper so we can wipe?"

"No catalogue here. Just this. It's called toilet paper. You just tear off a few sheets at a time. If you need more rolls," he said, indicating the cabinet, "you'll find them on this shelf."

I took a moment to examine the package that held four rolls. The name *Northern Tissue* was printed on the front with *splinter free* highlighted below it.

"Tonight, you should both wash your best dresses and undergarments. Hang them on the side of the tub, but not too close to the radiator."

"What's a ra-di-a-tor?" Katie asked shyly.

"Here," he said, pointing to the coiled iron unit. "It's used to heat the room. But it can get very hot, so be careful. Tomorrow, when we've finished breakfast, we'll meet the townspeople at the church. For tonight, though, I want both of you to bathe. We must all smell clean in the morning. And Nellie sent a special treat for you, a bar of lavender soap. It'll help you relax as you soak in the water."

"Did she put some out for the boys, too?" Katie asked with a snigger. "I bet they don't want to smell like lavender."

"No, for them she sent Lava," he said, and we all laughed.

Before the sandwiches were delivered, Katie bathed then snuggled under the covers and immediately fell asleep. I lay awake, still thinking that this castle wasn't where we belonged. We had no fairy godmother to make our tattered dresses look new. And although we erased cinders from our faces, nothing could subtract "orphan" from our identities—nor the possibility that we could be sent back.

That next morning, we gathered in the hallway outside our rooms and waited as Brother Andrew added some last-minute spit to Hans's cowlick. James couldn't keep himself from muttering *euwww*.

The murmur of voices drifted up from the dining area along with a smell of food that made my mouth water. The evening sandwiches had worn off and I craved a "Hilda breakfast."

At the front desk, the stern-looking man had been replaced by a young woman with braided yellow hair.

"Good morning," she said. "My name is Lillie. I've saved a table for you over there by the window."

I felt out of place as we weaved through the crowded room. Keenly aware that many pairs of eyes were locked on us, we all tried to be careful when pulling out our chairs and sliding onto the seats.

"Would you like a cup of coffee, sir?" Lillie asked Brother Andrew.

"Why, yes, thank you."

"And how about you?" Lillie directed her query to me.

"That would be wonderful."

Her simple question had acknowledged me as closer to adult than child, and it lifted my spirits.

"Number five is our special of the day," she said to Brother Andrew, pointing it out on the menu. "It'll save you five cents on each order."

"No need for menus," he said politely. "We'll each have an order of pancakes, bacon, and one egg. Oh, and a glass of milk for everyone."

I'd placed myself where I could see both out the window and into the full dining area. Always curious about my surroundings, I looked at each table. Some had well-dressed ladies and gentlemen. Others had fancy cowboys; their boots polished to a shine. No regular people like farmers or store owners, just the well-to-do. We didn't fit in. It made me self-conscious of every wrinkle in my dress, which Mother would have ironed before allowing me out of the house.

As for the room, my eyes took in the abundance of detail. Pressed white cloths covered every table. Built-in cabinets along the wall had glass doors. Inside them, the shelves held beautiful dishes and glassware. The wooden floors sparkled in the sunlight. An occasional brass-rimmed spittoon awaited a disgusting brown string of chaw-stained saliva sailing from a man's lips. I only knew of places like this in the books I'd read.

A rather tall man entered from the hallway and walked directly over to Brother Andrew. He tapped him on the shoulder and pulled him up into a huge bear hug.

"*God dag, god dag*," he kept repeating.

"Children," Brother Andrew said as he pulled the man in by his side. "I'd like you to meet my friend, Pastor Andersson. He's lived here in Pipestone City for many years and always comes to meet new arrivals."

Before anyone could ask a question or exchange any pleasantries, Lillie arrived with three cups of coffee and a large pitcher of cream. "Pastor, I know you enjoy your cream, so I filled the pitcher to the brim."

The man pulled an extra chair up to the table. After generously dousing his black coffee with circles of cream, he raised it to his lips and slurped loudly. The impolite noise startled the boys and Katie into fits of laughter.

"Now, see what you've done," Brother Andrew teased his friend.

"I know. I know. But really, Andrew. Where are your manners? Introduce me to these wonderful children."

"Well, the young man beside you is Hans. He's ten, soon to be eleven. James is the one with the big grin and he recently turned seven. Katie, with the beautiful red hair, is five. Next to her is Kristi, who turned fifteen a few days ago. She has been a huge help to me on this trip." Heat rose on my cheeks.

The pastor engaged each of us in conversations. We didn't wear our tags this morning, nor did he ask any questions pertaining to that basic information anyway. When he came to me, he asked, "What are your dreams, Kristi?"

"I want to be a teacher."

"Fantastic!" He slapped his knee. "We need teachers here. I'm hoping to convince the town to build a school that'll hold all the students through grade twelve. It only goes to grade eight now."

Before I could add to the conversation, Lillie came with the food and the pastor spoke the blessing.

"Father, we thank you for bringing these children safely to our community. Now, we ask your blessing upon this wonderful food. Amen."

We ate. He talked.

"At ten o'clock, we'll all meet at the church, which is just down the street a short way. Anyone interested in finding a child will be there. But you should know that folks from around here like to get to know you a bit before they decide. And I'm glad Andrew didn't have you wear your tags today. No one cares about that stuff."

He slurped more coffee. "I'll do the introducing and tell a few things about you. Then you can add more to the story if you'd like. Afterwards, everyone goes downstairs for coffee and sweets. There, people can ask more questions and mull over their selections. And you can find your new parents."

I couldn't get over his air of confidence and the way he left no doubt that everyone would have a home.

"But what if no one wants me?" James asked. "I can't hear well."

"And me," Katie chimed in. "No one ever likes my red hair."

"And my limp," Hans found the courage to say.

"Don't worry. You'll all fit right in."

I hadn't spoken. I needed air. So, when Lillie walked by, I motioned her over and whispered, "Could you tell me the name of the older gentleman who now stands behind the front desk?"

"Oh, that's Lester Braa. He's not a happy sort, so watch out."

I was trying hard to engage my mind in the conversation between the two men, but only noise without meaning rumbled in my ears. Every minute brought me closer to a yes or a no, stay or go back. My heart raced like a train whose engine had been fed too much coal.

"I need to be excused," I finally said without realizing I'd interrupted their conversation.

"Of course," Brother Andrew said without reprimand. "We'll leave here at quarter to ten. You can meet us out front."

I had no idea what I planned to do but, as I came around the corner of the dining area, I remembered my mother's words. *If you are unhappy or worried, make someone else happy.* So, I looked directly at the desk man and said, "Good morning, Mr. Braa."

"Humph!" he muttered without raising his eyes to meet mine.

I ignored his reply and stood for a moment to look around the lobby. We had rushed through it the night before, and I'd missed the painting that hung on the wall opposite the front desk. Simple, yet brimming with stories, it portrayed a quarry, open land, and a few Indians using tools to chip away at some red rock.

"Excuse me, sir. Could you tell me about this picture?" I asked politely.

He sprang to life like a teacher who'd just been given the opportunity to explain something to a wayward student. Raising his head, Mr. Braa came around to the front of the desk.

"That picture was painted by a man named Catlin. He came west many years ago to paint pictures of various Indian tribes. The scene is the quarry just north of town. The Indians carve out the best of the rock and make pipes with it. Because of this picture, the stone is often referred to as Catlinite."

I considered his explanation for a moment. Then I said, "I think I'd like to see this quarry."

"That wouldn't be possible," he said brusquely. "Only certain tribe members can enter the quarry. And besides, it wouldn't be safe for you."

I looked closer at the picture's details and mused further. "Somehow, I don't think it would be a problem. They let Mr.

Catlin stay long enough to paint this picture. And, besides, wouldn't it be nice to get to know some of the tribe?"

"Foolish girl!" he huffed, retreating to the other side of the high-gloss-surfaced counter.

Outside in the bright sunlight, I could see the busy street. Farmers stacked supplies in their wagons. A buckskin mare whinnied as she stood tethered in front of the watering trough. Two rowdy boys chased each other around the legs of another horse. A shopkeeper swished his broom across the wooden surface in front of the General Store, stirring up dust that made a sleepy dog sneeze. Two men, each with guns hanging from a belt draped across their hips, went into the saloon a few doors down. Nowhere did I see nor smell a factory. The fragrance of rose perfume wafted from a lady who walked by me on her way into the lobby. A moment later, a breeze replaced that scent with one of newly mown hay.

I jumped when Brother Andrew tapped me on the shoulder. "It's time to go, Kristi."

Instantly, my mouth went dry, and my body tensed. I faked a brave face as Katie gave me her hand and the two of us walked behind the others. Our last hopes lay only a short distance away.

CHAPTER 31

Our Last Chance

We crossed the street and headed toward the church with its tall white bell tower. James held onto one corner of Pastor Andersson's coat. Hans worked hard to hide his limp. And Katie just looked straight ahead. She had refused to allow me to braid her hair that morning, so her long red locks bounced as she walked. And me? I just felt out of place.

A group of fancy-dressed ladies stopped to look us over—or were they saying hello to the pastor? My mind couldn't focus. My legs felt wobbly. A train whistle wailed in the distance, but it didn't stop at the station. It wouldn't be the one to take us back.

The church didn't resemble our stave church back in Norway. This one had a white exterior and a steeple topped with a weathervane. Five wooden steps led up to the door, which the pastor held open for us. A burst of warm air, like a cuddly blanket, radiated from a wood stove just inside the sanctuary. Maybe the feel of autumn coming on scattered my thoughts, but for some reason I wondered how I'd find material to make a winter coat.

While the others walked to the front of the church, I held back to take in the entire room. Sunshine burst through the colored glass pieces on the wall behind the altar, including one that held an image of Jesus holding a lamb. Rows of wooden pews lined up on either side of the center aisle. On the wall next to each pew hung a picture of a Bible story. Mother had once told me that not everyone can read, so the pictures become their way of knowing the stories.

"I'd like the children to find a seat in the front row, over by the organ," the pastor said. He hurried off to greet an older couple who reminded me of the one that took Bernard.

"Don't let those folks take any of the children," I begged Brother Andrew. "They're too old."

"Don't worry," he said. "They aren't here for a child. They own the newspaper in town. They've come to gather information and write an article about all of you."

The room began to fill. Women and children talked quietly in the pews while their menfolk stood against the walls. The pastor took his time greeting each family. The talking died away when he made his way to the front of the room. I felt drops of sweat trickle down my brow and into my eyes, the salt causing them to burn.

Our last chance had begun.

He spoke, but I have no memory of what he said. I only know that it must have been something about us. He first motioned for James to come up on the platform, but the little guy wouldn't budge. Had he heard the pastor? I hadn't, but then again, my mind was reeling in fear.

Brother Andrew went over to James and got down on one knee. "These are good people," he said. "You go on up by the pastor now."

With a frightened look on his face, James, who'd been passed over so many times, slid off the wooden seat and climbed up to the platform. The pastor immediately wrapped his arm around the boy's shoulders, then began to speak.

"James recently celebrated his seventh birthday and wants nothing more than a good home for a present. Before he was born, his mother came down with measles, which resulted in a partial hearing loss for him. When he was only three, his mother died while giving birth to his sister. The baby had come too early and an hour later joined her mother in heaven. His da soon realized that caring for a child took more time than he could give, so James was sent to live with a spinster aunt in New York. Sadly"—and here the pastor paused to collect himself— "this aunt beat James and often locked him in a closet."

The people gasped, and I wondered how the pastor could know these things that I did not.

"So, one day, James ran away. Brother Andrew found him, hungry and cold, sleeping atop a steam vent at the corner of a tenement building. He took the boy back with him to the orphanage and tried to locate the father. Eventually, he learned that the man had died in an accident at the factory where he worked."

Silence. People were spellbound. I noticed myself breathing faster. No one had ever listened, truly listened, to anything about us before.

"So, you see, this young man has not had an easy start in life. But I am happy to report that he is smart as can be and loves science—especially bugs!"

That brought laughter from all the men and *eeews* from the women. James relaxed and stood a little straighter.

"I have a lot of bugs on my farm," hollered out a man dressed in coveralls. "Help yourself."

Hans, ever self-conscious about his limp, was next to be called to the front. His neck and face reddened as soon as he stood to approach the platform. Once again, he attempted to use the ball of his foot to even out the leg length, but it caused him to almost trip.

"Folks," the pastor began again, "this is one of the bravest boys you could ever want for a son. Hans is his name, and he is ten. Back in Norway, around age five, he fell from a haystack and broke his leg. No doctors lived anywhere near his home, so his da had to set the leg best he could.

"Like most farmers, his family's crops failed one too many

years, and that is why they came to America. While in New York, the entire family came down with influenza. Hans alone survived. For a while another family took him in, but they soon realized they had too many mouths to feed, so they cruelly rejected him with nothing but the clothes on his back."

I leaned toward Brother Andrew and whispered, "How does he know all of this?"

"I sent him a letter outlining something about all twelve of you because there could be no way to know who would make it to this stop."

He uttered this last phrase as if it were a badge of honor that came with getting here, to this town, no matter that we'd gone unwanted for so long.

Hans relaxed a bit as the pastor went on to tell everyone how much he loved numbers and practiced them every day.

When Hans started to come back to our pew, I grabbed Katie's hand and the two of us mounted the platform to stand next to the pastor. I looked back at Brother Andrew for approval, then faced the people of the town. My confidence was failing me. When I finally spoke, it was so soft that people had to lean forward to hear.

"My name is Kristi Monger," I began in a voice that gradually grew stronger, "and this is Katie, who is five."

"I'm almost six," Katie chirped with pride. The crowd laughed and Katie, without a moment of hesitation, told her story.

"My momma went to live with Jesus when I was two. Then Da married a lady named Evie. She was nice to me, and I liked her. We lived in Ireland but Da couldn't earn enough to buy food for us. Grandpa and Grandma wouldn't help us because Evie was a Prod'stant. They said she and the rest of us were damned to hell!"

"Katie, you mustn't use bad words like that," I said.

She just scowled at me, shrugged her shoulders, and went on.

"We came to America in a big boat. Da found work in a

factory but wouldn't let Evie work in one. We lived in a building with lots of other Irish people. One day, some men found out Da had changed to Prod'stant instead of staying Cath'lic. They hurt my da so bad he died a few days later. No one would help us. We had no money to pay the rent, so we slept in alleys, and I stole food for us."

Her next words got stuck in her throat, so she paused and looked down. After a few seconds, she lifted her head, took a big gulp of air, and charged ahead.

"The baby started coming and Evie cried. I yelled for help, but no one answered. Evie lay down and went to sleep with the cold baby below her. It was a boy. I named him Ian before I left and started walking. I was crying and hungry when Brother Andrew found me. He told me angels had come and taken Evie and Ian to be in heaven with Da."

Katie, consumed by hiccups and sadness, ran off the stage and threw herself into Brother Andrew's arms. A lump grew in my throat as I stood all alone facing the people. What could I say to make them understand my life? Like the others, I just wanted a home again. And a chance to go back to school and become a teacher.

Time stood still, or at least that's how it felt as I remained alone on the stage. Words that should have spilled out were locked inside me. I couldn't find the key.

"Kristi, would you like to tell your story?" the pastor inserted in my silence.

I nodded and swallowed hard.

"I recently turned fifteen." I stopped to organize my thoughts. "I'm not a young child, but I am a hard worker and I'm good with children. Brother Andrew found me hiding in a cardboard box after a night of pouring rain. My parents and little brother had died. I had no home. I had worked in a sewing factory, but I lost my job when I stayed home to care for my da. After Da died, I discovered that factories won't hire a person without a home."

My heart beat so loud in my ears that I was deaf to all other sounds around me. It took a little time before I could go on.

"I was a good student back in Norway. Miss Robinson helped direct my studies so I could go off to Oslo and prepare to be a teacher after I turned sixteen. I hope that the family who takes me will help me to accomplish that dream."

Recounting these events stirred a sadness that over-whelmed me, and my mind went blank of all else I wanted to say. So, I simply went and sat down.

Pastor Andersson moved to the center of the platform and said, "Now that you've heard something from all four children, it's up to you. Talk to them; there's more to learn. But for now, I can smell that wonderful egg coffee brewing. I think we should all go downstairs where our Ladies Aide has set up tables with sweets to go with your coffee."

Before he or anyone else could move even an inch, the cutest little red-headed girl ran up the aisle, full speed, screaming at the top of her lungs.

"Katie! I want Katie!"

She couldn't have been more than three, and we all laughed as her mother tried her best to catch the child.

"Fannie Mae, you get back here right now," she called out to no avail. Fannie had already clasped Katie's knees and wouldn't let go. By then, even her mother had to laugh.

"I'm so sorry, Katie. Fanny has been wanting a sister and when she saw your red hair, I couldn't stop her."

"But does that mean you want to be my new Mother and Da?"

"Yes, yes, yes!" crowed little Fannie Mae, jumping up and down.

Again, Katie looked at the woman, but this time she saw that Fannie's mother was signaling to her husband, who stood off to the side. He smiled and came over to squat down to eye level with Katie.

"We adopted Fannie Mae just a year ago, but we always wanted two children. So, Katie, we'd very much like to have you be a big sister to Fanny Mae. That is, if you'd like to join our family."

"Oh, I would!" Katie said, throwing her arms around her new da's neck. Then, without hesitation, Fannie snatched Katie's hand and the two went to play outside.

Brother Andrew stayed in the sanctuary to finish the paperwork. Everyone else headed to the church basement. I trailed behind the last person, feeling like a puppy begging to be noticed.

The room below had tiny windows close to the ceiling and walls that were made from blocks of cinder. A line had formed as people inched toward the counter where two women stood pouring hot coffee, and plates of sweets adorned tables off to the side. Each of the tables had bright-colored runners edged in tatting or crocheting, a small vase of flowers, a water pitcher, glasses, and napkins that looked as if they had been made from the same trees as our toilet paper.

Several couples spoke with the boys, but only two couples sat at my table. They told me that they had been hoping for a baby. So, even though they were polite, I knew they were passing me by. I felt invisible.

The pastor and his wife ended up taking James. They had no children, but that didn't matter to James. His new da understood the love of science and had been collecting bugs himself since a very young age. When the pastor finished signing papers, he took James outside for a time and the two came back with ladybugs in a jar and a bouquet of wildflowers for his new mother. Graciously, she accepted the flowers and acted excited about the bugs.

She leaned over to her friend at the next table and confided, "At least it wasn't bees."

But the real joy came when James ran up to Brother Andrew, tugged at his shirt, and said, "My new da is taking me to get hearing aids."

Hans found a family who lived on a farm about a mile outside of town. He made sure to tell me that they had a dog, horses, and some cattle. The farmer liked the idea that Hans was good with numbers. Not the slightest mention had been made of his limp.

"I can be the head bookkeeper," Hans told me. "And maybe someday I'll go to be a banker. My new da told me the banks need men who understand farming."

My worst fear had come true.

I stared in disbelief as people slowly left the downstairs area. Not one noticed that I stood alone. No one turned to look as I followed the last of them up the steps and out the back door. No one saw me turn away from, not toward, the hotel. Eventually, when I thought the sorrow would burst my heart and I could take it no more, I began to run and only stopped when my sides ached so bad I couldn't draw breath. A clump of scrub oak grew beside a field of corn and there I pushed aside the sharp branches, their thorns causing lines of blood to etch my arms.

The hem of my dress caught on a twig, and I fell to the ground, where I sat and sobbed. I felt like my heart had been dashed against a rock, smashed beyond repair. My stomach revolted and I fought to contain its contents. The wind caught a wisp of my hair and twisted it around a prickly low-hang-ing branch. Pulling it hurt, but I didn't care. My head buzzed from the crackling of windblown leaves in an unharvested corn field.

CHAPTER 32

Unwanted Again

"Kristi. Where are you? Come back. Don't be discouraged."

The voice seemed to come from far away and I couldn't trust it. I didn't answer. I kept my head buried against my knees as I shivered and tried to shut out everything around me. *Check! Check!* warned a red-winged blackbird from the top of a stalk. A dog barked and wouldn't stop.

"Kristi, you must come back."

The voice kept coming closer until footsteps stopped by where I sat. Mrs. Andersson, the pastor's wife, had found me. She'd brought a shawl.

"Oh, dear Kristi. Come out from those nasty trees and wrap this around you. I've looked everywhere. You must come back."

"I don't want to go back. No one wants me. I was a good daughter. I'm a hard worker. I wouldn't ask much in return. Why ... ?"

Before I could finish and she could reply, we both saw Brother Andrew at the edge of the grove.

"Kristi. Hannah. Come quickly. Dr. Samuelson is waiting."

"A doctor? But why a doctor? My scratches don't require a doctor."

"You must come. He wants to meet you. I'll run on ahead and tell him you're coming."

I entered the church from the side door. There in the back

pew sat a man caressing the brim of his hat as it lay in his lap. When he saw me, he rose and nodded. Without any introduction, he began to explain his tardiness.

"I'm so sorry," he said. "I wanted to be here to meet everyone, but I was helping Mrs. Jensen deliver a fine healthy boy, a big one—well over nine pounds, I'd say."

He chuckled a bit. Making no mention of my disheveled state, he gestured to me to come and sit so we could talk.

"My wife and I," he said, "well, we always wanted children. But for some reason, it didn't happen for us."

He took a moment to gather his thoughts, giving my mind the chance to go in a hundred different directions. "My wife is lonely. She needs the companionship of another woman, as well as some help around the house. I'm the only doctor in this area, so I'm often called out at odd hours and for long periods of time."

He lowered his eyes, still playing with his hat. *Maybe he's looking for inspiration in there*, I thought. It took all I had not to interject. Thankfully, he sighed and resumed the story.

"She's alone handling the animals, the garden, and the new trees we planted. It's a big job and much of it is heavy work. Brother Andrew wrote to me about you and how you lost your parents and little brother. I can't imagine the sadness you must feel. I lost my father when I was sixteen. He probably had cancer but in those days, they had no name for it. Mother raised us boys, all five, with the help of her bachelor brother. She worked harder than anyone I've ever known."

This man who sat beside me had begun to unwind my nerves. He understood my loss. When he spoke again, the voice came as if from a faraway land.

"You're older, Kristi. You have the right to accept or reject my offer." He swallowed, then looked at me with misty eyes. "Dessie and I would like to have you come live with us."

I started to shiver again. Should I believe him? Could I trust him? I didn't know. Yet I heard myself say, "I would be honored to come live with you and your wife."

"Oh, *mange tak, mange tak*," he kept repeating. "Dessie will be so excited. She's at home now tending to our dog. Poor thing tussled with a porcupine just before I left to help Mrs. Jensen. Ol' Red, that's his name. He's forever getting into trouble. One day he chases a skunk and the next it's the neighbor's goat."

I had no idea what a porcupine or a skunk could be, but his excitement spilled over in story after story. Then, right in the middle of a sentence, he stopped and belted out a hearty laugh.

"I've been negligent in my manners. I am Dr. Samuelson. Ben Samuelson."

"And I am Kristi Monger." I quickly corrected myself. "Kristi Ann Monger." Suddenly, for no reason I could name, I felt overwhelmingly shy in front of this man who had just said he would be my da.

"I think we should go back to the hotel and get your things. Dessie is eager to meet you. Hopefully all the quills are out of Red's nose because he is quite the greeter. Loves to give kisses. Never has been much of a watch dog, that's for sure."

My legs wobbled like newly poured jelly. I looked at this gray-haired man with hazel eyes and a closely trimmed beard. He smelled like a mixture of leather, horsehair, and just a hint of antiseptic. His suit needed a bit of pressing and his shirt had five small spots of blood on the front. His wife, I was sure, would soak it in cold water before washing. He reminded me of Dr. Fjelstad who'd set my da's leg and, years before that, had delivered Mother's dead baby. Both men had a kindness that put you at ease.

"You'll be the first, you know," he said, interrupting my reverie. "Andrew said he'll be bringing another group in the spring. Maybe we could find you a brother or a sister. At our age, that should round out our family."

The doctor's stories kept coming, but the one that held

the most interest for me centered around Brother Andrew. He told me that they first met two years ago in the lobby of our hotel.

"Andrew had just arrived with a group of children. As usual, he was talking to several people and not paying attention to his surroundings. He caught his foot on the corner of a scatter rug and down he went."

Dr. Samuelson chuckled again, adding, "The leg broke and the bone dislodged. I set it for him and over the weeks that followed he was forced—and I do mean forced—to stay in bed. I brought him home to live with us. I can tell you for certain that he is not a good patient. Nor is he a patient man."

Engrossed in the story, I hardly noticed we'd left the church and entered the hotel lobby.

"Ben, I'm so glad to see you found our Kristi," Brother Andrew called out from across the room.

"I did indeed. And what a wonderful young lady she is! Though it won't surprise you to learn that I took over the conversation on the way over here."

The two men conversed while I ran up the stairs to pack my things. I changed into my other dress because of the new rip in my hem. When I came back down, Brother Andrew guided me over to the settee—the very one he'd told us not to sit on the night we arrived.

"Kristi, before you leave with Dr. Samuelson, I have something for you. Please stay here. I'll be right back."

Just then, Lillie, the girl who'd waited on us at breakfast, came from the dining area and stopped in front of me. She held a handkerchief, folded to show off the small blue flower embroidered in the corner.

"This is for you."

Overwhelmed by her thoughtfulness, I felt tongue-tied. All I could get out was "Thank you," as she reached out to hug me and whisper in my ear, "Welcome to Pipestone City. I'm so glad you're staying."

Lillie politely excused herself when Brother Andrew arrived with a package wrapped in brown paper.

"You were a great help on this trip. I truly appreciate all you did."

I didn't know what to say. Too much had happened too fast. I looked from him to the package and back again.

"Well, open it. It's for you."

Carefully, methodically, I unwound the string and pulled back the paper. Inside, I found a new journal, some writing paper, envelopes, and enough stamps for six letters.

How did he know that my journal from Miss Robinson had but two pages left to fill? Every day, I'd written as if talking to Astrid or sometimes to Grandpa Carl. Those pages knew me, and I wanted to cry.

"The stamps are for when you want to write back to all of us at the Home."

His voice had broken through the rumble of my mind. My hands shook and I couldn't speak.

"Andrew. Kristi. We need to leave now. My Dessie will be waiting on us and by now she's worrying."

I rewrapped the package and stood up on my shaky legs. I choked back tears and embraced Brother Andrew. I'd not go back. Instead, I'd be going through Alice's looking glass into my new life.

CHAPTER 33

What Lies Ahead

I don't remember climbing into the buggy but there I was, sitting next to the doctor as he encouraged the mare forward. *Could all this be happening?* I wondered. The demons of worry snuck back into my head, sprouting all types of bad thoughts. But the *clip-clop, clip-clop, clip-clop* of the horse's hooves quieted my mind as I took in the surroundings outside the town.

"Where are the trees?" I asked in disbelief. "And the mountains?"

"This is prairie land. Trees are scarce here and usually only grow by a river or other body of water. Some folks, though, like my Dessie, plant them to act as windbreakers. Mostly it's farmers who disturb the land, till the wild grasses, and plant the wheat or corn."

"This land is so flat. It looks like it goes to the end of the earth and just falls off."

He chuckled. After a time, the two of us settled into a comfortable silence. We had passed by two sod homes when he began to speak.

"When Dessie and I first came from Norway, I thought we should live outside a town, have a few animals, and hopefully some children." He said this as if to the wind. "As it turned out, we do have animals. But when the children failed to arrive, I could see loneliness creep in on her. Sunday became the only time she had womenfolk to talk to. Not that she complains.

That's not in her nature."

It took a moment to twirl these observations inside my head and straighten them out before asking, "Do you think your wife will be disappointed that I'm not a baby?"

"Oh, no. Dessie and I wanted children, no matter their age."

The rocking of the buggy lulled my thoughts back to school—new friends, and my intense desire to teach. I felt as excited as Cinderella going to the ball. When we turned onto a narrow pathway outlined in wheel tracks with grass growing in the middle of them, I noticed that this man beside me had started to wave just as a red dog came racing toward us.

"It's Ol' Red," the doctor said. "Prepare yourself. He'll soon jump up and give you licks."

And he did. I'd never seen an animal so happy. He wiggled all over until sufficiently satisfied we'd been welcomed, then proceeded to find a way to sit between us. I laughed until my sides hurt.

"I warned you," the doctor said with a big grin. "And it looks like Dessie got all the quills removed. I wonder what he'll get into next."

The path ended in front of a white house, two stories high, outlined by late autumn flowers. A woman, most certainly Dessie, stood at the porch's edge and waved back. The wind whipped her pale-yellow braided hair into a frenzy. She swept it aside and looked straight at us while the mare came to a stop beside a fence that reminded me of a picture frame.

"Here we are!" the doctor called out. "I bet you've been baking all day, haven't you?"

"Oh pooh, Ben. I just wanted you to have a nice meal after a long night at the Jensens'. Now, tell me, who is this young lady you've brought home?" Her voice, low in pitch, smooth in delivery with a breathy sound to it, felt soothing.

"This is Kristi, and she is all ours," he announced with an air of pride.

At this, the woman stopped stock still. She covered her mouth and looked like she was about to cry.

My heart fluttered and I felt faint. "I hope you aren't disappointed," I said, still fearful that it may be the case.

"Oh, dear child! That could never be!"

"Dessie, you've left some flour on your cheek. Best wipe it away before it becomes the dough for your pie," the doctor teased to lighten the moment.

"Oh, Ben," she said, swatting the air then taking a moment to pull her apron across her cheek.

As if all this were normal as could be, she said, "Come. Let's go inside and get you situated. Ben, hand me her suitcase."

This woman with the wind-blown hair and flour on her cheek took hold of my arm, casual as you please, and folded it into the crook of hers. "We'll eat as soon as Ben has dealt with the horse and buggy."

As we neared the porch, the house seemed even taller. "We had a sod roof on our home in Norway," I said, tilting my head to examine the structure's covering. "Mother liked to toss seeds up there and when they bloomed it looked like an Easter bonnet."

Dessie stood still, her eyes searching as if for a long-forgotten memory. "We lived in Stavanger and had a sod roof too. But in this prairie the wind doesn't seem to sleep. If I tossed seeds up there, they'd not stay in place long enough to catch root."

That's when I first became aware of the wind. It couldn't be called a breeze. It blew and gusted enough to jostle the porch swing. Hair strands flew loose from my braids, and the skirts on both of our dresses swished around our ankles.

Once inside their home, my mouth watered at the aroma of fresh-baked bread and fried chicken. My stomach made a loud and embarrassing burble.

"Excuse me."

"Oh, don't worry. No doubt you are hungry. But first, you'll feel better after taking a moment to freshen up and settle in your room."

"My room?"

"Yes, of course. It will always be yours. You see, I knew that someday Ben would bring home a child, and I wanted to have everything ready."

Every board on the stairway to the second level creaked as if to say *welcome*. These stairs had no carpet, just time-polished boards and a handrail even Katie could grasp. At the top, she opened the first door and said, "This is yours."

What I saw before me was out of a storybook. The hotel had been castle-like—but this felt more like a forever home. Without hesitation, she immediately pointed out the wash basin, the closet—something I'd never had before—and finally the chamber pot that she'd hidden under the bed. It even had a crochet cover on both the pot and the lid.

I guess she read my questioning face because she explained, "I don't want any child of mine going to the outhouse in the night. I've always hated that." She slid the pot back under the bed. "And the cover I made because I hate sitting on cold metal." She'd said it emphatically and I knew what she meant. I smiled from ear to ear as she explained more things.

Dessie, I would soon learn, had always been one to say her piece, only stopping when she was done and acting as if everyone should have understood. There would never be embellishments.

She left me standing by the bed in this room she referred to as mine. *If this is a dream, don't wake me*, went through my head as I looked at the walls painted yellow and the two windows that let sunlight in through matching curtains she'd sewn from dotted Swiss material. I loved the feel of it. Back home, Mother had always passed that fabric by because of the cost.

I cleaned up as best I could before I went to sit on the bed upon which a beautiful quilt had been placed. It was made with new, not used, fabric patches. I soon realized that the mattress didn't have straw—it had been stuffed with rags. And the pillow had goose down. I knew that for sure because one feather thrust through the embroidered, ironed-to-perfection pillowcase.

The closet would hold only my dress with the torn hem. And the chest of drawers would be empty except for the top drawer where I'd put my underclothes, rags, and nightgown. The Bible, *Little Women*, and my journal would sit on the bedside table right next to the hurricane lamp, its wick soaked in kerosene and poking up just far enough to be lit.

Do people really need so many drawers? And who has clothes enough to fill a closet? The possibility amazed me. Maybe someday I could earn enough money to buy material for many dresses.

That evening, after the doctor gave the blessing, he recounted the day's events for his wife. I found it interesting to hear the details about the family with the new baby. When he'd finished, Mrs. Samuelson addressed me.

"I've been thinking," she said. "We should decide on the names you will use for us. If I were you, I'd want to keep Mother and Da just for my parents."

For a moment, everyone sat silent as we considered what was right. Then, as if from far away, her voice broke through.

"I have a suggestion. What would you think of calling us Papa Ben and Mama Dessie?"

Her question had come as a surprise, but only because I'd given no thought to the matter, even on those long train rides. I hadn't dared to believe, truly believe, that someone would take me in. But this soft-spoken woman had made a sensitive observation. No one could ever replace Mother or Da.

I glanced over at the doctor to see his reaction. Already, a big smile had begun to form on his face.

"I think it's a wonderful idea," I said, looking back at his wife before I added, "and thank you for thinking of it."

As hard as I tried, I couldn't stifle a sudden yawn.

"It's off to bed with you," Mama Dessie said.

"But I'm so sorry. I need to help you with dishes."

"No, tomorrow is another day and I have big plans for us. You'll need your rest."

She got up from the table and, with her arm around me, the two of us went upstairs to my room.

"Do you have a nightgown?" she asked.

I showed her the one Mabel had made and laid it on the bed. Then I saw Mama Dessie notice the book.

"That book has a story with it," I said. "You see, on the first night of our travels, we stayed with Mabel and Henry, who are friends of Brother Andrew. Mabel wanted to give this book to me, but I wouldn't hear of it. It wasn't until the next day when I opened my case that I found she had hidden it in this nightgown and included a letter. She knows how much it means to me to someday be a teacher and she promised to be at my graduation from Normal School."

Mama Dessie started to tear up and I worried I'd said something wrong. She fingered the title, and I reached out to stroke her arm.

"I didn't know you wanted to teach," Mama Dessie said. "No doubt Miss Torgerson will help you toward that goal. That means we'll need to send Ben tomorrow to get you registered. I bet you could start on Monday. That would give me time to make a new dress for you. We'll go shopping in the morning and get material, new leggings, and all the things you'll need when winter comes on. That'll be here before we know it."

She took hold of my hand before adding, "I always wanted to have books of my own. Maybe you can read this one to me while I'm making bread."

"Mama Dessie," I said hesitantly. "Could we go outside for a moment? I want to see the stars. Do you have Northern Lights here?"

"Seldom. But we won't know unless we look, now, will we?"

I felt wide awake as the two of us hurried back down the stairs and into the kitchen area where Papa Ben still sat.

"Ben, come join us."

"I thought Kristi would be tucked in bed by now."

"Well, Kristi wants to see the stars, maybe a Northern Light, but for sure we need a falling one to wish on. She wants to be a teacher."

Papa turned off the yard light and the three of us went to lie down on the blanket Mama Dessie placed atop the grass. The heavens sparkled with stars as we each pointed out a constellation, a planet, the Milky Way. When it happened, we all shouted. A shooting star had lit up the night, its brilliant long tail trailing over our heads and falling off the other side of heaven.

"That's your sign, Kristi. Remember it even in hard times. Ben and I support you and it's been written in the sky. Now, nothing can ever get between you and your dream to teach."

ACKNOWLEDGMENTS

Many thanks go to Alison McGhee, my professor at Metropolitan State University, who first suggested I write this book. Equally important was my writing group, The Headless Wonders, who were so kind as I struggled to find the right words, the right path.

Special thanks to my cousin, Valarie Anderson, who came with me to New York for research and has never failed to be my champion along the way.

To Susanne Dunlap, you proved to be the perfect writing coach, patient and kind always. And to Susan Leigh Babcock, many thanks for my first deep edit which was so needed and made the work better.

To the entire staff at Atmosphere Press who made this publication journey a joy, for you I could never offer enough praise.

And last, but never least, immense gratitude to my family and friends, my tribe, who have waited so long for this to become real. You never gave up on me.

ABOUT ATMOSPHERE PRESS

Founded in 2015, Atmosphere Press was built on the principles of Honesty, Transparency, Professionalism, Kindness, and Making Your Book Awesome. As an ethical and author-friendly hybrid press, we stay true to that founding mission today.

If you're a reader, enter our giveaway for a free book here:

SCAN TO ENTER
BOOK GIVEAWAY

If you're a writer, submit your manuscript for consideration here:

SCAN TO SUBMIT
MANUSCRIPT

And always feel free to visit Atmosphere Press and our authors online at atmospherepress.com. See you there soon!

ABOUT THE AUTHOR

SARAH FJELLANGER, born in southwestern Minnesota, had grandparents who immigrated from Norway in the late 1800s. Fascinated by stories told of these pioneers, she took on the challenge later in life to obtain a degree in creative writing. Now she writes about the young who were caught up in the rapid historical changes over which they had no control; a time when only the true warriors among them survived.

Sarah fills her spare time with reading, writing, travel, family, volunteering, and finger-knitting blankets for those in need.

www.ingramcontent.com/pod-product-compliance
Lightning Source LLC
Chambersburg PA
CBHW032018150726
47990CB00005B/2027